WHEN A PLANET IS STOLEN

Garda Nua Part 2

PALADIN SHADOWS SERIES, BOOK II

A Novel by **Aidan Red**

To my wife for her patience, tolerance and encouragement. Many thanks to my family and friends for their past and continued encouragement and assistance.

When a Planet is Stolen...

An entire planet's population disappears overnight. Shara and Greg thought they knew who had to be behind such a terrible deed, and if they were right, Shara knew history might have to repeat itself...

Chapters

One-Nineteen

"Aaah, here's Kiile now," Greg said, and looked up as the back door opened and Kiile walked slowly through the dining room and stopped at the edge of the living room.

"Coffee?" Greg asked. "Grab a cup from the table."

"Yes, sir," Kiile said, and stiffly picked up a cup and returned to the living room. "Thank you, sir."

Greg looked at Kiile, recognizing his disappointed manner and contrite air from their long association.

"Okay, Kiile," Greg said, and poured the coffee. "What's the problem? What's happened now?" He handed Kiile the cup.

"I'm glad you didn't ask what I've done now, sir," Kiile said, and tried to smile. "But the truth is that it's my fault and I will assume full responsibility for the incident."

He had their attention and stood rigidly at the end of the loveseat.

"I've lost Nikle." Kiile's face went completely ashen as he stared at Greg. "I don't know how, sir, but on our way back to Obscure, I realized he wasn't on the transport. I thought we had placed him with the body of the second man, where we had laid him just inside the aft portal."

"How could that happen...?" Greg asked softly, trying to keep himself from speculating.

"I really don't know, sir," Kiile said again. "When we stopped them on the rocks across the lake from the attack site, the man with him tried to run and was killed. My squad was veiled and Nikle tried to fire at the locations he thought our voices came from, but one of the remotes hit the Greymn in his hand and one of my marines shot him in the leg, knocking him

1

down. I remember he was screaming, and one of my marines administered an anesthetic to knock him out.

"We cleared the site of everything except their truck," Kiile continued. "I left the loading to the loadmaster and went forward. I ordered two of the troopers to put the body of the first man on the deck inside the aft portal and then to load Nikle. They would move him to Medical while we were en route.

"We met you beside the road when we landed, and Wally took Thom to see Deputy Reeds. He was still unconscious, and I was with the men moving the deputy's jeep to get it loaded. Colonel Mooren went back to base, leaving the patrol fighter to provide top cover. They alerted us to a car coming from the west, about ten minutes away, and we hurried to clear the site and move out. We were halfway back when I checked on the deputy and realized he was the only one in Medical. When I inquired, the loadmaster went aft and returned saying Nikle was not there. We checked Medical again and knew Nikle wasn't on board."

Kiile stopped and waited a long moment before Greg motioned for him to sit down. "Obviously you went back to search."

"Yes, sir," Kiile said, and sipped his coffee. "We ran infrared scans around the attack site and around the rocks on the north side of the lake. The truck was still there, but there was no trace of him. Our nav-com called Colonel Mooren, but they had already landed and deplaned. Franni checked for his *feel* after we got back, but couldn't sense him.

"My speculation is that the anesthesia stopped Nikle's pain but didn't render him unconscious. At some point in the hustle to clean the site, he must have seen his opportunity and he may have rolled into the brush. We stayed veiled, so he probably did not see us or the transport."

"I've said it before," Greg admitted. "Nikle has a knack for slipping away. I don't suppose you checked to see if he was wearing a cloaking transmitter."

"No, sir," Kiile said, and swallowed hard. "I see that we should have."

"I know," Greg sighed. "Check the data we got from Ahaar's complex to see if there is anything on Nikle—bloodline, origins, connections, past assignments, if any, with the Traders. Anything that might help us figure out where he goes, where he might hide, and who he might talk to."

"Yes, sir," Kiile said, and then touched his earpiece. He repeated Greg's request and nodded when the person on the other end of the connection confirmed the order.

Greg started to say more, then remembered Nikle's visit in town just before the attacks after Labor Day.

'Five, connection with Wally Lima, please.' He waited a moment and held up his hand when Nick started to ask a question. *'Wally, Greg. Do you know who Nikle might have been looking for when he came into town just after Labor Day? Someone that lives on Poplar between Amos and Cleary or on Birch, out above the college?'*

'Those are the homes,' Five said, repeating Wally's reply, *'of Abe Brownly on Birch and Mann and Ben Douglas on Poplar.'*

'Thanks,' Greg said. *'We need to see what those two know about Mr. Nikle's whereabouts and intentions.'*

'I'll get someone right on it,' Five repeated Wally again.

"Wally's going to check out Abe Brownly and Ben Douglas," Greg said. "Nikle tried to visit with them before the attacks in September. He'll let us know if he can find out anything useful." Greg turned back to Kiile. "Anything else I need to know?"

"Yes, sir," Kiile said, and set his cup down. "I told you Nikle and the man with him were going to go the Niles Reeds Ranch to meet someone named Buddy." Kiile hesitated and Greg nodded. "We stopped at the ranch and waited for anyone that might show up, but no one did. Nikle must have some form of communications, and my hunch is he warned this Buddy that we might be waiting for him or just rescheduled the meeting to another time or place."

"I'll see if I can find a Buddy among the Family or their support groups," Nick said. "It may be a name or a nickname, but I might be able to find something out."

Greg looked at him without smiling. "Okay. Just be very careful if you have to ask around."

"I know," Nick said, and forced a smile.

"That's all the bad news I have, Commander," Kiile said.

"Thank you, Kiile," Greg said, and turned to Hench. "How did our new cadet manage her first official week on the force?"

Hench smiled as if Greg were asking about Tayn. "Blaire has a knack for making friends. That's her first real talent. Your evaluation of her physical skills was spot on. She has learned all of the defensive moves and won nine out of ten one-on-ones her instructors have given her this week. Actually more like twenty-four out of twenty-five. I was told they would finish the self-defense syllabus next week."

Greg smiled brightly and nodded at Kiile and Nick. "I knew she would do well. Her sense of presence gives her a real advantage once she knows the basics."

"Yesterday," Hench continued, "I put her into the navigation class with the other new cadets and told Major Iims that she would be joining his flight training early next week. If she has the time and applies herself like she has this week, she might solo by week's end."

"Keep me advised," Greg said. "I want myself, Shara, and the girls to attend if there is a solo party."

"The girls too? Are you sure?" Hench asked in confirmation.

"The girls and Tayn are going to solo soon themselves," Greg said, and glanced at Nick's smile. "They should know what the celebration entails."

▲ ▲ ▲ ▲ ▲

"Sir," Kiile said after the discussions had strayed from the briefing topic and Greg had satisfied himself that Blaire was doing well after her first week as a cadet. He set his cup aside and stood. "I should return to Obscure. I will check on the data search and report anything we find out."

"Very well, Kiile," Greg said.

He stood and walked with Kiile to the back door, opened it, and stepped out with him.

"I have to ask, Kiile," Greg said, and stopped at the edge of the porch as Kiile stepped down into the yard. "Was the incident last night the result of our overall apathy due to the quiet eleven years, or could it have been partially influenced by an overriding personal problem?"

Kiile stopped and looked Greg in the eye. He started to rebuff the thought, but hesitated and then straightened his shoulders. "Possibly some of the latter, sir. My sincerest apologies—"

"Kiile! Stop," Greg said softly. "I assume your personal problem is Cheral." His statement came out as a question.

Kiile swallowed. "Yes. Yes, sir. I think I've acted poorly, but I am not sure what I should do. Her career has taken her to greater distinction, in a different direction than I thought she would go, while I'm still the same squad leader marching in circles on the same old parade ground."

"You dislike your assignment?"

"No, sir! I've never been disappointed supporting your command," Kiile said quickly. "But maybe I'm not ambitious enough..."

"You know you've never had to prove yourself with Cheral," Greg said, holding his attention. "She's always looked up to you—confident, assertive, in control, always on top of his game.

Well, usually." Greg chuckled. "She stepped away from just being a Shadow to take on learning to be a pilot so you'd be proud of her as well. But I will tell you, she's gotten tired of you taking her for granted, for becoming complacent with her. She needs to know how you feel about her, about you and her. She needs—"

"She's talked to you, sir?" Kiile asked in surprise.

"Of course not, Kiile," Greg said, and smiled. "But cousins do talk about things that concern them. And mates talk about things that concern them, especially personal things. If this didn't concern two of our best friends and family, I would never have mentioned it."

"Thank you, sir," Kiile said, and relaxed his shoulders. "But I still don't know what I should do."

Greg sighed. "I won't belittle you by telling you what I think is obvious," Greg said, his voice taking on a stern, authoritative tone. He straightened himself to his full height and looked at Kiile, using the height difference of the porch over the yard to his full advantage. "But I will only give you another twenty-four hours to face this issue face to face with Cheral and come to an understanding. You will settle on a solution that is best for the two of you, mutually agreed upon, by then, or I will personally lock the two of you in that practice room" —he pointed to the arena beyond the barns— "together, until you do find a solution. No matter how long it takes! Minutes, hours, or days! You have until tomorrow noon for both of you to report back to me, together, and tell me which way it'll be."

Greg did not drop his commanding stare, but waited, knowing that Kiile had never been the focus of his unrelenting, demanding countenance.

"Yes. Yes, sir," Kiile finally said. "By tomorrow noon. Sir."

Kiile saluted. Greg returned the salute and watched as Kiile turned and stiffly marched back to his waiting transport.

⏶

Greg watched Kiile for a moment, hoping he was doing

the right thing. He had never felt the need to be this stern with Kiile and now, as he watched Kiile walk back to the transport, he suddenly had second thoughts. Without Kiile's devotion and dedication to the campaign, they would never have gotten this far. Greg felt sad.

Greg pushed the back door open and walked back to the living room. He sat down heavily in the overstuffed chair, and Hench watched him closely but did not say anything. Greg looked up and Nick's confused expression stared back.

"Hench," Greg said softly. "I hope I handled that right."

"The issue of losing Nikle?" Hench asked. "Or of Kiile's relationship with Cheral?"

Greg poured himself another cup of coffee and took a sip before he answered.

"I have to admit losing Nikle surprised me more than I can say," Greg said, and sipped again. "To have him in our hands and then forget to lock him up..." Greg shook his head slowly. "Obviously there was a lot going on, but I wonder if Kiile might be holding the reins too tight—not letting his men do enough of their own thinking, not letting them act without him giving direct orders."

"Do you think it's that simple?" Hench asked, and glanced at Nick.

"No," Greg admitted. "But he used to empower Seventeen, Twenty-Two, and Thirty-One and a few others to take the broader orders and figure out how to get the job done. But something changed since summer."

"Do you think he and Cheral had words or a falling out?" Hench asked, and refilled his cup. He offered the carafe to Nick.

"Not from what Shara says," Greg said, shaking his head again. "Cheral is in the dark, wondering why Kiile started acting differently toward her. But something happened and I think it has influenced his relationship with her. He sees it, but I don't think he can figure out how to fix it."

"So his tighter grip on his command and his frustration

with himself concerning Cheral," Hench surmised, "may have caused him to be distracted last night?"

"He all but admitted it did," Greg said softly. "At least in part."

Hench sat in silence and sipped his coffee. "So for some reason he no longer trusts his leads or something has made him feel inferior—maybe insecure?"

"Greg?" Nick asked, and suddenly realized he was still holding the carafe Hench had handed him. He refilled his cup and handed the carafe back. "What are you going to do? I mean, we've all relied so heavily on Kiile and his men—you, especially. What happens if he can't get past this? Or you can't get past this?"

Greg sighed and sat back in the chair. "I gave him until noon tomorrow to talk with Cheral and work out their issues."

"Wow!" Nick said, almost to himself. "And if they can't?"

Greg closed his eyes and tried to compose his thoughts. "I threatened him with confinement. He and Cheral together until they can either agree on a solution or agree to disagree. If we have to, Shara and I will referee, like we had to do with Jim and Shelly many years ago. I cannot risk the operation by having my leaders distracted and unable to perform their duties." Greg looked at Nick and then at Hench. "If he cannot work this out, I may be forced to relieve him. And gentlemen, the option of going forward without him scares me a lot."

"But we still need to understand what changed," Hench said.

"Can any of our pilots put their ear to the ground?" Greg asked, and looked at Hench. "Maybe ask around, Seventeen or one of the others, to see if they've heard anything?"

Hench almost smiled. "We'll certainly try," he said, and turned his head and stared into the distance.

Greg didn't *listen* in, but knew Hench was asking Colonel Mooren for his assistance.

Greg led their conversation to the rigors of work, and the

few options they had to try to find and reacquire Nikle. They debated each idea, tossing aside those that seemed less apt to succeed and polishing those that seemed to have the best chance. Another hour passed before Greg straightened and stretched without getting up.

"We better look happy," Greg said as he glanced up, looking north beyond the confines of the great room. "Shara, Jill, and the children just dropped into the valley and are almost home."

▲ ▲ ▲ ▲ ▲

"Mom?' Cheyenne asked as she stabbed a piece of ham with her fork. "You said we'd talk about my 'official mission' name with Uncle Greg and Aunt Shara. Have you talked to them?"

"Not yet, dear," Jill said with a sigh, and looked at Greg and then at Hench and Leeana. "Sorry, but once Cheyenne found out Sedona and Sierra are to be registered as Caiti and Coli, she's been asking about her mission name."

Greg smiled and winked at Shara. "I think she ought to have one also." He leaned back in his chair and took a long sip of his tea.

"Our father's family name on Rygon," Jill continued, "was Taam, and Dad took the Terran name of Thomas when they immigrated here. He is Crl Taam. The Jordan family name was Dnar, and Bob was named Jadn Dnar. Obviously, you know I took Nick's family name for registration."

"We belong to Daddy," Cheyenne said proudly. "I have his Terran name just like Mom, so his other family name should be my mission name, too."

"I'm glad you agree," Jill said, and smiled at Nick. She reached over and squeezed Cheyenne's hand.

"But what about a first name?" Cheyenne asked seriously as she looked at her mom and then at her dad.

"Cheyenne," Greg said, and leaned closer to her. "I have

9

an idea, if it's okay with your mom and dad." Greg glanced up at Jill and smiled. "I think our favorite niece should be called Keely, because she's beautiful." He ruffled her bright red hair. "And Keely is an old country name for 'beautiful.'"

Cheyenne brightened and her eyes danced. "Keely is a beautiful name, Uncle Greg." She turned to her mother and dad. "Is it okay? Is it?"

Jill smiled at Nick and then at Cheyenne. "Yes, Chy. It's okay and it is beautiful. It's also very special because your favorite uncle gave it to you."

Cheyenne stretched up and hugged Jill and then quickly turned and hugged Greg. "Thank you, Uncle Greg. Thank you."

"You are very welcome, Cheyenne. Now, remember it's a name for when we are on official business. Not when we are here, among our family and friends. We have two lives, and now you have a name for each of yours."

Cheyenne turned abruptly and looked at Jill. "Mom? What's your official mission name?"

Jill smiled. "I'm Key-ray Dnar, spelled *C-E-R-A*. It means 'bright red.' And your dad is Jesi Dnar, from his grandfather."

"Wow," Cheyenne said softly, and looked around at all of the smiling faces. "Now I'm ready! I'm Keely Dnar!"

Greg chuckled and ruffled her hair again. "So are we."

▲

"Jill," Greg said as he pushed his lunch plate aside and set his cup and saucer on it. "I'm going to ask that you stay down with Nick while we take the girls up this afternoon."

"Okay," she agreed, but Greg knew she wanted to be there. She turned to Leeana. "Are you staying down too, or are you going back up?"

"I'm down for the rest of the day." Leeana smiled. "Hench is taking Tayn for this afternoon's session. I can keep you company if you'd like."

"Sure," Jill said, and flicked her eyes at Nick. "That'll keep

Nick in line."

"Are you sure?" he asked, and tickled Jill's side, enjoying her expected response. "But I will try to behave." He kissed her cheek.

"All right, young ladies," Greg said, and pushed himself back from the table. "It's time." He stood, helped Shara up, and waited as the girls followed.

Hench stood and guided Tayn to the backdoor. Leeana watched them leave and poured herself another cup of tea.

"Hench says they are all doing very well," Leeana said softly with a smile, "but Tayn will be very tired by the time this day is over."

⩓

"I can't believe he let Nikle get away," Shara said softly as she and Greg followed the girls out to STSX.

"Neither could he, love," Greg said, and took her hand. "I think telling me might have been the hardest thing he's ever done."

"It should be," Shara said sharply. "He knows how much you depend on him and his troops. Did he really admit he's over-controlling his men?"

"He did. That's why I asked if his issues with Cheral were causing him to be distracted."

"And you'd actually lock them in the training room if he doesn't work it out?"

"Sure would," Greg said, and smiled. "I have to get him back on track. Right now he's almost useless, and I can't let that continue."

Shara was going to ask another question, but looked up and saw the girls standing in a line beside STSX's ramp. She smiled instead, at their poise and proud stance.

Greg followed Shara to the aft portal and turned to the girls. "Please come aboard, cadets. Follow the captain to the upper deck."

Once they reached the central compartment behind the cockpit, Casi stood them in the nav-com compartment portal and waited for Stran to take his position in the aft-facing pilot's chair.

"Cadet Caiti," he said gently, "please take the right side jump seat." Then he smiled at the others. "Casi, please have the other cadets monitor our flight from the nav-com compartment until it is their turn."

Stran swiveled the chair to forward facing as Caiti settled into the jump seat and strapped herself in. He looked at her straps from his seat and smiled. "STSX, ignition ready. System status, please."

STSX replied with his usual litany, assuring that everything was mission ready.

"Is everyone secure?" Stran asked, and Casi replied they were. He glanced again at Caiti and smiled when he saw the anticipation in her eyes. "Hover at two hundred feet, please, STSX," Stran said, and began flipping switches along the right and left armrests.

Stran felt Caiti and Coli's excitement as STSX lifted, and heard Keely's soft "here we go" from the back.

"IGNITION," STSX announced as he leveled at the assigned altitude.

"Thank you, STSX," Stran said, and gently moved the thrust levers forward.

As STSX began to move, he pulled STSX's nose up and began climbing until he was just above the height of the North Spire. He leveled STSX, slowed to a hover, and turned his chair to aft facing. He stood up, stepped to the cockpit portal, and turned to look at Caiti, frozen in her jump seat, staring back at him.

"In the chair, Caiti. Please. You can't learn if you don't sit in the seat," he said, and started to help her with her straps.

She suddenly slapped his hand away and unfastened the clasp. "Sorry. I can do it." She looked at him, smiling, but the questions still flooded her expression as she stepped up and slid into the chair.

"You look a lot like your mother when I asked her to sit in the chair the first time," Stran admitted. "STSX, please adjust the back height, chair width, and stirrup length. When set, please record the settings for Caiti."

He leaned forward and showed her how the five-point security straps hooked up, slightly different from the four-point nav-com chair and the jump seat straps. He showed her the swivel controls and she turned the chair to forward facing.

"The chair controls STSX in the direction it's facing. When you're controlling forward flight, the chair must lock forward facing. When you're docking, having to back into a birth, it is easiest to maneuver if the chair's swiveled to aft facing." He then touched all of the switches on the armrests and the controls, describing their functions, knowing Caiti, like her mother before her, had been watching his and Casi's movements when she rode in the jump seat.

"Now look at the forward cockpit wall," he said. "STSX, please adjust the eye position."

Caiti inhaled as the mostly blank wall suddenly filled with displays, indicators, annunciator panels, and various status indicators.

"Wow. Where did those come from?"

"They're always there. You have to be in the right eye position. Only the one in the properly adjusted seat can see the necessary displays."

"I didn't know you were watching so much stuff. I thought STSX was watching everything."

"Well, he can," Stran said, "but the chair has first priority unless the pilot says otherwise."

She nodded while she scanned the extent of the displays and he pointed to each one, describing its function, how the display worked, and what information it provided.

"Okay." He directed her attention back to the controls. "You understand what the thrust lever is and basically how it works. Push forward to go faster. Treat it as gently as a Series Nine canister with two buttons pushed. ST-Class Q-Ships have the most powerful engines of any of the QShips.

"About the time your mom and I got married, I upgraded STSX's engines and," he pointed to the button at the base of the lever on the right-hand armrest, "when this button is toggled by squeezing your fist, the engine's thrust is increased by fifty percent."

Caiti looked around at him and smiled.

"We use the normal thrust range for our regular work," Stran explained, "but in combat, if someone is shooting at us, we use all of it to move quickly. And when we are on a long journey, we will use the higher thrust to go faster and get to our destination quicker."

"Are the ST-Class Q-Ships faster than the others?" Caiti asked.

"Normally, I would say yes," he said, and smiled. "But about eight years ago, I had all of the Apache Squadron QShips upgraded to the ST-Class engines and added the upgrade. I also had all of the Apache Squadron ships upgraded so the crews can converse with the ships empathically, like we can with STSX."

"Wow."

"Okay, Caiti. Add a little thrust with your left hand and guide STSX with the right. Everything should be within your reach and proper for your arm length."

Stran *felt* her chuckle as she eased the thrust lever forward and she felt STSX's push through the chair. She glanced aside and saw the spires slowly begin to move along the canopy sill. Then she added a little more thrust and watched the changes.

With the right lever, he showed her how to raise and lower the nose, how to roll STSX right and left, and how to slew his nose right and left. In the course of the maneuvering, Stran had her climb until the air was thin and the earth's afternoon crescent was vivid below the bright sun. He also had her roll STSX inverted so they felt like they were flying under the globe instead of over it.

"Many times when we approach a planet, we'll be in this attitude," Stran explained. "As you've seen before, it gives a better view of the planet and things on it."

Caiti was more excited than she had ever been and followed every direction Stran gave her, repeating them as he requested until she could manage his requests accurately and timely.

He sat beside her, grinning like the proud father he was, amazed that she could pick up and execute the basics as quickly as her mother had. She even managed the same complex maneuvers he had thrown at Casi.

"Do you know where we are?" Stran asked softly as she rolled STSX level and turned toward the sun.

"Yes, sir," Caiti said without looking at him. "We're between the Marshall Islands and Hawaii at an altitude of two hundred and six miles."

"Okay, Caiti," he said, smiling. "Take us back down to where we started beside the spires." He pushed his feelings of pride to her as she gently turned STSX's nose back to the east.

"Okay, Commander," she said politely. "STSX, please plot a course back to the spires and where we started." She turned to Stran and asked, "What are the atmospheric speed limitations you mentioned? So we don't create a shock wave."

"Very good," he said as he unbuckled and leaned close to her. He put his head beside hers and pointed. "See that indicator? When we enter the atmosphere, it will change to show only the acceptable speed range. Too fast and the needle and numbers will turn red, and like you said, we can be detected."

"Thanks," Caiti said, and focused on the indications and the unobstructed view out through the canopy.

~

When Caiti settled STSX above and beside the spires, she

noted the clouds beginning to spill over the northwest rim of the valley and down across the ranches.

"We'll probably land in snow," Stran said casually as Caiti unbuckled her straps. He turned to the nav-com compartment. "Keely, you're next."

Suddenly somber, Keely got up from the pull-out seat and walked forward. She smiled at Caiti as they passed and then slid into the pilot's chair at Stran's gesture.

"STSX, please adjust the back height, chair width, and stirrup length. When set, please record the settings for Keely."

He leaned forward and showed her the five-point straps and the chair swivel controls. Keely smiled brightly as she swiveled the chair around to forward facing and listened to Stran's explanation of the chair's authority, as he described the arrays of switches and finally the control levers at the end of the armrests.

Stran smiled as Keely quickly absorbed his words and meanings, knowing that she had also paid attention when she rode in one of the jump seats.

He adjusted the eye position for her and answered her questions about the displays, surprisingly similar to the ones Caiti had asked. He pointed to each display and indicator and explained how it worked, what information it provided.

"Okay," he said, and straightened up, stretched, and then settled into the right jump seat as he began his description of the thrust levers and the upgrades.

"We heard you telling Caiti about the upgrades," she said as she gently laid her hand on the thrust lever knobs.

"I'm glad, Keely," he said. "Now, gently add a little thrust with your left hand and guide STSX with your right. You should be able to reach everything easily."

Keely put his instructions into motion and giggled as the spires began to slip along the canopy sill. She glanced at Stran with a wide smile.

"Stay focused, Keely," he said softly. "Never lose sight of

what you're doing. Never lose focus."

"Yes, sir," she said, and he felt her determination and her elation.

They climbed again until the air was thin and he asked her to roll STSX inverted, explaining the different attitudes he used when he approached a planet and the benefits of each. He directed her through his list of maneuvers, including a few complex maneuvers, different from the ones he had given Caiti, and was very pleased when she executed them quickly and with reasonable accuracy for a first-timer. She stayed focused through the exercises and only hesitated briefly when she had to stop and remember where a particular switch or control was located.

Finally, Stran asked, "Do you know where you are?"

"Yes, sir," she said as she rolled STSX level and turned toward the sun, setting two diameters above the earth's crescent. "We're about four hundred miles south-southeast of Rio de Janeiro at an altitude of one hundred and eighty-eight miles."

"Very good, Keely," he said, and smiled. "Take us back to where we started beside the spires." Again, he pushed his feelings of pride to her.

"Yes, sir," she said, completely composed and with authority. "STSX, please plot a course back to the valley and where we started."

When she started to descend without the expected question on speed control, he asked, "Do you remember you have to watch your speed in the atmosphere?"

"Yes, sir," she answered with a touch of pride in her voice. "I *listened* when you explained it to Caiti."

Stran smiled and sat back to happily watch his favorite niece.

"Clouds are getting deeper," Keely said as she aligned STSX with the valley, approaching from the south. Then she absently added, "That man Nikle is somewhere southwest of Grants. He's moving west."

Startled at her comment, Stan looked at her, but her concentration was fully on STSX and the task she had to complete.

When she parked STSX beside the spires, Keely pointed out they could only see the taller, north spire as it peeked out of the tops of the cloud deck sliding across the valley. As she unbuckled her straps, Stran looked aft. "Coli, it's your turn."

Keely stepped down off the dais and turned to Stran. She quickly threw her arms around his neck and hugged him tightly. "Thank you, Uncle—Commander." She slowly straightened, and with a huge smile, high-fived Coli as they passed in the central compartment.

▲

Coli completed her session with the same ability and accuracy as the other two. Stran quizzed her more than once during the lesson on their position, and each time she answered almost flippantly and correctly. Stran was beginning to think the girls always knew where they were, even when they were not thinking about it.

"Take us back to where you started, Coli," he said, and was surprised when she turned STSX in the right direction and added thrust without asking for a plotted course home.

As she started her descent for the long approach, Stran interrupted her. "Vertical descent to the spires."

She glanced at him and he winked. "The bad guys are following you, so get there and duck down quickly."

She smiled and aborted the early descent, holding their altitude until they were over Clay, hidden beneath the cloud deck.

Coli pulled the thrust off and applied some braking as she rolled inverted and pulled STSX's nose toward the clouds. As the altimeter changed from a display of miles to a display of feet, Coli slowly began increasing the braking to keep their speed under control. At twenty thousand feet she increased the braking, and at about seventeen thousand feet STSX entered the cloud deck and the world outside the canopy instantly disappeared, replaced by unbroken white.

Stran *felt* Coli's focus and knew she knew where she was as she turned STSX to the west and settled to a hover in the spot they had left from. He sensed the taller spire to their west, off the right pylon and slightly below them, and smiled.

"Nicely done, Coli," he said softly with a wide smile. "Very nicely done."

One-Twenty

Kiile stepped out of the northeast hatch into the launch bay and saw Cheral and Keli as they came out of the corridor of steps and started across the bay to the northside hatch. He hurried to head them off.

"Major Haak," he said urgently to get her attention. When they slowed and he got close enough to speak in a more normal voice, he asked, "Major? May I have a word with you? Please. In private."

He watched as Cheral studied him, considering his request, her expression neutral.

"May I ask the subject?" Cheral asked.

"In private, please, Major," Kiile said, beginning to squirm.

Cheral inhaled deeply and then relaxed. "Okay, Kiile. Lieutenant Quil and I have just finished a four-hour stint and I have to wash the grime off and set my suit to clean. My quarters in an hour. That will give me time to clean up and eat something first."

"Thank you, ma'am," Kiile said, and straightened. "In one hour. Thank you." He proffered a quick salute, stepped aside to let them pass, and then entered the corridor of steps to complete the task he was on before he saw Cheral.

~

Cheral glanced back over her shoulder as Kiile quickstepped to the corridor and disappeared up the stairs.

"What was that about?" Keli asked as they resumed their walk to the north side of the launch bay.

"I'm not sure, Keli," Cheral said as they entered the long hallway and started toward Billeting.

"I know I've only been here a little over a week, but I think he's acting very strange," Keli admitted. "Were you two together?"

"We were," Cheral said. "At least I thought so until this summer, when he changed."

"Changed?"

They turned at the corridor leading to their apartments.

"We were together for over eleven Terran years," Cheral said when they stopped at her door. "I kept waiting for that man to make an offer, or something. Then suddenly, he seemed to grow cold, separate, unsure of himself." She sighed. "Keli, this is maybe the third or fourth time he has spoken directly to me in nearly two months."

"And now he is urgently seeking a moment of your time," Keli said, concerned. "He seems polite enough and courteous, and you obviously know him better than I do, but I'm nearby if you need help."

"Thanks," Cheral said, and smiled. "Meet me for a bite to eat in half and hour?"

"If you want," Keli said. "I'll be there."

⋏

Cheral was pacing, suddenly nervous as she waited for Kiile to come. She questioned her emotions, wondering why she was feeling this way after the way he had treated her. She told herself he had good reasons, but then questioned herself; no reasons were good enough to justify his actions.

She sat down on her loveseat and quickly stood back up. He had not seen her new arrangement with the loveseat and the two medium cushioned chairs flanking it, the small round coffee table and end tables with lamps, and she absently wondered if he'd like the homey touches. Then she reminded herself that they were not together anymore! He had turned a cold shoulder when she was considering the second most important and coveted decision of her career—to become a Q-Ship pilot, with all of the responsibilities that went with it.

He had not even congratulated her when she'd returned with not just a Q-Ship, but an ST-Class heavy fighter, Q-STSX12.

As she paced, she realized he had started acting the same way toward his troopers. He had stopped praising them for their efforts, taking more and more control of the daily details, immersing himself in his work. She had not seen him that way since Pitcarthy. Not since she was shot and he had started visiting her regularly, forced to leave the details to his troops.

"What has happened to you?" she asked his imaginary presence out loud.

Startled, she turned at the sudden portal chime. The hologram showed Kiile standing just beyond the closed panel, and she took another deep breath.

"Enter," she said, and her voice activated the panel and it slid aside. "Hello, Kiile. Please come in." She forced herself to hold her voice level. "Secure as private," she said to the portal controls. The panel closed and the illuminated pad beside the door switched from green to amber. Cheral turned and sat down in one of her new chairs. "Please sit down, Kiile."

"Thank you," he said, and took the chair opposite her.

She *listened*, sensing a definite quaver in his voice, a sincere nervousness that she had never felt in him before.

"Are you all right, Kiile?" she asked and leaned forward, caught completely off guard by the aura she was sensing.

"Yes, ma'am," he said, and looked at her quickly. "No." His shoulders sagged and he leaned forward with his elbows on his knees, wringing his hands.

Cheral waited and he slowly sat up straight.

"I owe you the deepest and most sincere apology," he began softly. "And I truly do not know how to mend the rift between us that I have caused." He looked at her and held her eyes. "You have done nothing to cause my behavior and...I became angry and then confused, unsure, and then one day I looked up and you were leaving, going to collect your new ship and shipmate."

"What happened? There were months in between," Cheral

23

said, "and you ignored me. Cut me out of your life, with no explanation. What was I supposed to think?"

Kiile sat quietly for a long moment. "I know I handled it wrong. I handled us wrong. When you left and I realized I had let you down, I didn't know what to do. I have worried about that so much." He hesitated and leaned forward again, elbows on his knees, and stared at the floor. "Last night, I realized I have let my worry and indecision interfere with my work."

"I know you have," Cheral said, trying to keep her tone compassionate. "Since the summer, you have been taking more and more control of the troopers' assignments. You have been giving them assignments and then telling them how to do every step. It puzzled me, like I was watching a different man—a man that was afraid someone was going to make him look inferior, inept."

"I think everyone except me has seen that," Kiile said, and straightened. "Last night, it all came to a head."

She waited as he looked at her, his eyes deep with contrition.

"We had Don Nikle last night, in our hands," Kiile said heavily.

Cheral felt her spirits soar, but quickly realized Kiile was looking back down at the floor.

"Then I lost him."

"Lost him?"

"I did not let my men do their jobs," he said, and slowly explained the events of the attack on Deputy Reeds and how Franni found Don Nikle and another man watching the progress. He explained his ineptitude, his fumbling the mission. "I explained the situation to the commander this morning, and I was surprised he did not ask for my bars and stripes right there and then. But he had seen my change also and asked if our relationship was part of it." Kiile nodded to no one in particular. "He gave me until tomorrow noon to make things right with you."

Cheral slowly bristled. "So the only reason you came was because the commander ordered you to come?"

"Not the only reason," Kiile said softly without rising to her challenge. "He was right that I needed to face this immediately. I should never have let it happen in the first place."

"Not let what happen? Us? Or waiting so long to tell me that I don't matter anymore?"

"No. No!" Kiile looked up in surprise. "I let my personal matters interfere with my ability to please you, to be the man you deserve, to do my job and support my men. You do matter... to me..." He sighed and sat back in the chair. "But maybe it's for the best that you have other things to fill your time, others to spend it with. I have proven I am not the man you deserve."

"Wait a minute," Cheral said, shaking her head, confused. "We've been together for over eleven years and you suddenly decided this summer what I do or don't deserve? I have given you my time, my affections, my patience, and that's not good enough? Now you're telling me I've wasted all of that as well as my hopes and dreams of a future?" Cheral got up and started pacing again. "Why, Kiile? Why have I had to wait so long?" Cheral asked, her voice pitched in distress.

"Because..."

"Because why?" Cheral demanded, pouncing on his word.

"Because" —he looked at her as she paced— "I have nothing to offer you. I have no place for us to live; I cannot offer you any kind of security—"

"What are you talking about?" Cheral asked, spinning around to look at him. "I am a fighter pilot and you are a combat marine captain. I have been wounded and have nearly died. Twice! We cannot offer each other security! We have no way to do that! But we have a place to live..." She spread her arms and turned slowly around. "...and I thought we had each other! Someday, if we live long enough, I thought we'd retire and have a family and a place outside of Obscure like everyone else. But I guess you don't want those things."

Her voice softened and she stopped, waiting on him.

"You have always been and are still the only love of my life," he said softly. "I have been a fool in many ways, but now, my past has caught up with me and I cannot offer you the man you think I am."

"What's that supposed to mean?" Cheral asked with her hands on her hips.

He looked up slowly. "In August, I found out that I have a fourteen-year-old daughter."

Cheral stared at him, suddenly unable to comprehend his words. She stumbled back and dropped into the chair. A long moment passed and she finally asked, "You...found out?"

He nodded and held her eyes. "A little over a year before Pitcarthy, I took Leave to go back home and visit with my folks and siblings on Nevar. They had a small farm business in our hometown of Turell. While I was there, I visited many families I knew from the time I lived there, growing up, many from my time as a child before I joined the Force." He paused, and she knew he was thinking. Then he looked at her and a twisted smile crossed his face. "One of them was an affectionate childhood friend, only she had grown up and was no longer the child I remembered. We spent a lot of my fifty turns of Leave together. We were involved, but there were no promises of futures or feelings. No commitments. I thought about her some after I returned to duty, until you and I met for the Pitcarthy mission. After that day and after you were shot, I never thought about Milna again—not until I received a message in late August."

Cheral listened, feeling the weight of Kiile's mood and words. "So she has finally found you and told you that you have a daughter."

"No," Kiile said, his voice still heavy. "One message was from the Force. Nevar suffered an invasion in June of this Terran year and our village, Turell, was leveled, destroyed in the initial attack. No survivors. The second message from the Force told me of Neila and that she was safe. She was visiting her grandfather in Belimoor on Somstri and he notified the Force, asking them to let me know. I received both messages—the formal assessment of the invasion and his request—on the same day when the supply freighter arrived."

"Does that mean you also lost your parents?" Cheral asked, suddenly afraid of his answer.

He nodded. "All of my siblings worked with them at the farm, and everything I have found out suggests they were killed as well."

"How terrible," Cheral said softly. "And I am hurt that after all of these years you would not share this terrible news with me."

"I thought I was being wise," he said, "by keeping it to myself and bearing it without troubling you. But I see that was wrong." He shook his head. "If I cannot make decisions as basic as these, how can I be trusted to make the right ones in combat, when people count on me?"

"That's a silly comparison," Cheral said, and waited a short moment. "What are you to do about…Neila? Is that her name? I assume her mother was killed in the attack."

"Yes," Kiile said. "She and her family were all killed. Part of Neila's grandfather's request was that I come and take the girl and care for her. Her grandfather is very old, in his fifty-third galactic year, and will not be able to support Neila for much longer."

"Have you decided?" Cheral asked.

"Yes," he said, and looked at Cheral. "I didn't know how to tell you, and you do not deserve having this burden dropped on you."

"Don't you think it is my decision whether to take up this burden or not?" Cheral asked patiently.

"She might not like you," Kiile argued.

"Well Kiile," Cheral chuckled. "She might not like you either. Especially if you act like you have been these past few months."

Kiile slowly smiled. "No, she probably would not. I know you don't, but Cheral, how am I going to raise her, support her, protect her? We are in combat."

"So, before I offer any suggestions on that," Cheral said, and leaned forward, "I want to know what you see ahead for us."

"What I see?"

"Yes. We are going to have to work together since I'm not planning on taking a different assignment," Cheral said, "and I don't think you want a different assignment, so how do you see us moving forward?"

"I would like us to be together," Kiile said.

"Like we have been?" Cheral asked and waited.

"I...want it to be more, but...how?"

"Kiile! You are exasperating! I know you don't have this much trouble making up your mind in battle. Do I have to ask for a joining? Or are you going to?"

She waited as Kiile's eyes widened and he stared at her. "Do you mean you will? After all the foolish things I've done? With all the uncertainty that I have facing me?"

"Are you asking? Or just wondering if I would?"

"No! I'm asking. Are you sure? Will you?" He was on his knees in front of her before she knew it. "Are you actually willing to watch me fail as a father, as a mate? I've never been either."

"God, thank you! Kiile, I haven't either," Cheral said with a wide smile. "I might not be very good at some parts too. We'll both have to learn how to be mates and still do our jobs, finding pleasure in our now. And, like Shara and Greg, and like Jill and Nick, and Rose and Doug, we will have to learn how to support your daughter, to become parents if that's possible, and to protect her."

Kiile stood up and pulled her to him. He kissed her slow and tenderly. When he relaxed his embrace, he said, "I think I am already mad at myself for being such a fool and waiting so long."

"You ought to be," Cheral teased, then turned serious. "I assume Neila had friends in Turell. Do you know if she was a social girl or if she spent a lot of time to herself?"

"I asked," Kiile said, but did not release his hold around her waist, "and I have been told she had a few friends, but not many. Life on Nevar was very different than here on Terra, and probably even different than on Feranni. Turell was a country village of only twelve families. They all worked from an early age and had no social time like you think of it. I am told she is an intelligent, spirited girl, moody, and of course has been depressed by the loss of her family and lack of a clear future."

"Do you have any tactical information on the threat situation around Nevar or Somstri?" Cheral asked. "Is the Zone still hot?"

"I understand it is no longer hot," Kiile said. "Marine command in the Rings said they have placed a combined force around Somstri and around Copus One, Two, and Three in the Colbr System. The Force also has two Watchers stationed near Nevar but no follow on activity has been detected."

"Have they confirmed the conditions on Nevar?" Cheral asked as a curious concern began to run around in her mind.

"Yes," Kiile said. "I also reviewed the limited video that is available. No one was left alive on the planet."

"No one? The whole planet?" Cheral asked, and stopped her questioning when he nodded. "Okay, we need to talk to Colonel Kooich about taking some time off. I want to see and *hear* Nevar and Turell first-hand before we pick up Neila."

"First," Kiile said, and checked his timepiece, "we will see the commander. If they are home and we go to the ranch, we can take care of both issues. Joining first and then the mission."

▲ ▲ ▲ ▲ ▲

"...and his jeep is full of holes from the projectile weapons they used," one of the cadets was saying when Blaire set her tray down and joined the small group taking their afternoon break in the Mess. "And the front glass is shattered and partially missing, three tires flat."

"Whose jeep?" Blaire asked as she slid into a chair and scooted up to the table.

"One of the local deputies," the man beside her said as the first speaker continued.

"They put it in a back corner of the storage area until a replacement comes."

"Which deputy's was it, Marc?" Blaire asked the man two years her junior. "All of the deputies have jeeps except for two."

"I didn't get a name, Blaire," Marc said, and glanced at her. "I heard about the incident and saw them moving the jeep on my way to our morning session. One of the deputies down south, I think."

"I'll find out," Blaire said, and started eating her cup of soup. "Dad will know who. Do you know if the deputy is all right?"

"Someone said he was wounded," Marc said, "and that Captain Kiile got him in Medical as soon as they got there."

'WL-One?' she asked when the conversation reached a lull and everyone was concentrating on their meal. *'Contact Mandy, please.'*

'Yes?' Blaire heard Mandy's words when she activated her earpiece.

'Mom. It's Blaire,' she said. *'I just heard one of the deputies got shot up last night. Do you know which one and if he's okay?'*

'Blaire.' WL-One passed Mandy's surprise to her empathically. *'It's good to hear you. It seems like a lot longer than*

30

just a week. Yes. Sam's dad down west of Grants. Your dad says the same fella that set up the attacks on the Malone and Jordan places set up an ambush. Thad's remote warned him and he ducked, but a couple of bullets hit him in the side. Everyone says he'll be okay in a few days.'

'That's good,' Blaire said. 'Does Sam know?'

'I'm sure he does. Wally picked up Betti and took her to be with Thad. Sam and Glory stayed here with their aunt.'

'Thanks, Mom. Please give them my sympathies. I've got to go. I'll try to talk with you later tonight.'

'Okay, dear. Whenever you have the time. Love you.'

'Love you too, Mom.'

"I hear you're going to start flight training Monday," Marc was saying when Blaire brought herself back to their conversation.

"What? Oh, yeah," Blaire said. "I got a note from Major Iims just before I got here. How'd you hear so soon?"

Marc smiled. "Just have to be in the right place at the right time. I heard Colonel Kooich talking with Major Iims at breakfast this morning."

Blaire chuckled. "I guess it's hard to keep secrets around here."

"Yeah," Marc said, and smiled. "Especially from cadets who are curious and nosy sorts anyway."

▲ ▲ ▲ ▲ ▲

"STSX?" Greg asked out loud to the great room as he helped Shara, Matti, Cara, and Kym straighten up the room. "Have you been able to get a connection with the director?"

'YES. HE IS AWAKE NOW AND WILL BE AVAILABLE AS SOON AS THE CAPTAIN AND THE MAJOR ARRIVE.'

"He woke the Director up," Greg said, and glanced at Shara, knowing she had *heard.*

31

"I'm glad the Director doesn't take offense when his subordinates decide to upset the normal order of things." Shara chuckled. "Matti? Can you let us use the communicator for the remotes?"

"Sure, Mrs. Shara," she answered. "Do you want it now?"

"When we do the ceremony. We will need to hear the director and I don't want STSX bellowing from outside."

'I DO NOT BELLOW.'

Greg and Shara looked at each other and laughed.

"What can we do?" Sedona and Sierra asked together as they stopped at the end of the loveseat.

"I think we have it under control, loves," Shara said as she stood up in front of the fireplace and stretched. "Oh, I know. Can either of you find the digital recorder? They might like a few pictures for keepsakes."

"Sure," they said in unison.

"We know where Dad put it last," Sierra said with a smirk.

"When he didn't want us using it anymore," Sedona added as they hurried down the hallway.

"We may be able to hide the words," Shara said, "but we sure can't hide what we do."

"Wouldn't want to, love," Greg said, and smiled at the hallway. "They need to know where we are every second, and we them."

Greg turned around at the sound of the back door opening and waved at Hench, Leeana, and Tayn as they entered.

"I'd call it spur of the moment," Hench said, "but taking twelve years to make up his mind isn't exactly quick."

"I thought marines were quick and punctual," Leeana said with a chuckle. "But it does look like your *clarification* this morning worked."

"Here it is, Mom," the girls said together, sounding like they were enjoying the ability to speak in unison. "Dad hid it in the vault we aren't supposed to know about."

Shara stopped, startled. "You know about the vault? And you can open it?"

"Yeess," they said, uncertain if they had said too much.

"For about a year now," Sedona said.

"We *watched* you," Sierra continued, "when you exchanged your Kaasprs for recharged ones. For a long time, we wondered what you kept in your front pocket, but as we began to *hear* and realize things weren't as safe as we thought, we *watched* you so we could learn more about what's happening. I hope you're not mad at us."

Shara hugged them both. "No, loves. We're not mad at you. Just surprised at how resourceful you both are. But when you have questions like that, come and ask us. Don't feel like you have to snoop around to find answers. That will also help us understand what you know and maybe help us tell you things you do need to know."

Leeana looked at Tayn, and Shara thought he suddenly looked a bit sheepish.

"The same goes for you, young man," Hench said gently. "There is no subject we can't talk about. And if we don't have the answer, we'll get it, for you or together with you."

Tayn nodded as the back door opened again and Jill, Nick, and Cheyenne came in.

"Did someone say there was going to be a joining?" Jill asked as they stopped in the living room.

"The happy couple isn't here yet," Sedona said bluntly. "Hey, Chy. What did you think about the lesson today?" Sedona asked and she and Sierra caught Cheyenne's arms and moved to the dining room table. "Hey, Tayn, want to play cards?"

⌃

Greg was about to ask STSX for a status on Kiile and Cheral's whereabouts when the back door opened and Cheral and Keli stepped in, wearing their Blues, with Kiile in camos behind them.

"Sorry we're late," Kiile said. "But Colonel Mooren called for backup and Cheral had to fly out and meet them."

"What happened?" Greg asked as he looked at Kiile and then at Cheral.

"Franni sensed that Don Nikle fellow and started following him west out of the south valley," Cheral explained as they found places to sit. "But somewhere west of the mouth, over near the state line, she lost him."

"Lost him?" Shara asked, surprised, and looked at Cheyenne, remembering her remarks during their afternoon lessons.

"Yes," Cheral said. "His sense went very mottled and weak and she called for backup. She called for me, since I can sense people too."

"Good," Greg said. "Any luck?"

"Very little," Cheral said with a sigh. "It was like he was underground again, but his sensations kept jumping around, over a large geographic area north of the highway west of Grants."

Shara sat down and slowly looked at each of them in the room.

"We set a remote out and gave it the sense to look for," Cheral said, and glanced at Keli's reserved smile. "It'll tell me if it moves."

"That's good," Greg said. "We didn't mind waiting."

Matti stopped at the edge of the living room and nodded to Shara. "Mrs. Shara. I have the communicator for you."

Shara got up quickly and crossed the space to Matti. "Thank you, Matti. I think we're about to begin. Will you tell Cara, Kym, and Annie to join us too?"

"Yes, ma'am," Matti said, smiled, and hurried back to the kitchen.

They all gathered in the living room with Cheral and Kiile in front of the fireplace and Sierra kneeling down with the digital recorder, Greg in the officiate position, Shara beside Cheral, and Hench beside Kiile.

"STSX, please connect with the director," Greg said, and then, surprised with himself, he looked at Kiile. "Kiile? Do you have a name other than Kiile?"

"Officially, no. On Nevar, I was Kiile of Beeli, sir," Kiile said, and smiled proudly. "My father was Beeli of Brin and my mother was Srah with Beeli. And under the circumstances, I am the last, of Beelis." He looked at Cheral. "I entered the Peace Force registered as Kiile of Beeli, but somewhere the records changed and some have recorded me as Kiile Beeli, and others as simply Kiile."

"I guess the more important question is," Shara said, "what do you wish to be known as, Cheral?"

"Kiile's," Cheral said, and laughed softly as she looked at Kiile. "In his family's tradition, I'll simply be Cheral with Kiile, but the records will probably show me as Cheral Haak-Beeli to honor the lineage of both of our fathers."

"COMMANDER. THE CONNECTION WITH THE DIRECTOR IS COMPLETED. YOU MAY START THE CEREMONY," STSX said through the communicator.

▲

Matti served champagne and heavy hors d'oeuvres after the ceremony. Keli joined Tayn and the three girls with juice in long-stemmed wine glasses for the toasts, and they all made deep inroads into the finger foods. The children finally tired of the adult talk and went back into the dining room, cleared the end of the table nearest to the living room, and resumed their card game.

The adult conversation had explored Cheral and Kiile's plans to continue living at Obscure with work as usual, but Cheral admitted there was a twist and had just told Hench they needed a two-week Leave. She was about to start an explanation when Sedona reached for a card on the pick-up pile in their game and Sierra slapped her hand, saying it wasn't her turn yet. When

Sierra's hand touched Sedona's, something flashed in their minds.

"Whoa!" Sedona and Sierra said loudly in unison, and locked stares and then slowly turned to look at Kiile and then at Cheral.

"What is it?" Shara asked, startled by their outburst and their sudden focus.

"Cousin Cheral?" Sedona and Sierra asked together.

"How could they steal all of the people from a planet?" Sierra asked. "Nevar is small, but not that small. Someone would've seen them and would have fought back."

"Is Neila going to live with you at Obscure?" Sedona asked.

Cheral's mouth dropped open in astonishment and she stared at her young cousins, unable to respond, unable to say anything, her mind frozen in disbelief.

"What are you saying?" Shara asked, and quickly crossed the room to kneel beside Sierra. "Stolen? Who's Neila?"

"That..." Cheral started softly. "...is exactly what I am concerned about. I haven't even told Kiile of my fears...that the invasion might have actually been a 'collection.' I want to go to Nevar and *feel* the land. I want to *feel* the devastation. Colonel" —she looked at Hench— "I want to know if Prince Lukré or his hand has touched that land. I want to take Ani and one additional Q-Ship to evaluate the situation."

Hench studied her for a moment. "I have not heard that Nevar was invaded."

Kiile nodded and explained the message he had received in August.

"After Cheral and I talked this afternoon," Kiile said, "I began to wonder the same thing. We have to go to Somstri anyway, and stopping at Nevar is not out of the way."

"Somstri? Why Somstri?" Leeana asked.

"Kiile's daughter is there with her grandfather," Cheral said, and glanced at Kiile. "He's been asked to come and take Neila with him, to care for her. We're going to try to give her a home."

Shara looked at Greg and then back at Sedona and Sierra.

"She's fourteen, Mom," Sierra said softly. "Almost Carrie's age."

"How do you know...?" Shara whispered.

"We just do," Sierra said, and then shrugged and looked back at Cheral and Hench.

"When do you plan on going?" Hench asked with a slight smile.

"With your permission, sir," Cheral said, "and yours, Commander, Kiile can have ST12 ready to carry Ani's fighter by late tomorrow. That would allow a departure early Monday."

"Who else do you want to go with you?" Hench asked, keeping his manner official.

"I cannot have who I want," Cheral admitted, "so I would ask that you assign someone else that can feel presences."

Hench looked at Leeana, and with a nod he turned back to Cheral. "I'll review the roster with Colonel Mooren tomorrow and let you know my decision then."

"Thank you," Cheral said, and smiled.

"Kiile?" Greg asked. "How are you going to be able to be away for two weeks?"

"Seventeen, sir," Kiile said, and grinned, catching Greg's tease. "He will have full authority over Obscure and all operations. I think he will assign Thirty-two, Lieutenant Mosl, to manage the daily postings and duty assignments."

One Twenty-One
Sunday, December 3

Jill glanced up from her instruments, peered at the blowing snow and fog that diminished forward visibility to a mere quarter mile, and quickly dropped her eyes back to the three-dimensional situation display.

"Chy?" Jill asked softly. "Call Obscure and let them know we're a flight of two and tell them when we're landing."

"It's Keely, Mom," Cheyenne answered from the second seat of Apache Fifteen, Jill's Class 2 patrol fighter. "Obscure Control," Cheyenne called in her very official voice. "Apache Fifteen is a flight of two, west northwest, four miles, inbound. IFF on. Landing in three point two minutes."

"We have you, Apache Fifteen," the Controller said in response. "Colonel Mooren requests Apache Fifteen land in the launch bay, west side. The portal will be partially open when you get here. Is Apache Sixteen the other half of your flight?"

"Yes, Obscure," Cheyenne confirmed.

"Thank you. Please have Apache Sixteen land outside, near the portal hatchway."

"Apache Fifteen will land in the launch bay as requested," Cheyenne said. "Apache Sixteen will land outside." Cheyenne switched the communications terminal to standby. "Mom? Why are we landing inside?"

"Because Colonel Mooren said for us to," Jill said with a soft laugh.

As Jill guided her flight through the shield dome over Obscure, the visibility instantly increased and the space inside the dome was nearly free of falling snow and completely free of fog. She flew Apache Fifteen toward the open wedge in the launch bay portal cover and gently settled into the still air inside.

"Dad has landed," Cheyenne said as Apache Fifteen settled onto its landing struts.

Jill secured the controls and deflated the canopy seals while Cheyenne followed the onscreen checklist and switched the ship systems either off or to standby. By the time Jill cycled the latches and the two canopy sections tilted open to allow them to exit, a ground crewman had rolled an egress ladder up to the side of the fighter and secured it in place.

"Good morning, Captain and Cadet Jordan," the ground crewman said as Jill stepped off the five-foot ladder and watched as Cheyenne started down. "Looks like it might have been a bumpy ride this morning."

"Good morning, Corporal," Jill said. "It was." Jill looked around at the two Q-Ships and another Class 2 fighter in the launch bay. She glanced up as the portal cover overhead slowly rolled closed and sealed with a soft hiss. "What are they doing?"

The corporal followed Jill's gesture and turned to the other ships. "STSX12 is being fitted with the repulsion pads so it can carry a patrol fighter," the corporal said. "Colonel Mooren has asked that Apache Fifteen also be fitted with the repulsion pads."

Jill instantly knew that something was afoot and she stopped her questions. "Where does Colonel Mooren want us to meet?"

"In the Flight Ops briefing room," the corporal said and turned as Nick entered the launch bay from the corridor of steps. "He requested your presence as soon as you both arrived."

"Thank you, Corporal," Jill said, gave him a quick salute, and turned to Nick as the corporal turned and headed across the bay floor to the other ships. "Looks like I'm getting fitted for a mission," she said, catching Nick's hand with one of hers and Cheyenne's with her other. She led them toward the appropriate hatch in the north wall.

⅄

"Colonel Mooren, sir," Jill said as she stopped in the briefing room doorway and snapped a salute.

"At ease," Colonel Mooren said as he returned the salute. "Good morning to you too, Cadet Jordan. Please take a seat," he said, and gestured to the seats. He grabbed a folding chair and set it in front of the table, then sat down facing Jill. He glanced at the open doorway and focused his thoughts. *'Franni, please bring Major Haak-Beeli, Lieutenant Quil, and Captain Tigs to the briefing room. Major and Captain Glean are already on their way.'*

Cheyenne smiled and looked at Jill. *'Must be something* big, Mom. *Two Q-ships and two patrol fighters.'*

Jill looked at Cheyenne and slowly shook her head. *'Chy, you're not supposed to eavesdrop, especially not on our superiors.'*

'I wasn't,' Cheyenne defended. *'He was broadcasting.'*

About to say more, Jill turned her attention to Major and Captain Glean as they stepped in, announced themselves, and saluted the colonel. Colonel Mooren quickly gestured to the seats and asked them to sit as he pulled out another folding chair and placed it beside him.

'I bet that's for Captain Franni,' Cheyenne said with a glance at her mom.

'Quiet please,' Jill said. *'Pay attention and listen.'*

'Yes, ma'am.'

Franni entered through the doorway in the opposite wall of the room, leading Cheral and Keli in, quickly followed by Ani. They immediately took seats behind and near those already seated.

"I believe congratulations are in order, Major," Colonel Mooren began. "So congratulations to you and Kiile. I'm very

41

glad he finally asked." Colonel Mooren smiled and covered his mouth at a thought. "However he might have been convinced or reminded of his feelings. Our very best to the both of you." He straightened his shoulders and looked at the group.

"I'll keep this informal in order to keep the meeting moving and to inspire conversation," Colonel Mooren said. "Cheral has been given permission to lead a special mission to the planet Nevar, Kiile's home planet. In August, the Force discovered the planet had been besieged and the population disappeared, assumed killed. We have checked and rechecked with the Rings, and they have confirmed no activity on the surface. STSX12 and LTVC21 are taking two patrol fighters with them to investigate. With Prince Kiese's replacement, Prince Lukré, taking control in Knobaal, we have reason to suspect the population may have been stolen, not killed." He stopped at the surprise in the room and he slowly looked at each of them as they waited. "At oh four hundred tomorrow morning, Apache Flight will depart for a minimum of one week. Depending on the findings at Nevar, we expect LTVC21 and one patrol fighter to return to Shadow Base and STSX12 and the other patrol fighter will complete the second phase of the mission."

Crem looked at Cheral. "Do you wish to discuss any of the second phase at this time?"

Cheral glanced around and nodded. "Since it will become obvious, I might as well dispel any gossip or questions now, rather than later. I'll keep it short."

"Very good," Crem said, and smiled at Cheral, gesturing for her to continue.

"Unknown to Kiile before the August messages from the Rings, Kiile has a daughter. We now have a daughter, since we are now officially mated." She waited for the smiles and murmurs to die down. "She is fourteen Terran years old and was conceived by accident, obviously, before Kiile and I met, and neither of us knew of her existence until recently. She was visiting on Somstri with her elderly grandfather when the attack came, and her mother and family are among those missing or dead. Our second phase is that Kiile and I will go to Somstri and meet the girl, and at the request of her grandfather we intend to bring her back to Shadow Base and this valley to live with us. We hope the meeting and adjustment time will only take another week, but we will extend if necessary, assuming what we find at Nevar allows us to."

Cheral smiled and waited for any questions.

"Thank you, Cheral," Crem said, and glanced at the group. "I am assigning Ani to Cheral and Keli for the duration of phase one and two of this mission." He turned and looked at Jill. "And because Cheral needs someone with certain perceptive talents, I have assigned Jill to Neel and Debira for the first phase. I'm sorry to pull you away while your daughter is in training, but the mission needs you."

"Yes, sir," Jill answered calmly, though her mind was racing.

"If any of you have questions regarding phase one of the mission, please ask them now," Crem said with a smile. "If you have questions about phase two, please ask Cheral after the meeting."

The group immediately began asking questions about the reported attack and the likelihood of whole planetary populations disappearing, the possibilities of encountering scouts or observers left behind to wait on rescue attempts and so forth, and a number of similar related topics. The session lasted another forty-five minutes before Crem felt they had covered the necessary details enough for one meeting.

"Sirs," Crem said, and held up his hand. "You will have full briefs onboard tomorrow's flight. Please review the details contained therein and we can answer any additional questions you raise at that time. It is almost time for my next meeting, so I'm going to adjourn for now. Take a break, visit the Mess, and discuss the overall mission with Cheral. She is the flight leader and mission commander on this one. Thank you."

Crem and Franni rose, thanked each of them for coming, and then left the room.

▲ ▲ ▲ ▲ ▲

Wally watched Carole walk Alyssa and Ridan out to the stables so they could spend some time with the horses, hoping to wear off some of the pent-up energy the two were displaying with the coming of cooler weather. When he could no longer see them in the fog and blowing snow, he turned and, with coffee in hand, walked to the front of the living room and sat down on the blanket he and Carole had left on the large, flat rock just inside the tall windows. He turned to face the southwest and tapped his earpiece.

"WL-One, please contact Greg Malone."

A short moment passed and Greg's voice answered.

"Hey, Wally. What's up?"

"Do you have a few minutes?"

"Sure," Greg said. "Let me refill my cup. There. Shoot."

"We talked to Abe Brownly last night," Wally said softly. "It seems our man Nikle keeps coming back to Abe for information."

"What sort of information?"

"Mostly about me and the deputies. Our whereabouts and routines and so on," Wally said. "Abe claims that he hadn't seen Nikle since just before the night Thom and Eddie caught Chief Parks down by the school, the same night we captured the freighter down at the farmstead. Abe said Parks was collecting those women for Nikle." Wally paused and took a sip of his coffee. He figured Greg was doing the same. "Anyway, a few days before the attack on your ranch and the Jordans' ranch, the day after you saw him wander through town and the day we talked about him in the office, Nikle paid Abe an unexpected visit. He had just returned to the valley and was looking for information on Jill and Shar, specifically. Abe said Nikle told him he had made contact with the slavers and had promised new shipments."

"How was he going to ship them out?" Greg asked.

"Like you surmised," Wally chuckled. "Abe said he had two converted fighters they were going to use to meet a small freighter somewhere where they wouldn't be seen. He said somewhere like the backside of the moon.

"He told Abe about the death of a prince that was their prime customer, and that market had just reopened with the seating of a new prince. He talked a lot about some large battle somewhere and the prince's ship and armada was destroyed."

"Yeah," Greg said in a neutral voice. "We heard about that."

"Abe said Nikle sent four guys into town just before Thanksgiving to 'pick up some things' for him. Nikle called Abe the night before Thanksgiving to see if he had seen the 'Copper boys,' as Abe called them. They didn't return and Nikle wanted to know if he had seen them."

"Okay," Greg said. "At least we have confirmation that Nikle was the one trying to collect the children."

"Yeah," Wally agreed. "But Abe said that when Nikle started explaining what the Copper boys were doing, he told Nikle he would not help him anymore; he said he didn't want to know what Nikle was doing, and when Nikle started to ask him to go looking for them, he hung up on him. He hasn't heard from Nikle since, but thinks he probably made Nikle mad."

"Might need to keep a tail on Abe," Greg said. "I get the feeling that Nikle learned from Bernice and doesn't like anyone to disagree with him, and especially doesn't like anyone telling him no."

"Yeah. I also found out that Nikle hid out at his sister's place over the long years since we released his captives," Wally said, and took another sip of his coffee. "He only knows her first name was Bessie, probably Elizabeth, and she was a widow still using her husband's name."

"Where does she live?"

"Somewhere in the Chicago area," Wally admitted. "We've just started looking for leads to find her. Anyway, like I said,

Nikle claims to have made contact with the new slavers and is trying to set up the 'family' business again. I'll let you know if we find out any more."

"Thanks, Wally," Greg said. "We'll do the same."

▲ ▲ ▲ ▲ ▲

"They sure do make good burgers, don't they, Mom?" Cheyenne asked, more to keep the conversation going than anything else. She smiled at Sedona and Sierra.

Jill nodded and sipped her cool tea. "Are your mom and dad going to break for lunch?" Jill asked, looking at Sedona.

"They're supposed to break," Sedona said.

"But Dad said these physical tests can sometimes run long," Sierra added.

"We wanted to watch," Sedona said, "but Mom felt too many people standing around could be a distraction."

"We were getting hungry anyway, and this way we didn't have to wait on them." Sierra took another bite of her burger.

"I like the potato strings," Cheyenne continued. "But they don't really taste like potatoes."

"They aren't," Nick said softly. "They're issls, a tuber from Copus Two, one of the agricultural planets in the Colbr System. They're specially shipped in at the request of the troopers."

"What does issl mean?" Cheyenne asked without skipping a beat.

"'Bread root' is the closest translation I can get." Nick smiled at the three girls.

"They're sweeter than a potato. I like that," Sedona said. "And they fry up nice and crunchy."

"Annie says they bake up wonderfully as a substitute in gratin potatoes," Sierra commented and then chuckled. "She should call them gratin issls, instead."

46

Cheyenne looked at Jill as she swallowed a bite. "Are you going to get to go to Somstri? STSX says it's a planet in the Botuni System. But bread boot doesn't come from there."

"Will you please slow down, Chy?" Jill asked, lowering her voice as if to give Cheyenne an example. "Too many questions, too quickly."

"Sorry, Mom," Cheyenne said, and sipped her drink. "It's just exciting that you're going to get to go."

"I'm sorry I'm not as excited as you are for me," Jill said. "The problem is, it's a mission, Chy. A mission to find out what happened to a lot of missing people, and if they happen to still be alive, we'll try to figure out how to get them back home."

"Then it could be dangerous," Cheyenne said softly, and Jill nodded.

"It could be."

"Is it far away?"

Jill hesitated and looked at Nick before she answered. "Yes, dear. It's a long ways away. So far that it isn't visible in any direction in our night sky."

Cheyenne stared at Jill a long moment. "Will I still be able to *hear* you?"

"Yes," Jill said. "I understand your uncle Greg and aunt Shar talked to each other regularly from much farther away. You'll be able to *hear* me. And if I can, we'll talk every night. That way you can tell Dad what I've said."

"That's good," Cheyenne said. "And STSX can show me where Nevar and Somstri are on the star maps."

"We'll help," Sedona and Sierra said together.

Cheyenne smiled and reengaged her meal.

Suddenly the room lights dimmed and switched to red, and a soft, pulsing wail filled the room.

"What's happening, Mom?" Cheyenne asked, but Jill noted there was no fear in her tone.

"Intruders," Sedona and Sierra said softly, and glanced at

each other.

"It's a combat alert. There's a threat to the complex nearby," Jill said, and slowly started feeling the walls and beyond, turning slowly until she was facing southwest. "There are unfamiliar people in the tunnels coming from Clay and the Niles Ranch." She looked around. "Have any of you seen Kiile or Seventeen?"

"They've been dispatched, Aunt Jill," Sedona said.

⋏ ⋏ ⋏ ⋏ ⋏

Blaire closed her lesson's zippered case and started back to her apartment. She passed the large window in the wall common with the launch bay and noticed the sleeker Q-Ship was hovering in the middle of the bay, and one of the patrol fighters was slowly approaching it, closer to the floor. She hurried and stepped out through the first hatchway she came to and crossed the bay until she was only the length of a Q-Ship away. She stopped and watched, recognizing Colonel Mooren and Franni on a remote following the movements of the patrol fighter. Then the fighter turned and she saw the commander and Shara on a second remote as they slipped under the Q-Ship's pylon, checking wing clearance as the patrol fighter lined up under the QShip.

The ballet was slow and graceful and she was mesmerized, watching as the patrol fighter slowed and seemed to jiggle slightly when it stopped. Then it turned gently to its left and began to rise.

Absently she stepped forward and stopped when the fighter seemed to bump into the QShip, even though there were still a couple of feet of clear air between them. Blaire smiled when she heard Colonel Mooren comment pleasantly on the docking and then asked Captain Tigs to deplane through the belly hatch.

Blaire waited, enthralled as the belly hatch slowly withdrew inward and Captain Tigs dangled her legs through the opening.

"Just as good as all of the other dockings," Captain Tigs said to Colonel Mooren. "Do want a full deplane or are you satisfied?"

"No, you're good," Colonel Mooren said. "You've transferred to the host ship and back so many times I know you can do it in your sleep. And Major Haak has joined just as many times. I think we're all good. Alignment is good and the rigid air is set right. Do you agree, Commander?"

"Yes, Colonel," the commander said, and Blaire smiled, feeling strangely happy to have gotten the chance to see an actual docking and the preparations for a very hush-hush mission. She knew the commander and Colonel Kooich did not want any information leaks in case there had been a collection and someone was waiting for the Force to arrive.

She turned, and was almost back to the hatchway when she felt the sensation of the room shift slightly. She grabbed the jamb, steadied herself, and quickly *felt* her surroundings.

'Oh my!' she said when she touched the source of her disturbance. *'Has anyone seen Kiile or Seventeen?'* she asked suddenly without thinking. *'There are unfamiliar people in the tunnel coming this way. They are armed!'*

'Where, Blaire?' She felt the familiar touch of Shara's voice in her mind. *'I'll pass the information to them!'*

'Southwest about a third of the way to Clay. Near an intersection? Is there an intersection in the tunnels?'

'Yes. How many?'

'Twelve coming from Clay and fourteen coming from some ranch to the south.'

Suddenly the bay lights dimmed and changed to red, and all of the exit signs around the bay began to flash. Softly, a low, pulsating wail rose above the calm of a moment before.

'Thank you, Blaire. I have alerted Kiile and Seventeen and they have alerted the security checkpoints in the tunnels and dispatched three squads to drop into the tunnels behind the men.'

'Well done, Cadet,' Greg's warm voice said softly. *'Thank you.'*

49

She turned around and saw the patrol fighter had parked and Ani was on the ground running. The aft portal of the QShip was open, and Cheral and Keli were quickly following her to the hatch in the northeast bay wall. The remotes were gone but Blaire could *feel* Colonel and Captain Mooren and the commander and Shara inside the complex as they entered Security Control beyond the northeast portion of the bay walls.

'Blaire,' Shara said, '*come to Security with us.*'

▲ ▲ ▲ ▲ ▲

Seventeen hung onto the remote's handhold and peered intently into the fog and blowing snow as he led the three squads through the forest above the main tunnel shaft. Even though he could not see more than fifty feet ahead, he trusted his remote's ability to miss trees and boulders and he trusted Captain Shara's ability to lead him and his squad directly to where they needed to be. Nothing in the forest around them even hinted at the presence of the tunnel beneath their path, much less their destinations.

"Seventeen?" Shara's clear voice said in his earpiece. "Who are your squad leaders?"

"Thirty-two and Forty-two," he said in reply. "Twelve is leading the squad from Obscure down the tunnel to meet them head-on."

"Thanks," Shara said. "I'll monitor yours and Twelve's positions, Captain Tigs will monitor Thirty-two's position, and Cadet Lupis will monitor Forty-two's position. We'll let you know when you've passed the men in the tunnels. You're almost to the intersection."

"Roger that," Seventeen said, and in the next couple of minutes, his remote slowed and came to a stop among the densely spaced pines. Seventeen turned his attention to his men. "Thirty-two, Riggin leg. Forty-two, Niles Ranch leg. I'll take the Clay leg. When we've passed the intruders, enter through a maintenance hatch and close in from the rear. Twelve is coming down the main tunnel from Obscure. We want them alive if we can, so plan to use a Series Two sleep canister. Defend yourselves if necessary. Away then." Seventeen gave an appropriate hand signal, pumped his right arm, and drifted southwest into the foggy, snow-filled forest.

▲

The squads followed their leaders on their assigned legs. It seemed only a minute or two when Thirty-two heard Captain Tigs' alert, his men were clear, and he was free to enter the tunnel.

▲

Forty-two had barely gone another half mile when he heard Cadet Lupis call. "You have passed the group from Nile's Ranch. There are thirteen in a cluster, approaching the intersection. One is lagging behind. Seems to be laboring, out of shape or ailing in some manner. He has just passed the first maintenance hatch on your leg."

▲

"Seventeen," Shara's voice said suddenly. "You have passed your group of twelve."

▲

Thirty-two dismounted when his remote stopped. He scanned the ground with a hand probe, knelt down at the indication, and began shoveling the snow aside. A second marine scraped the dirt and uncovered the hatch, and the third spread a double-lined tent over them, providing a light baffle to keep the outside light from spilling into the absolute blackness of the tunnel below. He was glad it was not a bright, sunny day.

Thirty-two brushed the joint clear of debris and unlatched the panel. The second marine shorted the wires to the hinge sensor and together they slowly lifted the panel and swung it open; thankful the hinges did not give testimony to their presence. Thirty-two signaled for night-vision gear and respirators on, and then led the way down the rungs cast into the silo wall.

At the bottom, he waited as the others joined him in the small work space beside the tunnel shaft and the hatch was closed behind them. He motioned for them to follow, stepped forward into the Riggin leg of the tunnel, and started back toward the intersection.

▲

Forty-two cautiously led his squad of four into the tunnel from the Nile's Ranch and turned toward the intersection. The youngest squad leader at Obscure at only twenty Terran years old, he did not want to mess this mission up. So far, he had worked very hard in his three years at Obscure and had stayed in the commander's good graces. He sincerely wanted to keep it that way.

Knowing communications in the tunnels would not be sharp and clear, Forty-two focused on watching for the straggler between them and the main group. He listened as attentively as he could for any new orders.

Minutes passed slowly as they walked, trying to move himself and his men quietly. Cadet Lupis' voice startled him, sounding as clear as if she were right beside him, whispering. *'Fifty feet ahead. He's kneeling down, winded. A little closer and a throwing dart would do the trick.'*

Forty-two motioned to his number two and explained what Cadet Lupis had told him. He and his squad waited and watched as his number two slowly moved forward, becoming a mere shadow at the extent of their night-vision.

Finally the marine flashed his faint red signal beam and Forty-two led his squad closer; his number two was retrieving the dart when they joined up. His number three shackled the man's wrists and ankles to ensure he would still be there when they came back for him, and Forty-two signed them forward.

▲

Seventeen and his two marines followed the group from Clay, staying about fifty feet behind until they stopped at the intersection and met the group from the Nile's Ranch leg and the Riggin leg. He cautiously moved his squad closer, listening to the soft murmurs as the groups' leaders happily congratulated each other on reaching the intersection and confirming their speculations that the tunnels were no longer in use; they had not seen anyone.

"We still have ten miles to go," one of the three leaders said to the group clustered together in the wider expanse of the intersection, which had curved sections that allowed the tunnel cars to change directions and turn into any of the adjoining legs. "We need to hurry it up a little. It will be after nightfall when we get there. We will stop and rest and eat when we get to the last maintenance area, and then set a time to make an entrance."

"All three of your squads are near the intersection," Shara's voice said softly in Seventeen's earpiece. "Twelve has set up a barrier thirty feet up on his side of the intersection. If you seal each of your shafts, one Series Two from each of you will incapacitate them."

Seventeen absently nodded to himself and touched his number two. He touched the long container he was carrying and motioned for him to set it up. The marine nodded and moved forward, closing their distance to twenty feet from the intersection chamber.

▲

"Thirty-two," Captain Tigs' voice said in his earpiece. "Set up your baffle and seal the shaft. One Series Two on Seventeen's mark."

Thirty-two signaled for his number three to bring his container and set the baffle up; the marine moved forward, closing the distance between the squad and the intruders.

▲

'Forty-two,' Cadet Lupis' voice said again. 'Twelve, Thirty-two, and Seventeen are setting up their baffles as close to the intruders as they can. Use a Series Two sleep gas canister on Seventeen's mark.'

53

Forty-two looked around, still a little shaken at the clarity and closeness of the cadet's smooth, rich, confident voice.

He motioned for his number four to set up the barrier and the marine quickly moved forward, unfolded the umbrella-like baffle, expanded it until its smooth edge touched the surface of the tunnel shaft all around, and then he jerked it back to lock it in place, producing a virtually airtight barrier across the shaft. Number four opened a small flap in the barrier and punched the first two buttons on his Series Two canister.

▲

The leader of the intruders finished giving his instructions to his group and had just turned to start up the tunnel toward Obscure when someone in the group asked, "Where did these walls come from? They were not there when we came through there." He flipped a hand light on and illuminated the baffle, seeing what looked like a steel door closed across the tunnel.

"What the—?" someone started to ask when they heard a voice beyond one of the barriers yell, "Mark!"

Confused, they watched as a slender silver object shot out of a small opening in each of the barriers and dropped into their huddled midst. Someone yelled in surprise and the canisters burst within a second of each other, filling the sealed chamber with a blue haze.

Within seconds, the twenty-six intruders wilted and slumped to the floor.

▲

"Twelve," Seventeen said into his earpiece. "Intruders are sleeping. Keep your respirators on. Four minutes," he said, citing the time needed for the gas to degrade and for the air to become normal again. "Do you have sleds ready?"

"Affirmative," Twelve replied. "We have four sleds. Three for our guests and one for the squads."

"Thank you. A 'well done' to all squads and members," Seventeen said, then focused on Shara. "Captain, the tunnels are secure."

"Four minutes," Thirty-two finally announced.

"Remove and stow the baffles," Seventeen said. "Let's get our guests loaded and back to Detention and see who we have."

▲

'Nicely done, Sergeant Stial,' Cadet Lupis' voice said softly, and Forty-two turned quickly, again feeling she could be standing beside him. Puzzled, he sniffed the air, thinking he could smell her perfume. *'I'm certain the commander will agree.'*

Forty-two tapped his earpiece. "Thank you, Cadet Lupis," he said, thinking he needed to meet his cadet.

One Twenty-Two

C.3486.741

Terran Date: Tuesday, December 5

"The Rings' Dispatch says they have two Watchers parked in orbit around Nevar's only moon, Major," Keli said as Cheral guided QSTSX12 for a gentle lunar insertion. "Shall I hail them?"

"Not yet," Cheral said. "They are on the planet side of the moon. We'll drift around and see if they are veiled. Keep us sensor-blocked and IFF off."

Ani watched from the jump seat as they drifted closer to the moon and settled about the same distance out as the Watchers. Hearing the conversation, Kiile came up into the cockpit and stood on Cheral's left, backed against the cockpit bulkhead.

"Hey, Kiile. They are in formation," Cheral said. "About five spans apart, side by side. I'm not hearing any conversation."

"QKVJC5 and QMMRT17," Keli said. "Older IDs."

"They're sensor-blocked but not cloaked," Cheral said as their dark, silver-gray dots appeared, drifting above the arc of the moon. "Send an optical message to LTVC21. Let them know we're going to slip quietly into formation with the Watchers."

Keli rechecked the optical alignment and sent the message as Cheral maneuvered her flight into a left echelon position at eight o'clock.

"Very nice," Cheral said when she relaxed her grip on the controls. "ST, hold us in position. Shields full in case they get startled." Cheral smiled at Ani and then quickly scanned the *feel* around them. "We seem to be alone, Keli. Give them a hail. Whisper."

"Yes, ma'am," Keli said, and smiled. "ST, coms please." The monitor on the right-hand console brightened and Keli formed her message's words in her mind.

"Greetings, Q-KVJC5 and QMMRT17 from Apache Squadron," Keli said, and the words immediately formed in the space in front of the monitor. "Apache Four, QSTSX12 mission commander with Apache Five, Q-LTVC21 mission wing second and Apache Ten and Apache Fifteen are with you."

"G...greetings," QKVJC5 replied sleepily, and after a few moments added, "Apache... Aaah...we do not have you painted. What is your position?"

"Q-STSX12 and Q-LTVC21 are in left echelon, three spans out and one length behind," Keli explained. "We are surprised you are not cloaked."

"There has not been any activity since we arrived seven turns ago," Q-KVJC5 said. "The previous two Watchers were here fifty turns and dropped cloaking to save energy after the first twenty turns."

"IFF on," Cheral said to Keli. Then to Q-KVJC5, "I am Major Haak-Beeli and Lieutenant Quil of STSX12. I report directly to Apache Squadron Commander Stran Geaardt, and my fight-of-four was sent to investigate the planet Nevar and what happened here. Do you have any information? Or are you waiting to see if the attackers come back?"

"Thanks for the IFF, but we only see two targets. You said you are four."

"We are," Cheral said. "Back to my question?"

"We are the latest of the Watchers assigned to see if anyone returns," QKVJC5 said. "The only official information we have is that on C.3486.575 all communications with Nevar ceased. The Rings sent a recon ship out the next turn and found no signs of the population or their communications satellite infrastructure. Most of the cities and towns are rubble. On the tenth turn after the loss of communications, Headquarters dropped two remotes to fly low over the cities to determine if anyone was still alive. No people were seen."

"What about traces of them?" Cheral asked. "Clothing, bodies, vehicles?"

"No bodies, but some tatters that could have been clothing or large pieces of fabrics were spotted. If they are of clothing, the bodies that wore them would not look very good. Most of the transportation vehicles are in ruins—twisted, torn, and burnt."

"Did they find anything else?"

"Two rovers landed in two different cities," Q-KVJC5 said. "When they spotted something that interested them and went to investigate, they were destroyed."

"Mines?" Cheral asked.

"Maybe," Q-KVJC5 said. "Headquarters decided no more rovers and authorized only flyovers."

"Any other forms of life detected? Specifically animal?"

"None," Q-KVJC5 said. "We thought we might sense some of the wildlife in the wooded, non-arable land, but nothing. No flitters, no marine life, nothing."

"Did they run soil samples or crop samples?" Cheral asked.

"We do not have any information on any, if they did."

Cheral looked over her shoulder at Keli, and Keli smiled. "I'm getting an answer from the Rings now."

"Okay," Cheral said. "I think we will unpack and then go see what we can find out. Thanks for the help."

"Certainly," Q-KVJC5 said.

"Looks like the Rings initially ran daily checks on the crops," Keli said as she scanned the monitor, "while they looked for survivors. Then...Whoa!"

Cheral turned her chair to look at Keli, and Kiile drifted back to look over her shoulder.

"There were no crops!" Keli said, rereading the report page. "Sometime during that forty-five days, every edible crop on the planet disappeared. It looks like they harvested the land and left it untilled."

"Well," Kiile said as he looked at Cheral and shook his head. "You wanted to know if they were stolen. They wouldn't need food for dead people."

"Ani," Cheral said softly. "You and Jill need to suit up. We're going to go down and look around. Major Glean..." She turned her head and looked at the void where she knew Q-LTVC21 floated behind its veil. "...let's prepare to release the patrol fighters."

Tuesday, December 5

A stocky man and a slender man slipped across the yard, dim in the twilight. They stopped beside the cabin situated on ten acres just west of the highway out of Riggin where it passed the North Butte as it headed south to the Buck Canyon Switchbacks and Clay. The slender man quickly compromised the basic lock on the back door and pushed the other man in.

"You sure this is where the ex-wife of Abe Brownly lives?" the stocky man asked as he hurried into the front room and looked out through the sheer drapes at the front drive.

"Yes. Her name is Pat and he gave her this place in their divorce, over fifteen years ago," the slender man said as he checked a picture on the mantle. "I understand he even gives her money every month to make things easier for her."

"Why would he do that?"

"You figure it out," the slender man said. "If Abe did not still care about her, Mr. Nikle would not want us to send pictures to Abe of what we do to her. Mr. Nikle wants Abe to know in great detail the pain and suffering that is caused when someone refuses his demands."

Headlights flashed through the front window and the slender man took a video recorder from his jacket pocket.

"Get in the coat closet," he said to the stocky man. "Be ready when she hangs up her coat. I'll set the recorder."

The stocky man opened the closet, pushed the few coats aside, then eased himself in backwards and closed the door. The slender man chose a hiding place and set the recorder on an end table facing the closet. When the back door opened, he pressed the button on the recorder and slipped down behind the large chair.

The woman closed the door behind her, switched the dining room light on, and slowly looked at the mail she had retrieved from the box by the road. Finished, she dropped the stack onto the kitchen table and slipped her heavy coat off and went to the closet.

When she opened the door to reach for a hanger, the stocky man's right fist slammed into her face. Her head snapped back, her knees buckled, and she tumbled backwards, collapsing in a sprawl on the floor.

The slender man picked up the recorder, moved for a clear view of the woman, and followed the stocky man's movements as he pulled her arms up, rolled her over, and quickly tied her wrists behind her. He straightened her legs and tied her ankles, then rolled her onto her back again, stuffed a rag in her mouth, and tied another around her head, the bulky knot holding the first deep and secure.

The slender man smiled, still recording. "Put her in the truck. There's a good place for us to spend some time with her, up in the rocks just north of the South Butte."

"Should I get her coat? That thin dress won't keep her very warm."

"I do not want her to be warm." The slender man stared at the stocky man and shook his head. He handed him the recorder, keeping it pointed at the woman. He reached down and grabbed the neck of her dress and, with a jerk, tore the front open to the hem. "Now she does not even have a thin dress. Put her in the truck."

▲ ▲ ▲ ▲ ▲

On their way home from Obscure, STSX had just crossed the Deerskin River north of the Double J when Shara turned at a sudden sensation. They were all looking at each other and Sedona said, "Someone screamed. *Feels* like a woman in trouble."

"Yes," Greg said, and swung STSX's nose to the southwest. "Sedona, take the chair. Follow us. Sierra, contact Twelve. Get some of his troopers and a medic."

"We're on it," they said in unison.

Shara jumped down the rungs to the lower deck and hurried to the aft portal. "Release Seven and Eight. We're going down to help."

Sedona was in the chair, strapped in and focused on the desperate woman's cries before Greg reached the lower deck. "Open the aft portal," she said.

▲

Greg and Shara *saw* the men before they reached the small clearing trampled out of the snow between the rocks where they brought the woman and beat her. Seeing her bared, tormented, and abused by the men, Shara felt a surge of fiery indignation, remembering the night many years before when two men had dragged her into the woods east of the ranch and joined up with two others, knowing they would have had their way if Greg had not rescued her. And now, filled with an overwhelming sense of urgent purpose, she was paying them back.

They both stepped off the remotes behind the men and unveiled as they jumped forward. Greg grabbed the slender man and jerked him up, tossing him aside. He crashed headfirst onto a large boulder. The man's yell was short, accompanied by a second yell as Shara grabbed the stocky man and jerked him up, tossing him back over her head. He hit a smaller boulder with a loud snap and fell limp.

Shara moved forward, knelt, and whispered softly to the frantic woman. Shara touched her forehead, *sensing* her condition and pain.

She gently untied the rag around her head, removing the wad from her mouth, and then turned the woman sideways and cut the cord around her wrists. The woman leaned forward, gasping for air, and hugged Shara with all of her strength, trembling in cold, fear, and pain.

Shara glanced at Greg and saw him jerk the pants off the slender man. He turned and handed them to her. *'Have her put these on. I'll get his coat.'*

Shara helped the woman stand, and had the pants on her when Greg wrapped the man's heavy coat around her. He turned back, bound the slender man, and as he stood up, Twelve and two marines stepped out of the darkness.

"Thanks for coming, Twelve," Greg said. "Is one of these your medic?"

"No," Twelve admitted. "Our medic is on his way. Should he come here?"

"No," Shara said, and turned to look at the woman. "You're Pat Brownly, aren't you?"

The woman nodded slowly, uncertain.

"We'll take her home," Shara said. "You take care of these two. Can you do a mind scan on that one?" she asked, pointing to the slender man.

"No," Twelve reluctantly admitted.

"Okay, Greg" —she looked at him— "do a scan and then come and meet me at her place. It's a very short remote ride. Twelve, have the medic come there. Greg, help me get Pat onto Seven."

Greg turned back to the two men and glanced up. *'Caiti. Follow your mom and hover over Pat's place. Stay cloaked and listen to the surroundings—for anything that shouldn't be there.'*

'*Yes, sir,*' Sedona and Sierra said together.

Greg checked the man Shara had thrown aside, confirmed his broken neck, and then turned to the slender man. "All right. Let's see who sent you and why you were doing what you were doing."

▲

Shara, followed by one of the marines, propped Pat up and half carried her into the cabin and to the one bedroom across from a bath in a short hallway. The marine closed the door behind them, turned, and took a stance at the mouth of the hall.

Shara asked and Pat told her where her nightgowns were, and Shara dressed her in one and laid her back on the bed.

"I want you to close your eyes now and sleep," Shara said as Pat stretched out on the bed. Shara pulled the spread over her and placed the palm of her hand gently over Pat's forehead. "The medic will be here in a few minutes to care for you, but now you need to sleep." Shara pushed the *command* to sleep and felt Pat relax and gently go limp.

She waited, and in a few minutes she *felt* the medic as he arrived by remote, dropped from a transport that stopped beside STSX. The marine knocked on the door and let the medic in when Shara answered.

Greg arrived, and they sat in the living room holding each other's hands until the medic finally came out of the bedroom and sat down with them.

"She's very lucky, Commander," he said. "Very bruised, but surprisingly, no broken bones. They were thorough, mistreating her in all of the usual, brutal ways people like them demean a woman, but she will recover physically. Mentally, I am not sure. I suggest you minimize her memory. She'll know she was attacked and raped, but you should remove the memories of the brutality and the pain, leave that hazy and unfocused, vague."

"Certainly. We can do that," Greg said softly. "I'll explain

64

what happened to Wally and have him bring Abe here to be with her when she wakes up. I think they are still on good terms with each other."

"Very good," the medic said, and stood up. "I did a quick blood check to be sure, and gave her a time-release medication. By morning the meds will have done what they can and the rest will be up to her."

"Thank you," Greg said, and shook the medic's hand.

The marine escorted the medic out the back door and Shara went in to see Pat. Greg looked up and checked on the girls. *'I know you were listening, and I wish there was a way to spare you the details of something this brutal, but I can't, loves. Stay focused and we'll be up as quickly as we can. Let me know if you have any trouble.'*

'Who else?' they asked together, and Greg, hearing them repeat Shara's usual response to him, felt their spirits lift a little.

He refocused his thoughts and said, *'Five, contact Wally.'*

▲ ▲ ▲ ▲ ▲

Deputy Thom Baine was waiting at the cabin when Wally and Abe arrived. He gave Abe the rundown, omitting those of how Pat was rescued and other details Abe should not know when Wally led him inside and took him to Pat.

In the shadows cast by the trees in the first moonlight they had in days, Greg walked Shara toward the remotes. Shara stopped, feeling Greg's troubled thoughts.

"What is it, love?"

"Obviously," Greg said with a sigh, "the men were sent by Nikle. He was going to use the videos we found, and more, to show to Abe—to coerce Abe into doing whatever he asks, demands of him."

"What more were they going to do?" Shara asked, not certain she wanted to know.

"I think the slender man had a hand in your mother's death," Greg said heavily. "The scan revealed he was planning on the same tortures and dismemberments you found in Bernice's scan. They were going to kill her in the same brutal way they killed your mother."

Shara sighed and looked at him, forcing herself away from those memories. "I'm sure glad we *heard* her in time."

"I am too," he said, and hugged her. "Now let's go up and congratulate Caiti on her first, though short, solo."

"Does that mean Coli takes us home?" Shara smiled at the happier thought.

"Yes, Bren. I think it does."

▲ ▲ ▲ ▲ ▲

Sergeant Stial saw Seventeen in the corridor outside the Mess, finishing a discussion with another marine. He stopped and waited at a discreet distance, and when they finished and the marine walked away, Sergeant Stial stepped forward.

"Seventeen? May I have a word with you?" he asked.

"What do you need, Sergeant?" Seventeen asked.

"Sunday afternoon, when we were in the tunnels," Sergeant Stial began. "My contact was a Cadet Lupis. First, sir, I was surprised at being given a cadet as my contact, but then I was more surprised at her clarity and confidence in knowing where we were, where the intruders were, and what everyone else was doing."

Seventeen chuckled softly. "So you were surprised. Because she is a cadet? Because she knows what she's talking about? Because she is a she? Or because she has a pretty voice?"

Sergeant Stial smiled. "Maybe all of the above, sir. I have not met the cadet and I am wondering if you can tell me anything about her."

"Aah," Seventeen said, and gestured to the Mess. "Coffee?"

"Sure."

They got their coffees and Seventeen led him to a small table.

"I have to warn you, Forty-two, Cadet Lupis is special," Seventeen said as they sat down. "Cadet Lupis? What can I tell you about her?" He smiled and looked at the Sergeant. "She is the daughter of a local deputy under State Marshal Wally Lima. She grew up influenced by law enforcement and has a very high sense of moral right. Captain Casi began her physical hand-to-hand training and let our marines finish the lessons. Cadet Lupis scored ninety-eight to one hundred percent in all hand-to-hand combat scenarios, armed and unarmed, and completed that phase of her training in a week. Captain Casi trained her on Kaasprs, Brekshiirs, Caldite Darts—"

"Brekshiirs?"

Seventeen nodded and continued. "And she is deadly accurate. As accurate and quick as Captain Casi and Captain Cera Dnar. Since last Friday, she has devoured all of the pre-flying navigation lessons and holds a score of one hundred percent in testing, completing that syllabus on Sunday. Yesterday she started flight training with Iims, and he expects her to solo this week. The commander plans to move her into Q-Ships as quickly as he can after that."

"Are you serious?" Sergeant Stial asked, disbelieving. "All of that in less than two weeks?"

"Oh." Seventeen smiled. "Cadet Lupis is the first one that knew we had intruders Sunday. She was watching the commander and Colonel Mooren preparing for their mission and sounded the alert."

Sergeant Stial stared at Seventeen and slowly questioned his decision to meet this cadet.

"If you're wondering if you're in her league?" Seventeen continued. "Just remember she is a young woman that will not suffer fools. She may enjoy the company of polite and intelligent sergeants, and again she may not. She'll see through you in a heartbeat if you're not honest, truthful, and respectful. I think there are a lot of our fellow marines that are beginning to think she measures up to Captain Casi very well. Give her the same courtesy and go and talk to her. She's really very nice."

"She seemed so," he said softly. "Do you know where I can find her? What she looks like?"

Seventeen finished his coffee and returned his empty mug to the used dishes bin. "Judging by the time, I suspect she's studying advance flight combat maneuvers." He smiled at the sergeant. "She is most likely the only redhead in the flight training library dissecting Captain Casi's infamous maneuvers. Good luck, Sergeant."

Seventeen smiled and walked out of the Mess, turning down the corridor toward Billeting.

Sergeant Stial swallowed, straightened his shoulders, and followed the corridor in the opposite direction toward the flight-training areas.

▲

Blaire was deep in the descriptions and details recorded from Shara's attack on the Kyddellan battlecruisers and the firing sequence she devised for the quad-cannons to break through their shields and open a clear path for a destructive shot into the ship. The sequence saved a canon for lesser, normal targets like fighters. She glanced from the first monitor to the second, comparing notes and similarities between Casi's different combat engagements. She recorded her own thoughts and memory notes in her personal digital pad.

Blaire was not sure how long he had been standing behind her in the portal when she first noticed he was there. She did not turn, but continued reading and writing notes, but *felt* his debate as he waited, trying to decide if he should interrupt her not. Finally, without looking up from her reading and without turning around, Blaire asked out loud, "Sergeant, are you just going to stand in the portal and make everyone wonder what you're doing?"

"I'm sorry," he said softly, surprised, and clasped his hands behind him as he stepped farther into the room. "I wasn't sure if I should interrupt—"

"That's obvious," she said, and slowly sat up from her hunched position and turned in her chair. She extended her hand. "It's nice to finally meet you, Sergeant Stial."

"Thank you," he said, and shook her hand in return. "How'd you know?"

Blaire chuckled and pushed out the chair beside her.

"Sit," she said, and smiled at him. "I don't bite unless I have reason to. I probably need a short break anyway."

He pulled the chair out a little more and sat down, not letting his posture completely relax.

"Thank you," he said again. "After the incident in the tunnels on Sunday"—he smiled—"I wanted to meet you and say thank you for your assistance."

"Oh," she said, and waited.

"Well," he said after a moment of awkward silence, "the whole experience Sunday surprised me some."

"How was that?"

"Listening to your very polished and confidently delivered information," he said, and she felt him thinking, trying to say what he wanted to say correctly, "I was surprised when I remembered you were a cadet. You sounded like you have had a lot more experience than a cadet is expected to have."

"I grew up an only child in an adult world, in a family where clear and knowledgeable communications were essential," she said, and smiled. "If you didn't know what you wanted, were talking about, or explaining, the discussion was over before it started."

"I heard you are the daughter of Deputy Lupis in Riggin," he said. "I can see where that would have its own set of rules and circumstances growing up. My parents and older siblings were military. Maybe similar."

"Maybe," Blaire said, and smiled as he inhaled deeply. "Something wrong?"

"No. No," he said, and looked puzzled. "Your fragrance."

"You don't like my perfume?" Blaire asked, and looked at him, curious.

"No, it's very nice, but I swear I smelled that same fragrance in the tunnels Sunday," he said, his expression still puzzled. "It seemed like I smelled it when you spoke to me, and somehow, I figured it had to be yours. But how?"

"Being an empath," Blaire said, "you'll *smell* and *feel* as well as *hear* someone when they talk to you."

"An empath?" he asked, startled, and slowly smiled, shaking his head. "I'm not. That's why I use the earpiece and links to the remotes."

She shrugged and turned back to her monitors. *'Okay, if that's what you think. Do they work good underground?'*

"You know underground communication is sometimes garbled and distorted," he said, and realized she had turned back to her work.

'Yeah, our conversation was very garbled on Sunday,' she said, and smiled to herself, feeling him as he stared at her, remembering how clear her words were.

"Wait a minute," he said, confused.

She turned her head and looked him in the eyes, holding her lips together, and asked, *'Was it as clear as it is now?'*

He did not answer immediately and she knew he was still watching her lips. His thoughts drifted from surprise in hearing her words to a pleasant feeling as he watched her, and then he remembered himself.

"How'd you do that?" he asked.

'Do what?'

'That?'

Slowly she curled her lips into a soft smile and warmed the tone of her thoughts. *'I think my lips look nice too.'*

She switched off her monitors and closed her digital pad and slowly stood up. *'I'm Blaire,'* she said. *'I'm tired and need to call it a day. Give me your first name and I'll have dinner with you in the Mess tomorrow evening. We can talk then.'*

He stared at her and formed his thoughts. *'Blaire? That's pretty. I'm...I'm Luc. Named after my father's father. Dinner with you would be nice. May I walk you to Billeting now?'*

'From one empath to another empath,' Blaire said, and smiled as she picked up her pad, *'I think I'd like that.'*

▲ ▲ ▲ ▲ ▲

"ST," Cheral said, "please drop our veils. Remain sensor blocked and shielded."

Q-LTVC21 coalesced in the space beside and behind Q-STSX12 and they *felt* Q-KVJC5 and Q-MMRT17's surprise when they saw the ships and the red stripes, instantly confirming they were indeed Apache Squadron fighters. Cheral also knew they had never seen Q-Ships carrying patrol fighters.

"Keli, take the chair, please," Cheral said, and unbuckled. As she drifted to the central compartment, she gave Kiile a quick kiss and then hurried down to the lower deck.

"Excuse me, sir," Keli said as she slipped past Kiile and settled into the pilot's chair.

Kiile made room for her to pass and smiled, watching her as the seat adjusted and she fastened the straps.

"Have you had your celebration for soloing yet?" Kiile asked as she looked at LTVC21. "I should know without asking, but I've let myself be a little distracted and can't remember."

Keli smiled but kept her eyes focused on LTVC21's aft portal. "No, sir. It should have been today, Terran time. Maybe when we return to Shadow Base, unless the excitement has worn off by then."

"Seal the inner airlock panel, please, ST," Cheral said from

71

the lower deck.

Keli saw Major Glean and Captain Dnar slip out of LTVC21's aft portal and drift to Apache Fifteen, knowing Cheral and Ani were doing the same beneath STSX12, monitored by Captain Debira.

In four minutes flat, Cheral announced she was back inside and STSX12 sealed the outer airlock panel. Another two passed as Cheral unsuited and drifted up through the floor portal into the central compartment.

"Fighter status, ST," Keli said, knowing it would be Cheral's first request.

"APACHE TEN AND APACHE FIFTEEN ARE READY FOR POWER UP."

Keli nodded absently and relayed the 'Power Up' order.

"Power coming online," Ani said. "Apache Ten is ready to run the initializing checklist."

"Apache Fifteen is powered and commencing initialization," Cera's voice said in response.

After a short moment, Ani announced, "Apache Ten is mission ready."

"Apache Fifteen is mission ready. We're ready when you are."

"Release them, Keli," Cheral said, and smiled, seeing her still focused on LTVC21 and Apache Fifteen.

"Disengage," Keli said, and immediately they felt the gentle push as the repulsion pads pushed Apache Ten away from STSX12. She watched as Apache Fifteen slowly separated from LTVC21 and drifted into its place in the echelon. Apache Ten drifted into view as Ani maneuvered into her place between Apache Four and Apache Five.

"APACHE FLIGHT IS MISSION READY, LIEUTENANT."

"Take us down for a closer look, Keli," Cheral said, and smiled as she turned back to the coms. "KVJC5, Apache Flight is breaking formation. Alert us if you see anything we should know about."

"We will," KVJC5 said. "It was a pleasure to meet Apache Flight. Your squadron is much talked about and it's an honor to be of assistance. Good hunting."

"Thank you KVJC5 and thank you MMRT17," Cheral said, and switched the coms to standby.

"My thought is a wide line abreast for a first pass at moderate altitude," Keli said, thinking out loud as she turned the pilot's chair to forward facing. "Apache Flight, Apache Four will lead. Mark." She gently pushed the thrust levers forward and Apache Flight slowly drifted up and away from the Watchers.

Keli checked their separation as they moved forward. "Cloaking on," she said, and Apache Flight quickly faded and disappeared, as if absorbed into the vast field of stars.

⋀ ⋀ ⋀ ⋀ ⋀

"Apache Fifteen," Captain Debira said sharply. "There's a bright glint from that mound ahead and to our left. About forty miles. Did you see it?"

"Yes," Cera said. "I'm headed over that way now."

Debira waited, watching the distant mound as LTVC21 steadily flew forward, scanning a wide swath of the planet's surface. Together, the two Q-Ships had been able to scan a hundred-mile-wide swath, focusing on the land masses and skipping the water covering about forty percent of the surface. Resting two hours between passes, they had completed six passes parallel to the planet's equator at different latitudes and were now completing their third polar pass. The glint was not abnormal, as the ships had seen one city or town in ruins after another. In most cases, the shiny glints were unbroken windowpanes or painted signage that had somehow escaped the soot and soil of the attacks.

They had passed over the small town of Turell, almost not

recognizing the widely scattered debris on the scorched land as the town. It was more than just disheartening to see so little of the town left, and Cheral watched, feeling Kiile's growing despair. He turned more and more somber and withdrawn with each unfruitful hour of searching, and Cheral tried to console him but knew there was little she could give him. Her own despair slowly turned into a growing yet contained rage as the hours of unchanging desolation drifted past them.

"I guess if you wanted to tell the worlds that you had the power," Keli said softly from the nav-com compartment, "this would be a convincing banner to wave at them." She looked forward. "Major? Do you want to take a break? You've been up for almost three hours."

"Sure," Cheral said, and swiveled the chair to aft facing. "But Keli, why would anyone think taking over an undefended world was flexing any kind of real power? This was just sneaking in, unseen in the dark, and taking what you can. No one seemed to object. No one stood up in their defense. No one has responded until now, and that's only to look around and see what they left behind. No one's being held responsible for this atrocity." Cheral stopped, realizing she was becoming too emotional. She wanted to blame it on fatigue, but knew it was more—a lot more. "Let's finish this pass and then go up and settle into a suitable orbit for some needed rest." She caught Kiile's hand and started down the rungs to the lower deck. "I'm about done and I know everyone else is. Do you want some tea?"

"That would be good," Keli said as she took her place in the pilot's chair. "We've only got about another hour, then we can go up and recover Ten and Fifteen. They have to really be tired."

"It's nothing," Cera's voice said in the coms. "Large city, more shiny debris. I'm joining back up."

"You sound funny," Cheral said. "What is it?"

"I'm not sure," Cera said. "There was something about that city. I felt the same...same...I'll call it oddness, when I checked on the last big city. I can't put my finger on it." She hesitated a

74

long moment. "Ask Kiile how many big cities there are."

Cheral did and then answered. "Twenty, planet-wide. And he said there was a space port, a huge shipping depot on the equator, opposite side of the planet from Turell. We went over it on our first pass today, but we'll do a deeper scan of it and the cities tomorrow."

ᴧ ᴧ ᴧ ᴧ ᴧ

Greg and Shara sat down on the loveseat in front of the fireplace and motioned for the girls to join them. Sierra settled on Greg's lap and Sedona on Shara's.

"We are so happy for you two," Greg said softly, and hugged Sierra. "You took command of STSX like you've done it all your lives."

"Thanks, Dad." Sedona smiled. "But it wasn't really a real solo was it?"

"It was real," he said. "I gave you specific things to do and you did them. You're right, though, it wasn't like the tests we normally give, but it had all of the necessary elements. If you want the normal check ride, we can do that tomorrow when I solo Cheyenne."

The girls smiled and looked from Greg to Shara and back to Greg.

"Chy's going to solo tomorrow?" Sedona asked.

"That's great!" they said together when Greg nodded and put his finger over his lips, reminding them to not say anything to Cheyenne.

Shara pulled Sedona close and Greg reached out and took Sedona's hand as he hugged Sierra again. Sierra took Shara's hand and they sat quietly for many long moments in their family embrace.

"We want you to know we are very proud of you two," Shara finally said. "You were both very professional tonight, credits to yourselves, your training, and to your family. We—"

"They were going to kill her, weren't they? The men?" Sierra asked, suddenly looking Shara straight in the eye.

Shara gave the barest nod. "Yes, love. I'm afraid they were."

"Why?" Sedona asked. "What did she do? I thought she just worked at the school. No social life and not many friends, but she's okay."

Greg explained that she had not done anything wrong except once being married to Abe, who had made a few mistakes in his life. He tried to be delicate as he explained how Abe had helped the Family and the Council of Elders over the years, had straightened out in the last ten years or so, and that he had told Don Nikle he would not help him anymore.

"That made him mad, right? Mister Nikle?" Sierra asked. "And he knew Abe still liked Pat, right?"

"Yes, love," Shara said.

"So he wanted to force Abe to help by taking away something he knew was important to Abe," Sedona summarized.

"Basically, yes," Greg agreed.

"I'm glad you got there in time," Sierra said, and squeezed Greg again. "It was scary at first—"

"But we knew you could stop them," Sedona finished. "When you went down, it wasn't scary anymore. We knew you could make her safe again."

"And the medic said she would heal quickly. That's good too," Sierra said.

"I knew you would be listening to us and the medic," Shara said. "Did you understand everything he was saying?"

"Yes, Mom," they said softly together.

"They were very bad men and deserved to be punished," Sierra said, "for what they did to her."

"Yes, they were," Greg said. "Are you two going to be all right? After seeing everything tonight?"

"We think so," they said together. "We know we're as safe as you can make us. We know there's bad in the world and you've taught us to defend ourselves and our friends and you're always close by, always here for us."

Sedona yawned suddenly and Sierra laughed.

"Okay, you two," Shara said, and helped Sedona up. "I think it's time to call it a night."

She got up and helped Sierra up from Greg's lap. When Greg stood, they each hugged a daughter and guided them to the hallway.

"The ranch is secure, all locked up," Shara continued. "Meara and Matti and Dusty are in for the night, Hank and the hands are in, the shields are active, our ships are listening, and the remotes are on patrol. I want you two to dream about soloing and flying tomorrow and nothing else."

One Twenty-Three
C.3486.742

"Neel?" Debira asked as she leaned closer to the monitor. "Zoom, please, LT. Neel, have you looked at any of these images?"

"No," he admitted with a yawn as he floated up into the central chamber.

"Yesterday we scanned three of the major cities and a number of the smaller towns and villages," Debira said, and re-centered the image LTVC21 had enlarged for her. "And Cera mentioned the strange reflections she saw when she checked on the city near the end of the day. Look at this one."

Major Glean stepped into the nav-com compartment and leaned over Debira's shoulder, catching her other shoulder and hugging her gently.

"What have you found, Deb?" he asked, and looked closely at the image.

"This is near city center, best I can tell, of the third city we scanned," she said, and pointed to a bright spot. "Enhance, please, LT."

The image sharpened and cleared some, but was still fuzzier than she wanted.

"If this is the best resolution we can get, we shouldn't be here," she said disgustedly, and leaned closer.

"THIS WAS FROM HIGH ALTITUDE USING THE LOW-ALTITUDE IMAGER WHEN THE PASS WAS FINISHED. THE SCAN WAS NOT OPTIMIZED AS MAJOR HAAK-BEELI PLANS FOR TODAY," LTVC21 said in justification.

"Thanks, LT," Neel said. "What's the bright spot?"

"It looks like a little more than half of an octagon," Debira said, "with five surrounding panels showing out from under the rubble. About thirty feet in diameter. Previous city, please, LT."

The image changed and Debira had LTVC21 zoom in on another bright spot.

"This one, Neel," she said softly, "is the same size and shape. Another octagon with surrounding panels. The rubble covers less than a third of it. LT? Does the pattern repeat? Is it completely regular?"

"YES."

"In the first city," Debira said, "I only saw two of the surrounding panels, but after seeing the other two and from the shape, I'm sure it's another unit like them. LT? Can you pose any purpose or identity for these units?"

"NO," LT said.

"Compose a summary for Cheral and send her your thoughts, Deb," Neel said. "I think we can justify a thorough scan of the cities today."

⚓

Jill rolled over, constrained by the netting over her light blanket. She opened her eyes slowly, blinked, and stared at the empty berths across the aisle from her. Puzzled at first, she slowly remembered where she was and that she was Cera today. She gently reached out, searching for Cheyenne's *feel*, and was surprised to *see* the forward view out of a Q-Ship, a fully displayed instrument panel in front of her and a three-dimensional map display to her right, almost to the panel. She *felt* Cheyenne's mind in full concentration as the view before her rolled inverted and the nose of the ship tucked toward the planet.

Suddenly, she realized her daughter was flying a Q-Ship! She was soloing! She was flying exercise maneuvers!

Cera threw the containment net off, slipped out from under the blanket, and pushed herself to the central compartment. She looked up and shouted, "Keely's soloing! Right now! She's flying STSX1!"

Neel's face appeared in the opening, looking down at her. "Really? She's soloing?"

"Right now! I was going to talk to her, but she's so full of determination and so focused! I just had to watch! My little girl is flying STSX1!"

"Oh, that's so wonderful," Debira said, her head appearing beside Neel's. "We have another member of the Ladies' Brigade! Come up, Cera, we have something to show you too!"

Cera started to climb the rungs and stopped. "In a moment. I just got up and nature's calling."

"Grab some clothes and something to eat and come up as soon as you can," Neel said, and their heads moved away from the opening.

Wednesday, December 6

"Calm down, Chy," Nick said as Cheyenne, dressed in her Blues, fidgeted on the loveseat beside him. "Relax. Making yourself nervous will only make it harder."

"I know, Dad," she said, then leaned back against the cushions and glanced at Sierra, patiently waiting, sitting in her dad's favorite overstuffed chair.

Sierra looked away from the fire in the fireplace at her dad and mom, calmly sipping their coffee at the dining room table.

Cheyenne turned without getting up and asked, "Uncle Greg? Is Tayn flying this morning too?"

"I believe he is," Greg said cheerfully. "Hench said he had something new to show him today."

"New?" Cheyenne asked. "What?"

"I'm not sure. She's back," he said, and looked up.

Sierra and Cheyenne got up and moved to the dining room table. They were sitting down in their normal places when Sedona pushed the back door open and burst into the room.

She tried to force herself to stop and regain her poise, but when Greg stood up she hurried forward, jumped up, and hugged him.

"Well done, Cadet Caiti," he said, holding her tight. "Very well done."

He gently set her feet back on the floor and she pulled her chair out and sat down beside Sierra.

"We'll debrief in a few minutes," he said with a huge smile, and then turned to Shara. "Please pick another envelope."

Cheyenne and Sierra watched intently as Shara reached out and held her hand over the two envelopes lying face down on the table. She glanced at the two girls and then put her finger on one of the envelopes. Greg smiled and turned the envelope over. Cheyenne exhaled, releasing the breath she had been holding when she saw her name, *Keely*, clearly visible on the envelope.

Greg picked it up and handed it to her.

"Stay calm and you'll remember everything we've practiced," Greg said. "When you hover over the ranch, open the envelope," Greg explained as he had to Sedona when her envelope was chosen earlier, "and follow each step that is outlined in it. STSX will record everything and we'll debrief when you get back. Have a safe flight, Cadet."

Cheyenne slowly stood up, and with a smile that stretched from one ear to the other, looked at Greg and said, "Thank you, sir. I will do my best."

Nick sat down at the table as he watched a suddenly calm and poised Cheyenne-Keely walk to the back door and step out.

⋏

"Please close the aft portal and retract the ramp," Keely said as she walked up the aisle through the sleeping area to the central compartment, accompanied only by the soft hum of the ship.

She heard the hiss of the seals inflating as she climbed the rungs to the chamber above. In the central compartment, she stopped and listened to the soft murmurs from the equipment in the nav-com compartment and realized that it was her very first time onboard STSX by herself.

"WELCOME ABOARD, CADET KEELY," STSX said softly.

"Thank you, STSX," Keely said, then smiled and turned to the pilot's chair. As the chair adjusted to her, she secured the straps and turned the chair to forward facing. "System status, please."

"ALL SYSTEMS ARE MISSION READY. CLOAKING ON, SENSOR BLOCKING ON. SHIELDS ARE ON FULL. PASSIVE SCAN INDICATES NO TRAFFIC. WEAPONS ARE PEAKED AND ON STANDBY."

"I hope we don't need those today," she said, and smiled.

"A FIGHTER AND HIS PILOT MUST ALWAYS BE READY FOR THE UNEXPECTED. THE COMMANDER ONCE TOLD HIS MATE THAT DANGER CAN COME FROM THE MOST UNEXPECTED PLACES."

"That's very true. Please hover at two hundred feet and set ignition on," she said, and tucked the envelope under the seat's waist strap. She scanned the panel of displays in front of her and watched the changes as STSX put her command into action and gently lifted up through the shield dome.

The blustery winds caught her by surprise and she smiled, remembering her uncle's comment during one of their training sessions—that if the weather was always good, anyone could do this. She absently reached out and *felt* the valley around her, the ranch below and the morning activities taking place, and the people below, completely unaware that Sedona had, she was currently, and Sierra would be completing the most important thing they had done yet in their young lives.

STSX leveled and settled just outside the ranch's veil and Keely took a deep breath and slowly opened the envelope, extracting the folded sheet from within. She smiled and exhaled when she read the first of the three tasks.

"STSX, please bring up the cockpit three-dimensional display," she said as she *felt* the sky above and back to the west. "Plot the current location of the space station. Calculate and display an interception course from here, vertical ascent to an unseen formation join-up. Veiled and sensor blocked."

She unzipped the front of her Blues and slid the envelope and sheet in against her chest as the display coalesced between her and the front cockpit wall, just to her right. She resealed her Blues as she watched the space station's dot appear east of Australia, its path bringing it across the Pacific toward her current position.

"BEST INTERCEPT IN EIGHTEEN POINT THREE MINUTES."

"Okay, STSX. Let's do it," she said. "Ignition ready. Is cloaking still on, sensors blocked, shields full?"

"AFFIRMATIVE."

Keely gently but aggressively pushed the thrust levers forward as she pulled STSX's nose up to follow the green line plotted on the display globe. She checked her speed and altitude against the display notations as they climbed and began the push-over to exchange her vertical speed for horizontal speed.

"SIX POINT EIGHT MINUTES TO INTERCEPT."

Keely reached out and sensed the station, the personnel inside, and the supply ships tethered at its space side docking portals. Then she felt another ship, following the station in a two-mile loose formation. She felt deeper.

"STSX, please confirm there is a hidden fighter escorting the station," Keely said. "Origins unknown."

"CLOAKED AND SENSOR BLOCKED FIGHTER CONFIRMED. ORIGIN IS NOT UNKNOWN. IT IS, OR IS SIMILAR TO, THE FIGHTER YOU DISCOVERED WHEN YOU FLEW OVER AUSTRALIA ON 18 NOVEMBER, C.DATE 3486.724."

"Record all pertinent information concerning the fighter,"

Keely said. "I don't like knowing it is here, stalking our station."

"PLEASE *VISUALIZE* THE FIGHTER, CADET KEELY. I WILL RECORD WHAT YOU *SEE* AND *FEEL*."

Keely focused on the details and feelings of the fighter as she maneuvered closer, stopping her closure at five hundred feet to the fighter's right. Staring at the seemingly void spot in space, Keely ducked under the fighter, slowly rolling STSX to keep the fighter 'above' her, in the canopy's view. She rolled completely around the fighter and STSX recorded every detail she could discern.

"The pilot seems too young," Keely said absently. "Uncle Greg—sorry, the commander mentioned that these fighters were hidden by the crews when they captured the IO facility eleven years ago. This one doesn't feel old enough to have been one of the pilots back then." She shook her head. "Something isn't right here, STSX. Please send this information to the commander. I'll want to talk to him about it when we get down."

"DONE, CADET KEELY. INFORMATION SENT."

"Thanks, STSX," Keely said, and glanced back at the station. "Please record our formation with the station for flight confirmation. Whoa! STSX, the station's shields are down."

Caught in the dilemma of needing to remain unseen and undetected as ordered for her solo flight credit and knowing that protecting the station was one of the Force's purposes on earth, she took a deep breath and decided.

"STSX," she said slowly. "Please open a communications link with Apache Watch."

"LINK OPEN."

"Thanks. Apache Watch, this is Apache One."

"Apache One, Apache Watch here," the woman's voice answered. She hesitated a moment. "Apache Watch does not have you painted."

"Apache One is not visible at this time. IFF off," Keely said, trying to hold her youthful voice level and professional.

"If I may ask, Apache One," Apache Watch said. "You do not sound like Apache One."

"Apache One is hosting a training flight this morning. I am not his usual pilot," Keely admitted. "For reasons I cannot say, my mission is supposed to be clande...clan...secret. I have contacted you because you are being stalked by a veiled and sensor-blocked enemy fighter. How long he's been tracking you I don't know, but I realized your shields are down and you need to know the situation. I will try to light him up for your scanners and call for an Apache escort."

"Thank you, Apache One," Apache Watch said, and the station's shields activated.

Keely switched the coms to standby. "STSX, please try the transmitter codes. If he lights up, maybe it'll rattle him enough he'll leave. If not, we should still call for an escort."

"AFFIRMATIVE, CADET KEELY. FORTH KYDDELLAN CODE SUCCESSFUL. VEIL MALFUNCTION?"

Keely laughed out loud, remembering her Aunt Casi's trick. "Yes! A veil malfunction would be grand."

STSX transmitted the diagnostic command and the fighter suddenly winked into view. Keely could *feel* the surprise and sudden fear in the fighter's cockpit. The pilot quickly added thrust and broke formation.

"Apache Watch," Keely said to the coms. "You will be able to follow him for about five minutes." Then to STSX, she asked, '*Any word on an escort?*'

'*YES. ESCORT WILL BE UP IN TWENTY-THREE MINUTES.*'

'*Thanks.*' Keely turned back to the Coms. "QuickSilver should have an Apache escort in formation in about twenty-three minutes. Apache One out."

"Thank you, Apache One. Safe mission. Apache Watch out."

Keely pulled the envelope out, read the second item on the list, and then put the envelope back inside her Blues. She slowly added thrust and broke formation.

"STSX," she said happily. "Plot a course to the Indian Ocean Facility. Vertical approach from directly overhead."

A new green line appeared on the globe and Keely realized her formation flight had actually brought them closer and STSX'S course was ahead and a little to the right of QuickSilver's orbital path.

"Let's get there," Keely said, and pushed the thrust levers forward.

▲

A little more than an hour after Greg received Keely's information on the enemy fighter, he turned to Shara and Nick and smiled. "She's back."

The weather had deteriorated and he knew Keely had to navigate and land in a light snow with about five miles of visibility. But her safe arrival without STSX's assistance confirmed his faith in her abilities and that she had listened during training. He sat back in his chair and sipped his coffee, and a moment later, Keely pushed the door open and stepped through. She was happy with herself, but she held herself in reserve.

Greg stood up and smiled, holding his arms out to her.

"Well done, Keely," he said. "Very well done."

She ran to him and jumped up and hugged him. She held him a long moment and then softly said, "I'm sorry, Uncle Greg. I know I was supposed to keep the flight secret, but I just *had* to be sure they knew. They didn't have their shields up or anything."

Greg knelt and set her back on the floor and, still holding her, he said, "You did the right thing, Keely. And you did stay veiled and sensor blocked. No one knew where you were that wasn't supposed to know. And you're very right. They needed to know." He relaxed and pushed her back enough so he could see her face. He smiled. "We'll debrief in a few minutes, but before we do, don't you think you owe someone else a thank you?" He nodded aside, toward Nick. "For letting you train early."

"Yes, sir," she said, and pushed herself up, standing straight. "Thank you, sir."

Greg stood up and smiled down at Cheyenne. "At ease, Cadet Keely. Go see your dad."

Cheyenne hurried around the table and Nick caught her in a full jump into his arms.

"Daddy? Did you see?" she bubbled with delight. "I flew STSX! I soloed!"

"You certainly did," Nick said as he stood up and held her. "Too bad your mom wasn't here to see you."

"She knows, Dad," Cheyenne said proudly. "We didn't talk to each other, but when I started my descent to the IO facility, she listened in. I could tell she was happy for me, but she stopped listening so I could do my job."

"That is really wonderful." Nick smiled. "But now your uncle has more business to take care of."

"Okay," she said as Nick set her down. "Thank you for letting me train." She smiled hugely at Sedona and then at Sierra. "You're going to do great, Coli. I know it." Cheyenne composed herself and walked around the dining room table and sat down in her usual chair. "Thank you, Uncle Greg, Aunt Shara. I'm sorry to keep you waiting."

Greg nodded to her and looked at Shara and then at Sierra. He picked up the last envelope and gave Sierra the same speech he had given Caiti and Keely. She took the proffered envelope. "I'll do my best, Commander," she said, then smiled and winked at him. She smiled at Shara and Sedona, then turned to the door and slipped out into the snowy yard.

Greg waited, still standing beside the table, until STSX lifted in response to her command to hover. He relaxed his stance and smiled at Cheyenne.

"Okay, Cadet," he said. "Let's go into the living room and see what STSX recorded."

⋏

"And why did you say you thought the pilot was too young?" Greg asked, and glanced at Shara, Sedona, and Nick.

"He's only nineteen or twenty Terran years old," Cheyenne answered, expressing that it should be obvious with her gestures. "Eleven or twelve years ago he would have been younger than me."

"You also told STSX there was something funny about him, the pilot," Greg persisted.

"Yes, sir. He didn't have the same sort of feel I get when I sense that man Nikle or someone that's helping him. This one almost *felt…*"

"Like what?"

"Well, like I should know him," she said, and wrinkled her nose and skewed her mouth. "Like he was familiar somehow."

Greg began to chuckle and Shara smiled. Cheyenne looked at them and shook her head in wonder.

"Cheyenne," Greg said, trying to stop his soft laughter. "You amaze me more every day. Just like your cousins do. You are correct on all counts. You did exactly the sort of things you should've done under the circumstances. And I'm very glad you decided to scare him off rather than go offensive."

Cheyenne looked at his smile and then at everyone else.

"Cheyenne," Greg continued. "I contacted Seventeen after I got your information, and it seems the fighter you discovered was the same fighter Kiile and his men captured when we picked up Coleen and Brendan before Thanksgiving. A young lance corporal has the assignment to evaluate the captured fighter and produce a capabilities report. His report will educate Headquarters, our fighter pilots, and even our own Apache Squadron pilots on what we know about the enemy fighter. The lance corporal you scared out of his mind today is one of our marine pilots."

"He is?" she asked, suddenly thinking about how easily she or the station could have decided to shoot at him.

89

"Well, one good thing came out of this," Greg chuckled. "He knows you found him, revealed him, and he won't be stupid enough to stalk the station again in an enemy fighter. He knows he could have been shot down for simply being there."

"We wouldn't have ever known he wasn't an enemy pilot."

"Not really, Cheyenne," Greg said, and continued to smile. "I think your *feel* of him kept you from doing anything like that. You said you felt like you could know him."

"Yes, sir. He didn't *feel* like I thought he would."

Cheyenne saw everyone smiling at her.

"That's because you can *read* his GPF tag," Greg said softly. "Everyone in the Peace Force has a tag so we all know who each other is."

"Everyone?"

Greg nodded, and when she looked around, they were all nodding.

"Just like your secret mission name," Shara said. "We all have secret tags so the others in the Force know we also belong. When you meet one of Kiile's marines, you know immediately he's a friendly. When you *feel* people from town, most of the time you get no sense of who they are. But if you *feel* any of us"—and Shara pushed her tag to the front of her mind—"you automatically *read* our tag, whether you realize it or not."

Cheyenne's mouth dropped open. "You have two tags. HQZL09-SS2 and IAL02-SS2."

"Yes. Very good," Greg said.

Cheyenne looked at her dad. "IAL36-SS." And then at Sedona. "IAL02-SS2.1. Wow."

"That's why Dad used to call us his two-points when we were younger," Sedona said. "Two-point-one and Two-point-two, and how everyone at Obscure can tell us apart."

"I did wonder, especially before we could *talk* to each other," Cheyenne mused, "how I always knew which of you was which. Besides being family, of course."

"When you are registered," Greg said, "and since you will all be qualified Q-Ship pilots, you will probably be given director's tags to go with the ones you now have."

"Another besides my Two-point-one?"

"Yes," Greg said, and straightened in his chair. "Now, let's look at another thing STSX recorded. When you descended to the IO facility..."

⋏ ⋏ ⋏ ⋏ ⋏

Cera in Apache Fifteen followed STSX12 as it slowly passed over the rubble that was once a busy space port, importing food and material supplies and exporting agricultural products, sowing and reaping equipment, and woven goods produced and created on Nevar. It was hard for Cera to fully grasp that only one hundred and sixty-eight turns past, this sprawling plain of ruins was a thriving, admired metropolis. And from all they could tell, the scene stretching out before them was the same metropolis one day later.

Behind her on her left, she took note of LTVC21 flying an overlapping, parallel course. The combined data would be resolved into a thousand-foot-wide, high-resolution pictorial swath of the port. It was the third pass they had made that morning, and Cheral estimated they would do another seven before moving on to the next large city.

Cera sighed. *At least a pass across the city only takes about twenty to twenty-five minutes, Terran time.* They would have their ten passes done before it was time for their midday meal.

"STSX12," Cera said into her helmet mic. "I'd like to take Apache Ten and do our escort from a higher altitude."

"That's acceptable, Apache Fifteen," Keli said. "Look around for another one of those octagon features. They could be important."

"Will do that," Cera said, and signaled Ani in Ten to break formation. "We'll fly back and forth over you and look for anything unusual."

"Ten's with you, Fifteen," Ani said as she joined up.

Cera set an altitude about a thousand feet above the Q-Ships and reached out past the edges of the port.

"Ani, do you *feel* anything unusual?" Cera asked. "I keep getting a tingle, like there's something here, watching us."

"Yeah," Ani said. "Not often or most of the time, but every once in a while. It feels mechanical, but with a faint aura of life. I'm not sure I'm explaining it right."

"I think you've explained it very well," Cera said, and turned back toward the Q-Ships, drifting farther across the city with each pass.

"I think I feel explosive devices of some kind," Ani said suddenly. "Around that launch dish ahead and left of the Q-Ships."

"Yeah," Cera agreed. "Similar to a mine, but different. STSX12? Can you look at the sensation Ani and I are projecting?"

"YES. IT FEELS LIKE AN ACOUSTICAL MINE. CAN YOU LOOK INSIDE?"

Cera focused like Shara had taught her to do when they went after Ahaar many years ago.

"YES, CAPTAIN DNAR. THE DEVICE SENSES CHANGES IN VIBRATIONS IN THE AIR, SOUNDS, AND IN THE GROUND, FOOTSTEPS. I DETECT SEVEN HUNDRED AND SIXTEEN UNITS IN THE PORT CITY."

"Why would someone spread mines like that across a ruined city?" Ani asked. "There's no one here to set them off."

"What if there are?" Cera asked, suddenly wondering. "If we suppose there are people here, hiding, the mines would keep them from coming out. They will either die in hiding or die trying to move through the city."

"Do you suppose there are underground places where people could hide?" Ani asked, studying the piles of rubble beneath them.

"It's possible," Cera said softly. "A planet without defenses might have a way to hide if they were attacked. It's certainly possible."

The Q-Ships reversed directions and began flying back on a parallel course, offset from the previous enough to provide a suitable overlap at the edges of the scans. Apache Fifteen and Ten continued weaving overhead until Cera and Ani crossed over the city center.

"Whoa! Did you feel that?" Cera asked, and slowed Fifteen to a hover.

"Yeah," Ani admitted. "Very strong."

Cera tapped a series of instructions into the side console of Apache Fifteen and waited as the scanners began sweeping the area around them.

"Ani," Cera said softly. "Behind us. There's an energy column. Near ultraviolet spectrum. I think we flew right through it." Cera slowly turned Apache Fifteen to face the column, and she tilted her head back as far as she could. "It looks like it stops, about..." She glanced at the display on her right. "At about thirty thousand feet."

"STSX12, Cheral? Are you listening to any of this?"

"Yeah. LTVC21 is listening also."

"I'm *feeling* a stationary object, cloaked at the top of the column," Cera said. "Ani, watch the base of the column. Run a spectral series on it. I'm going up to see what might be at the top."

Cera pulled the fighter's nose up and added thrust, spiraling around the column as she climbed. As she neared the top of the column, she could sense a larger object, similar to a remote. She focused and felt its mass, its construction, and slowly she felt the insides, electronics and scanners.

"It appears to be shielded and is obviously cloaked," Cera said. "It's about the size of Apache Fifteen, but circular, full of data sensors, processors, and a bank of transmitters. Looks like it's observing the surroundings and sending data down the energy column."

"Captain Dnar," Ani said. "There's another one of those octagonal units at the bottom of the column. It's about ninety percent covered with loose debris. It looks like lightweight material. Do we have any way to clear it off?"

"Yes," Cheral said, "We can use remotes. But first, we need a soil sample to see if the ground is poisoned. If not, then we can consider letting a remote scrape the debris away."

"Are there any of those acoustical mines nearby?" Cera asked. "I'd hate to lose a remote trying to clear an octagonal whatever it is."

"YES," STSX12 said. "TWO NEARBY."

"ST12's released our Remote Six for a soil sample," Keli said.

"Good," Cheral agreed. "We'll keep our scanning on track and you two watch the octagon for signs of...well, of anything."

"Will do," Cera said.

It took Remote Six two minutes to reach the surface and another four to decide on a suitable soil source. It scooped up a small sample and drifted back to STSX12. They waited another ten minutes before Remote Six announced to STSX12 that the soil was not toxic, at least not within the parameters it could test.

While Remote Six did its analysis, Cera settled near the octagonal feature and slowly drifted around it. It sat higher than the surrounding rubble, projecting a man's height out of a stone like paved surface, poured in the center of a raised section of a city plaza or square.

Behind the piles of loose gravel-like rubble, the feature looked like special windows forming the eight segments of a slanted wall around a horizontal, upward-facing octagonal window, emitting the energy column at the cloaked object above. It was obviously a communications link. *But what is it communicating? And to who?* Cera asked herself.

"STSX12?" Cera asked. "Has Kiile seen anything like

94

these before? They seemed to have survived the attack and destruction, and this one appears to be active, communicating with the cloaked object above."

▲

"Kiile, come up here please," Cheral said as she studied the images Cera was sending. She turned when he climbed the rungs and stepped in and sat down on the pull-out beside her. "Cera is looking at one of these structures up close. Were they here when you were a boy and living here?"

Kiile studied the images and reviewed video segments recorded earlier. He shook his head.

"I'm not remembering them," he said softly. "Check the Rings for any historical information the Force has on Nevar. I remember my *pada*, father, telling us about the Guardians and how they watched the skies for the supply ships, passenger ships, weather, maybe even intruders. He said they could even help change the weather, seeding clouds and things like that. From Turell, when the meteorological conditions were right, we could see the faint purple glow of the Guardians in the night sky."

"Where was that one?" Cheral asked.

"In Wiibsa, the large town about forty Terran miles northwest of Turell," Kiile said. "My *pada* went there for supplies every ten or fifteen turns."

"And you and your brothers?"

"No. We never went with him. We worked the farms," Kiile said, and smiled at some memory. "It was better that way."

"But you obviously learned enough about the world to decide to leave," Cheral said, trying to understand him, "and join the Force."

"Not as much as you might think," Kiile said, and smiled at her. "I was eleven when the Recruiters first came to our village. I was too young, but I remembered the stories of great need they told, and when they came back the following year, I remembered the stories and I was eager to join. I was tired of wrestling and fighting with my brothers over everything, and nothing, and I wanted to do something for the good of someone else."

"Your folks were all right with that?"

"No, but I went anyway." Kiile sighed. "There were no confrontations or harsh words, and I left. We visited when I could, but we were not tight to each other like your culture or your cousin's culture. I have been trying to learn how to be more that way."

Cheral smiled, then sobered. "Okay, back to the Guardians and the city. If the Guardians saw a threat, storms of weather, or maybe intruders, what did they do? What did the people do?"

"The Guardians alerted the whole area under each one's authority if bad weather came," Kiile said, "and people would take shelter."

"Where, Kiile? Where would they go to take shelter?" Cheral asked softly, suddenly sharing Cera's feeling that some people might have taken shelter during the attack.

"If we had time," Kiile said, his expression turning somber, "the people would go to the nearest town with a storm shelter. But usually the people did not have time." He thought about something a long moment. "We only had one storm that hit Turell while I was here and before I left. We did not have time to go to Wiibsa and had to take shelter in our village, in our homes or in makeshift 'safe rooms,' which usually weren't. Seven died in that storm. My father said the shelter in Wiibsa could hide double its population, thus plenty of room for those that could get there from the farms. They were stocked to support the sheltered people for many days while farms were rebuilt and resown."

"Underground shelters?"

"Yes," he said, and looked at Cheral's startled expression as she spun around to the console.

"ST12, contact the Rings. I need all of the information you can get on the storm shelters in the cities on Nevar.

Anything you can find from the libraries and archives." She switched to the coms, trying to keep the anticipation out of her voice. "Apache Fifteen, I am trying to get suitable descriptive information, but Kiile remembers there are underground storm shelters in each of the larger towns and cities. We think the communications system you found alerts the population of dangerous storms and tells the people when to take cover. I'm sending Remotes Six and Five to start uncovering and clearing the debris away from the feature you have found." She turned to look at Kiile. "What can we do about the acoustical mines?"

"May I?" he asked, and turned to the coms. Cheral nodded and Kiile composed a message to the major general in charge of the Peace Force Marines in the Rings. When he finished and the screen cleared, he smiled at Cheral's curious expression.

"What did you say, Kiile? I couldn't read it."

"Oh, sorry," Kiile said, and wrinkled his face. "I forgot and used our battle language. We have specialized equipment and men to handle acoustical explosives. I explained the urgent need in case there are survivors trapped by these mines and requested two squads of suitable explosive handlers be dispatched to us on Nevar to attempt whatever rescue efforts we can."

"That's wonderful," Cheral said as she leaned forward and hugged him. The console beeped and she looked around. "A reply?"

Kiile looked at the scrambled message and smiled. He asked for a clear display in Galactic Standard and the message promptly changed and drifted in front of the monitor screen.

"Two squads of explosive specialists will arrive on Nevar midday 3486.743 here at the Space Port. That's tomorrow. He is also sending two squads of marine regulars with medical personnel to provide manpower assistance in searching for survivors."

Cheral started to say something but hesitated before she found the words. "Kiile, it's been five and a half Terran months. I hope we're not too late."

▲ ▲ ▲ ▲ ▲

Kiile strapped himself into the forward-facing double-wide cushion chair in the alcove across from the two sleeping bunks and stretched, pushing his legs as far out in front of him as he could. Restrained by the chair's belt and with the table folded and stowed out of the way, he reclined and let himself relax in the freedom of weightlessness. He was nearly asleep when Cheral positioned herself, stretching out beside him and gently slipping her arms and legs around him.

He blinked, smiled, and responded by curling his arm around her. "Taking a break?" he asked, and kissed her.

"Yeah," she said, and laid her head against his shoulder. "I saw you and it looked like such a good idea. I'm sorry we haven't had much time alone."

"Me too, but I know how the job works," he said, and smiled. "We will have."

"Are you ready?" she asked softly.

"Ready?" he questioned, unsure of her point.

"Neila?"

"Aah, yes. No," he said, and laughed at himself. "I'm scared to death. Like I always am when I prepare for a skirmish or a battle." He turned his head and looked at her. "But I don't want this to be a skirmish or a battle. I really want her to like me. And like you. I suddenly feel like I've missed so much by not knowing, yet I'm anticipating the learning of 'who' she is and 'what' she is. Seeing what she can become."

"Well, Mr. Kiile of Beeli," she said, and gently poked his abs, "I think you need to let them know we're here and that we'll be arriving on Friday, ah, 3486.744. Probably late morning."

"You're right," he said, and kissed her again as he unstrapped and righted himself.

"Find out where we should land and any other information

we may need," she said as he started drifting along the aisle toward the central chamber. "We want to make a good first impression."

"We certainly do," he said, then stopped and looked back at her as she took a blanket from the storage drawer under the right medical couch.

"I have two hours before I have to relieve Keli," she said, and smiled, looking at him sideways. "Don't take too long."

One Twenty-Four

Sergeant Stial was waiting near the start of the food serving line when Blaire came into the Mess with two other cadets. She smiled when she saw him and introduced her friends, Cadet Bri Litl and Willa Endr, when they stopped beside him.

He smiled and greeted Blaire's friends pleasantly and then gestured for them and Blaire to precede him through the line. When they reached the end of the line and picked up their drinks and desserts, Bri and Willa again said it was a pleasure to meet Sergeant Stial and then went to a table by themselves.

"I guess, Luc, you'll just have to endure my company alone," Blaire said as she led them to a small empty table.

"I was fine with your friends," Luc said as he set his tray down, "if they wanted to join us."

"Thanks, that's nice of you to say," Blaire said, and sat down, knowing he wasn't.

"Did you have a good day today?" he asked.

"Actually, it was very nice," she said, her excitement seeping into her words. "We flew combat maneuvers and I got to try out some of the maneuvers Captain Casi invented or perfected, depending on whose point of view you're listening to." She took a small bite of her breaded cutlet, but quickly realized she had to chew and swallow before she could continue. "Did you know all of the codes we have for lighting up a cloaked target came from her and the commander? In combat, the records credit her with being able to destroy a Kyddellan battlecruiser with three shots. And she's the only pilot in the Force's recorded history to singlehandedly take out a Kyddellan battleship." She stopped and sipped her drink.

"I can see you are definitely a fan of the commander and his mate," Luc said, and smiled politely. "But I would prefer to hear about your exploits instead of hers."

"Sorry," she said. "I'm just decompressing after four hours of intense flying. I hope you can understand and don't take offense at my ramblings. I'll refrain."

"I didn't mean to sound like I don't want to hear about your training," Luc said, and she *felt* his sudden concern.

"Okay." She smiled and took another bite. "Tell me, Luc, where are you from? Your family and kin?"

He smiled. "Small place on Antheria in the Tunst System," he said, and sipped his tea. "Like I mentioned last night, my family was military. Everyone was or is in the military somewhere. My grands were local marines and integrated into the Peace Force during their careers. My parents went into the Peace Force as early as they could, and met when their respective squads put down the rioting in Aridont on Listera."

Blaire ate quietly and sipped her drink, listening to him as he explained.

"I lost them two years ago when their squad leader led their mop-up team into a minefield on Angels Five. None of the team survived." He took a deep breath as his mood saddened, but he continued. "My two older brothers—I'm the youngest— they were part of the elite squad that goes in and softens targets before an attack begins. They were both marine pilots and I lost them in the Pordenl Uprising of 3485.203, just over four Terran years ago."

"I'm sorry," Blaire said honestly. "I can only imagine how difficult it is losing both your brothers and then your parents. And you've been here for just over three years and in the Force for only five years. Was this your first assignment?"

"Thanks. It's my second," Luc said. "The first was basically a dry run doing long-distance surveillance and data reduction for some of the field squads. And here, I've helped in the facility security, but no big engagements—not like you were speaking of, anyway."

"Were you with Kiile's group last Friday?" she asked, and sipped her drink.

"Yes." He smiled, his sadness easing. "We were pretty evenly matched in numbers, but the deputy took out nearly a third of the attackers before we landed. Shooting in the dark, from under his jeep, and wounded, Squad Leader Kiile said he only missed two or three times out of two clips."

"I know Deputy Reeds and his family," she said softly, smiling as she continued eating. "We were very relieved when we knew he was going to be all right. I first met them when my mom and I came to the valley about eleven years ago. Our families have been friends ever since."

He nodded slowly and ate more of his dinner.

"I understand he has a daughter and a son," Luc said, almost a question.

"Yes." Blaire smiled. "Glory is a couple of years older than I am, and Sam is six years older."

"Sam," Luc repeated softly with a smile. "Is he competition?"

She looked up sharply at his quizzical smile. "You think this is a competition? Are you on some kind of a quest?"

"No," he backpedaled, seeing her stare and *feeling* her sudden defiance. "I didn't mean it like that. I was just kidding around. I...I was wondering if you and Sam have some sort of an arrangement is all."

She watched him for a long moment before she relaxed. "We do. We're friends." Knowing now what Sergeant Stial had in the back of his mind, she *listened* to more than just his words as they continued to talk. "Riggin is my 'back home.' Like everyone has a place they're from, Riggin is mine. I have a lot of friends there—some closer than others."

She knew Luc was trying to reevaluate his position with her, but it was too soon for her to decide if he would be more than a casual friend, if that.

She finished her main course and started on her dessert before Luc engaged in conversation again.

"What do you like to do?" he asked. "When you're not studying or training?"

She smiled. "I think sleep is all I have time for anymore." She heard the question *'Alone?'* flash through his mind, but he suppressed the urge to tease her.

"That intense?" he said instead. "It's been a long time since I applied myself that completely to work."

"Right now, it isn't work," she said. "You should remember how it was when you started. I want to do everything the commander thinks I can do. I want to do it as well as Captain Casi did when she started out. Do you know she's the only person *ever* to enter the Force as an officer, an under-lieutenant? She was never a cadet. And she was promoted to upper-lieutenant in mere months, when she got her pilot's ribbon."

"And you want to copy her?"

"Not copy," Blaire admitted. "I'm already a cadet so I can't join the Force as an officer. But, like everyone else, sans one, I have to work hard to get there. The commander has told me what he wants to see happen, and I want to make it happen. Just like you told yourself in the tunnels, I want to stay in his good graces too."

"You were *listening*?"

"Of course." She smiled. "It was my job to *listen* and to *tell* you what you needed to know. Because we felt the same way about the commander, and how he sees us, I figured you might be worth meeting."

"Aah," he said slowly. "And am I?"

"I don't know. I'm still thinking about it," she said without smiling, then took the last bite of her dessert and a long sip of her drink.

"Please let me know," he said, and smiled a cautious smile, "when you know."

"I will."

Thursday, December 6

Sam stepped out of the blustery, snowy morning and into Connie's Deli. He waited as a woman ahead of him ordered, and when she finished, he stepped up and ordered a breakfast wrap with bacon and a cup of Connie's dark roast coffee. He paid the girl behind the counter, took his coffee, and stepped aside to wait and saw Deputy Lupis sitting at a table near the side wall of the shop.

"Morning, Deputy Lupis," Sam said, stopping beside his table. "May I join you?"

Dan looked up and smiled. "Good morning, Sam. Sure. Certainly." He quickly closed his digital pad and slipped it into his coat pocket. "I don't know why I read the local paper," he said as Sam hung his coat on the back of the chair across from him. "I get better reports in the office."

Sam nodded and saw the man behind the counter hold up a small bag and nod in his direction. Sam went back to the counter, grabbed his order, and then settled into the chair across from Dan.

"How have you been?" Dan asked as he sipped his coffee and Sam opened his bag. "I haven't seen you around in a couple of weeks or more."

"Doing okay, Dan," he said, and began to eat. "Still working long days for Marty."

"I hear your dad's doing okay," Dan said. "I'm glad he was able to get back on his feet quickly."

"We are too." Sam smiled. "Mom especially. If Dad's not working or doing something, he gets anxious and can be a real bear. He doesn't relax and sit around home very well."

Dan chuckled.

"Say, Dan," Sam said, becoming more serious. "How's Blaire

doing?"

"Oh, she's actually doing pretty well," Dan said. "Staying really busy, I hear."

"You hear? Where is she?"

"She's training for a new job, Sam," Dan admitted.

Sam cocked his head, wondering if Dan was being more reserved than usual.

"Did she get into the Law Enforcement Academy after all?" Sam asked. "I thought you didn't want her to."

Don nodded, but said, "She hasn't told us what she's actually training for, but she says she's very happy and pleasantly exhausted trying to learn all she can."

"Well," Sam said softly, and sipped his coffee. "I'm glad for her."

"You don't sound very happy about it," Dan said, and watched him.

"We sort of had words before she left," Sam admitted. "I was still holding a grudge over her not coming to my graduation. And when she asked for my help, my support, I didn't give it to her. I was a total jerk, and she stormed off like she should've. I haven't been able to talk to her since."

"She'll be back when her training is done," Dan said, "or when she has a break. At least for visits."

"Visits?" Sam stared at him. "So she really did decide to change and put all of this behind her."

"She hopes to get back for Christmas," Dan said. "You might be able to catch her then."

Sam exhaled a long breath. "I doubt she'll want to talk to me either. If she gets back, and I don't see her, tell her I was asking if she's okay. Maybe that won't make her any madder at me than she already is."

Sam wadded the paper wrapper around the last of his breakfast wrap, stood up, and slipped his coat on. He picked up his cup of coffee and looked at Dan.

"I just worry about her and want her to be happy, you know. I always have. Ever since we first met that night Kiile and Wally brought Glory and me up to my folks." Sam smiled weakly. "Just tell her hey for me when you talk to her."

"I will, Sam," Dan said.

"Thanks." Sam turned and tossed his trash into the bin as he left the deli.

▲ ▲ ▲ ▲ ▲

Major Iims walked Blaire out to the Class 2 fighter like he always did at the beginning of a training flight. He handed her the "Mission Flip-File" and gestured for her to get on board.

"Plug in as soon as you get strapped in," he said, and watched her scamper up the ladder and drop into the front cockpit. He slipped his earpiece on and tapped the boom mic. "Do you hear me?"

"Yes, sir," Blaire answered absently as she fastened the straps and started the preflight preparations. She looked up at a movement beside her, expecting to see the major as he slipped over the rail into the aft cockpit. She stared as she realized the ladder was moving away and Major Iims was looking up at her from the ground.

"Cadet Lupis," he said with a grin. "Follow your mission plan, step by step, and report to me when you have completed it and have returned to Shadow Base. Good flying, Cadet Lupis."

He saluted her and waited as the reality that she was about to solo soaked in and she finally returned his salute. Then he turned smartly and left as if he had not a care in the world.

Quickly bringing herself back to the moment, she lowered the canopies. The seals hissed as she toggled the "Flip-File's" cover open and read the mission items listed on the summary page. She smiled and turned to finishing her preflight checks. When the systems status reported satisfactory, she toggled ignition on and watched the start progress indicators.

"Shadow Base, Apache Patrol Seven is departing with Information Charlie-Six-Six-Niner," she said into her helmet mic as she sealed the faceplate.

"Cleared for departure, Apache Patrol Seven," the controller's voice replied.

She saluted the ground crewman and slowly lifted the fighter. The gusty winds jostled the ship as she emerged through the shield dome, and she made a quick glance around at the near whiteout conditions. She entered the first coordinates into the navigation computer and watched as the three-dimensional display coalesced in front of her and the green course line extended from her current position to her first destination.

Sure wish you could talk like the Q-Ships do, she said to herself as she added thrust and pulled the fighter's nose up to follow the green line.

⬥

Two hours after takeoff, Blaire turned Patrol Seven north toward the valley. With the completion of the Flip-File, she had swung wide to the south, following a subtle sensation she had picked up when she overflew the valley earlier. It was similar to the sensation they had followed on Sunday, and she wanted to investigate it on her return leg.

Caught in a dilemma as the *feeling* got stronger, fully aware of the interdiction against communicating with unauthorized persons, she knew she had to tell someone. Then she remembered STSX!

'STSX, *please record what I'm seeing and feeling,*' she said in her mind. '*Please do not reply. If you can confirm the ID of the sensation, please show this file to the commander and Casi.*'

She slowed Patrol Seven and drifted down into the cloud deck, knowing she had about five thousand feet to play in before she found the valley floor. But then she *felt* the valley— the shape, the contours, the trees and the rivers and the lakes. She slowly drifted east of the river, and when she was east of

Hawthorne on a line from Grants to Obscure, she passed over the sensation.

'STSX, he is here with another twenty men. He is at the Niles Reeds Ranch and they are discussing two men that were supposed to kill someone, a woman, last Tuesday. The leader is upset and is looking for the men he sent and someone named Abe. I think he is planning something.'

Blaire took a deep breath, suddenly realizing what she was overhearing. She forced herself to stop thinking about the content of her *hearing* and focus on her task; she had a ship to fly. But she knew she would contact the commander as quickly as she could after she landed.

Blaire focused on her mission, slowed Patrol Seven, and settled low over the obscured trees she *saw* beneath her and followed the rising terrain as she approached Shadow Base.

"Control," she said with an accomplished voice into her helmet mic, "Apache Patrol Seven is approaching from the south with Information Delta-One-One-Three, landing in two minutes."

"Welcome back, Apache Patrol Seven. Approach heading is two-six-five," Control said. "Your spot is still open."

"Thanks, Control," she said.

As she settled above the shield dome, approaching from the northeast, she felt an increased tension, and as Patrol Seven passed through, the intense activity caught her by surprise. Two marine transports were loading at the east side of the launch portal, and three patrol fighters and two Q-Ships were powering up. Marines in full combat gear were running to the transports and jumping in through the open hatches and aft portals.

Blaire drifted over the launch portal and landed in the same spot she had taken off from, and the ground crewman slid the ladder up beside the cockpit as she unsealed the canopy and switched it to open.

"What's going on?" she asked the ground crewman when she jumped off the ladder. She looked around, expecting Major

Iims to greet her.

"They're going after a group of the slavers," he said, and climbed the ladder to close the canopy. "They just got the alert a few minutes ago. Oh, there's the commander."

She looked up and saw Q-STSX1, with the double red stripes, descending through the shield dome and another Q-Ship in tight formation. She figured it was Colonel Kooich in KKLC14, suddenly realizing she had sounded the alert and caused all of this.

"Major Iims asked for you to meet him in the Flight Ops briefing room," the ground crewman said, and began pulling the ladder away from the ship.

Blaire turned, suddenly feeling very conspicuous. If she were wrong, she would be—

'Thank you, Blaire,' Casi's calm and pleased voice said in her head. *'STSX confirmed your identification. Maybe, if we're lucky, we can catch Nikle this time.'*

Blaire looked back at STSX1 and saw Casi's black-haired head with a red headband tied around it. Blaire smiled and absently saluted Casi as she watched from the cockpit. Then she turned and started down the curved corridor of steps.

C.3486.743

"How will we find the entrances to the underground storm shelters?" Ani asked Cheral as they transferred Ani to Apache Ten.

"I'm not sure," Cheral answered as the remote slowed beneath the patrol fighter and Ani grabbed the handhold.

Ani punched a code into the belly access controls, and the belly door responded and slowly swung inside, leaving the portal open for entry. She floated to the opening and pulled herself in. Cheral waited until the panel swung back into place and was aligned with the ship's skin.

"Portal secure," Ani's voice said in Cheral's earpiece.

The remote carried Cheral back to ST12's aft portal and docked as she stepped in. The outer airlock closed and sealed and the chamber refilled with breathable air. When the inner airlock panel slid aside, Cheral broke the EV suit's helmet seal and began removing the suit.

"Kiile," Cheral said in a normal voice. "Ani had a good question. Does any of the information we received show us where the entrances are for the storm shelters?"

"Yes," he said, "but it appears they are controlled by a computer system. I'm assuming that as long as the computer system thinks there is a threat, the entrances will remain closed and sealed."

"So if we get the mines taken care of," she said as she drifted up through the ceiling portal to the upper deck, "we still may not be able to get the entrances open. The computer system has to be convinced the threat is gone?"

"I'll interrogate the archives," Kiile said. "Maybe there's something we haven't been told."

"Major," Keli said, and Cheral turned to face her. "Apache Fifteen and Apache Ten are ready for separation."

"Okay," Cheral said with a nod. "Separate. Let's get back down and see what more we can find. ST? Do we have an ETA on the marine transports?"

"They should enter orbit," ST12 said, "in two Terran hours and twenty minutes."

Keli gave the command and the flight began its descent to the space port.

▲

"MARINE TRANSPORT MT-6643M AND MT-4386R ARE IN ORBIT AND WILL PASS OVERHEAD IN TWELVE MINUTES," ST12 announced.

"Thanks ST," Cheral said. "Which one is the flight leader?"

"MT-6643M IS THE COMMAND SHIP."

Cheral turned to the coms and said in Galactic Standard, "MT-6643M, welcome to Nevar. This is Apache Flight, Apache Four speaking. We are a flight of four."

"Good day, Apache Four," the heavy masculine voice of the transport's nav-com replied.

"We have USL15, Marine Captain Kiile Beeli, the commandant of the marine installation at Apache Base with us," she continued. "He has been monitoring our activities as we investigate what has happened here on Nevar."

"Very good, Apache Four," the nav-com said. "I am Corporal Prta and we are under the command of Lieutenant Bostl. Do you have details you can supply on the current status?"

"Affirmative," Cheral said. "Complete video and data files are being transferred. At this time, it appears the storm shelter protection system is still active. We think the Guardians still see the conditions as hostile. We also feel the situation is caused by the acoustic mines scattered across each of the population centers on the planet."

"That is reasonable."

"We have also ascertained," Kiile said, "by soil samples and analysis, the grounds are not toxic."

"Thank you, USL15," the nav-com said. "The flight commander wishes to descend as quickly as possible and begin removing the mines."

"Apache Fifteen, IFF on," Cheral said, and then turned back to the coms. "I have announced our position at the base of the Guardian. Please descend on our IFF position. Captain Dnar in Apache Fifteen will be your eyes and ears if you need them. I have also transferred a map showing the locations of the known mines in and around the space port."

"Thank you, Apache Four," the nav-com said. "We have your IFF position. Flight of two descending.

~

Cera watched as the transports came into view and slowly

circled the space port. Staying sensor blocked and shielded, she switched her veil off and flashed a visual light beam at the lead transport.

"6643, Apache Fifteen has your visual," Cera said into her helmet mic. "The Guardian systems are unchanged. No signs of activity." She *felt* the surrounding area and *touched* STSX12 scanning the next city to the northwest.

"6643 has your visual, Apache Fifteen," the now familiar voice of the nav-com said. "From your map information we will hover and start with the mines closest to the base of the Guardian. We will then work outward in concentric rings. 4386 will focus on the area around the port's launch basin. May I ask how you knew about the Guardians?"

"This is USL15's home planet," Cera said. "He was born and raised in a small farming village about one hundred seventy degrees east longitude and two and a half degrees north latitude from the space port. He remembered and led us to the information in the historical archive in the Rings."

"That would certainly be a help," the nav-com chuckled.

"ST12," Cera called. "Please send a copy of the archive data we have on the Guardians."

"TRANSFER COMMENCING."

"6643, Guardian data transfer has begun," Cera said.

She watched as 6643 settled beside the Guardian's base and four marines dropped onto the square beside the octagonal feature. They moved to the side nearest the first mine, some distance away from the square. One moved down to what she assumed was street level and set a boxy piece of equipment on the ground, just off the poured, stone like material surrounding the square. He adjusted some controls, stepped back onto the square, and followed the other three around to the far side of the square, nearer to the second mine.

With the second boxy piece of equipment in place, the marines returned to look at the sloped walls of the octagonal feature.

"6643?" Cera asked. "Since your men seem to be waiting for something, may I ask what the equipment does that they placed beside the square?"

"Yes, Apache Fifteen," the nav-com said. "They produce a sound and vibration that slowly increases until they reach a level that will mask the sounds of the men's movements and the vibrations of their footsteps. When they can reach the mines, they can either turn them off or disable their sensors. The process is usually simple if they can gain access."

"Sound simple enough," Cera said. "Does it always work?"

"Seventy percent success rate," the nav-com said in a somber tone.

After about half of a Terran hour, the marines started moving toward the first mine. Three stopped short and the fourth continued until he settled beside it and slowly opened his tool kit. Cera lifted Apache Fifteen and diverted all the ship's shield power to the forward shields, and she turned the fighter's nose to face the marine and the mine.

Within five minutes, the marine stood up and closed his tool kit.

"All clear," 6643's nav-com announced. "4386 has the first neutralized at the port basin. Two down."

Cera watched the process through the day as the marines slowly worked their way around the Guardian in expanding circles. They physically removed the disarmed mines and created a munitions dump in a clear plain some forty Terran miles from the city.

By nightfall, the cleared area was almost halfway from the Guardian to the outskirts of the city, three hundred and twenty mines were disabled and removed with no accidents and no losses, and 6643 finally called for a stop to the day. They recalled their troops and lifted to a low orbit, where Apache Flight joined them and transferred Ani and Cera back to their respective host ships.

Settled on her bunk, Cera thought about the day and the

Guardians and wondered, '*Cheral? How would the Guardians normally know if ships within their planetary space were friendly or not?*'

A long pause ensued before Cheral answered.

'*Normal protocol would be like at home: ships arriving announce themselves and their intentions to Approach Control and ships leaving would coordinate with and be guided by Departure Control.*'

'*So,*' Cera said, '*if we didn't announce ourselves and just flew in without warning or clearances or following any normal procedures or protocol, we could be considered an unknown, likely hostile entity.*'

There was another long pause.

'*And since the Guardians are still active, a fact no one realized, they would also see unannounced ships,*' Cera continued, '*in orbit or parked near their moon, watching, and could construe their silent presence as potentially hostile.*'

'*Wait a minute,*' Cheral said, and Cera could feel new activity on STSX12. '*Keli has just downloaded the Approach and Departure Charts for the Nevar Space Port. If I'm getting what you're thinking, we will announce ourselves and follow these procedures in the morning for our descent. Maybe we can explain the recent activities.*'

'*It's worth a try,*' Cera said. '*The space port Guardian did not change in any way after the mines were removed. Are you going to join the descent, or will you depart for Belimoor before we test the procedures?*'

'*We'll make the initial contact,*' Cheral said, '*and hope the Guardians understand we're here to help recovery. Then we'll follow protocol and depart.*'

'*Good luck with Neila. I hope you have a good meeting and she's accepting of the change.*'

'*Thanks, Captain Cera Dnar, Jill,*' Cheral said softly. '*I've sent a copy of our conversation to LTVC21 and Ani and copies of the protocol and procedures to 6643 and 4386. Get some rest and we'll see how tomorrow goes.'*

▲ ▲ ▲ ▲ ▲

Blaire smiled at the twins, Cheyenne, and Tayn as they entered the preparations room with Casi and Leeana close behind. She and the other three older cadets had just finished dressing for the occasion: sweatpants, "Soloed"-emblazoned T-shirts with pertinent data, and bare feet.

"I heard you four soloed yesterday," Blaire said as they picked lockers and hung their equipment belts on hooks inside. "Congratulations. I'm very happy for you."

"Thanks," Sedona said as she slipped out of her Blues and hung them up.

"I'm glad your mom warned you about the ceremony," Blaire said, smiling at them each wearing swimsuits under their Blues. "I heard that someone, a long time ago, didn't understand and got very embarrassed during the Cutting Off."

Cheyenne giggled and the twins and Tayn smiled as Casi opened the girls' carrysacks and Leeana got his sweats out.

"And you, Cheyenne," Blaire said, turning to her. "I am so very pleased you were able to keep up and succeed."

"Cadet Keely Dnar, please," Cheyenne said with a wink and a wide smile as she extended her hand formally. Then she leaned closer and whispered, "Uncle—er, the commander said we should be polite and formal while we're at Shadow Base."

"Thank you, Cadet Keely," Blaire said, her eyes dancing as she shook Keely's hand, "for the reminder. And what do we call your cousins?" Blaire glanced past Keely at the twins.

"Oh," Keely said, surprised, and then straightened up and turned to Sedona and Sierra as they finished dressing. "I must present Cadet Caiti Geaardt and Cadet Coli Geaardt. And you already know Cadet Tayn Kooich."

Keely laughed when Caiti, Coli, and Tayn bowed to Blaire.

"Do you have a registered name yet?" Keely asked, looking at Blaire.

"Not yet, Keely," Blaire admitted. "Everyone knows me as Blaire, so I might have to stay with that."

When Casi and Leeana had the carrysacks in the lockers and turned to the room, Blaire realized all eight of them had taken standing positions, silently facing their co-commanders, waiting for them to finish their tasks.

Casi stood up and closed the three lockers, and when she saw the cadets, she smiled. "You certainly don't have to wait on us. We're just proud and happy moms tonight, making over the accomplishments of our wonderful children."

"Thank you, ma'am," Blaire said with a smile. "You may not be our actual moms, but we all owe you a large amount of gratitude for all you've done for each of us and those that have trained and graduated here before us. A very heartfelt thank you, Captain. From each of us."

Casi looked at each of the four older cadets and then at the children as she smiled. "Thank you, but you have put in the work and the hours that have brought you here tonight. This is your night, your celebration, honoring all that you have accomplished. Please tolerate this time-honored celebration and the brash and sometimes raucous accolades of your peers in the happy vein they are meant and 'welcome' to the most prestigious career in the Galactic Peace Force."

Casi smiled at the group and turned to Leeana. "I think we should let the cadets visit while they wait to be called to the ceremony," she said, and looked back at the cadets. "At ease, cadets. We'll see you for the celebration." She pushed her happy thoughts to the girls and Tayn and winked at Keely. Then they turned and left.

One Twenty-Five

Stran, Casi, Hench, and Leeana stood to one side, their backs against the wall of the rearranged flight briefing room as Major Iims called each of the cadets by name. Hearing the calls, the cadets came into the room and took places in front of a long, plastic-lined trough positioned in the middle of the room.

"Cadet Huml," he said, and the first young man entered to the clapping of their peers and took his place at the end of the trough farthest from the door. "Cadet Huml soloed in Patrol Two, a Class 1 fighter."

"Cadet Milik," Major Iims said, and the second young man entered and took his place beside Cadet Huml. "Cadet Milik soloed in Patrol Three, a Class 1 fighter." The clapping continued.

"Cadet Ilistr," he said next, and the young woman entered and took the third position. "Cadet Ilistr soloed in Patrol Four, a Class 1 fighter."

"Cadet Lupis," Iims said, and Blaire entered the room and stood beside Cadet Ilistr. "Cadet Lupis soloed in Patrol Five, a Class 2 fighter."

"Cadet Tayn Kooich," Major Iims said with a proud tinge to his thoughts, and Tayn entered and stood beside Blaire. "Cadet Kooich soloed in heavy fighter Q-KKLC14." Someone whistled amidst the clapping.

"Cadet Caiti Geaardt," he said with the same pride, and Caiti entered, smiling hugely, and stood beside Tayn. "Cadet Caiti Geaardt soloed in heavy fighter Q-STSX1." More whistles and the clapping continued.

"Cadet Coli Geaardt," Iims said, and smiled at Coli as

she entered and stood proudly beside her sister. "Cadet Coli Geaardt soloed in heavy fighter Q-STSX1." The peers' enthusiasm grew.

"Cadet Keely Dnar," he said, and Keely, chin high and shoulders back, entered and stood beside Coli. "Cadet Dnar soloed in heavy fighter Q-STSX1. For the record, Cadet Dnar is the youngest person to ever train as a cadet and is the youngest cadet to ever solo in the Force. And she is the youngest cadet to ever fly a heavy fighter." His smile for Keely was contagious and the applause and the whistling grew in volume.

Major Iims waited for the enthusiasm to abate, then turned and faced the room full of pilots. "There is another that cannot be here tonight for this honorable celebration of Passage. Lieutenant Keli Quil soloed on Monday in a heavy fighter Q-STSX12. She successfully completed the nav-com-to-pilot transition training just before Major Haak-Beeli led Apache Flight on an attempted rescue mission to the planet Nevar. We will include Lieutenant Quil in our next celebration, even if we have to have one just for her.

"Each of you," he said to the now quiet room, "gave the same effort these cadets have given. Each of you faced the same trials and doubts that these cadets have faced. Each of you has stood before your peers, pilots and instructors alike, just like these cadets are doing now. Each of you have been honorably celebrated the same as they are about to be."

Major Iims turned to the cadets. "Cadets, please step into the trough."

Everyone watched in silence as the cadets stepped in and turned to face the major.

"Please turn in pairs to face the one beside you," he continued, and then nodded to the two stewards standing at the end of the trough. "Cadets, please take a cup of Champagne from the Stewards." He waited until the cups had been distributed and then continued. "In the time-honored tradition, each cadet will now 'anoint' his or her 'partner' by pouring the Champagne over their heads. Mark!"

The room cheered as the cadets followed the captain's order and upturned the entire cup of Champagne on the head of the cadet facing them. The second steward passed slowly in front of them and collected the empty cups. Major Iims smiled and shouted, "Cadets. Attention!"

The eight cadets snapped to attention, facing the major. Without causing themselves to be noticed, sixteen previously chosen pilots stepped out of the group of celebrants and stopped behind eight large, nondescript buckets. In pairs, they quickly lifted a bucket and together, the sixteen simultaneously poured the cold water over the cadets.

Again, the room cheered loudly, their voices carrying over the sudden shrieks, yells, and gasps as the surprised and drenched cadets dissembled into laughter, hugging each other or slapping each other's backs.

"Scissors please," Major Iims said, and stepped forward, stopping at the edge of the trough in front of Cadet Huml as another officer stopped behind the cadet, opposite the major. Two others stopped in front of and behind Keely. "Each of you wears a shirt with the official details of your accomplishment printed on the front and back. A cutting from the front is for the School's Records and a cutting from the back is yours to keep in your personal effects. Beginning with Cadet Huml on this end and with Cadet Dnar on the other, the Cutting Off will begin."

▲

Blaire waited patiently and nervously at the same time as the Cutting Off moved from each end of the line of erect and motionless cadets, each unable to think of anything other than the scissors sliding slowly through the fabric as the front and back of their T-shirts were carefully cut away, removing the printed portion as Major Iims had described.

When the officers reached Blaire and Tayn, Blaire heard Luc and his friends somewhere nearby. At first, she thought it was nice that they were thinking of them and the ceremony, but then she began to *listen* to the rude comments Luc's friends were making about cadets having their clothes cut off in public.

Luc did not respond to their comments and innuendos, but she heard a laugh at their lewd and suggestive thoughts. When they brought her into their conversation, specifically speculating and pointing out Luc's ulterior intentions and desires, Blaire interrupted.

'Keep it clean, Luc. You have no claims and I am not a trophy you can set on a shelf to fondle as you desire, or to discuss in a rude or vulgar manner with your friends when I'm not around. Thank you for letting me see your true and crass self.'

Blaire felt him start to respond, but she closed her mind.

⬥

"Who was that?" Caiti asked when the major dismissed them to go, dry off, and change into partying clothes.

"Sorry you heard that," Blaire said softly, and dried her hair with a towel. "It's a sergeant that I helped in Sunday's incident. I thought he might be different."

"He sounds just like the boys at school," Caiti said with a knowing smile. "They think that as we change physically"—she gestured to herself—"that we suddenly have sex on the brain. They forget we grew up on a ranch and know all about sex and the ramifications of prom...promiscuity."

Blaire laughed. "I don't think their thinking gets any better as they get older—just more explicit."

Caiti laughed and then turned serious. "Mom had a lot of trouble with that when she grew up here. She said that with so many girls in the valley, out numbering the boys something like two to one, maybe more, the boys think they can just pick and choose and that the girls have to go along with them." She looked at Blaire. "Is that the way it works?"

"No!" Blaire said sharply. "I don't believe you are obligated to pair up with any boy, unless he suits you. And I mean completely suits you! No matter the pressure. Just look at your aunt and uncle, Wally and Carole, Thom and Eddie, and your folks. You will probably have to wait a bit for the right one, but no one can tell you who or when, or even if, you have to choose. At Thanksgiving, I saw how much your dad is still in love with your mom. It's forever! Your dad waited a long time, against all odds, to be with your mom. And your mom defied her mom, her great-aunt, and a whole society to wait for him. She was willing to give her life to wait. She didn't know who he was, but she was ready when he came and showed her how he felt about her, how he cared for her, how he protected her without asking for anything in return. None of these men—your uncle Nick, Wally, Thom, or your dad—acted or thought about their women like Luc, his friends, or the boys you know in school. Remember the history and trust your *feelings*. There are real, honest men out there, and maybe one of them is looking for you."

"Thanks," Caiti said, and smiled.

"Hey, do you have your good clothes in your bags?" Blaire asked, suddenly changing the subject.

"Yeah, we all do," Caiti said, looking at Coli and Keely.

"Okay," Blaire said, and smiled. "Sorry, Tayn, but you girls grab your towels and your bags and follow me. We'll shower, change, and fix our hair in my apartment."

ᐱ ᐱ ᐱ ᐱ ᐱ

"Thanks for the help, Forty-two" Seventeen said as he entered the Mess and saw Sergeant Stial sitting alone at a corner table, sipping a beer.

"Hey, Seventeen. Glad to be a help," he said, and raised his mug to the lieutenant.

"Mind if I get a beer and join you?" Seventeen asked.

"No," Sergeant Stial said. "You must be off duty for the rest of the night."

Seventeen ordered his brew and then returned and took the chair against the other wall from the sergeant. "Yeah. I'm off for the next forty-eight hours." He leaned his chair back, rocking up on two legs, and leaned against the wall. "Unless we have another major crisis. Don't get time off very often."

"I know," Sergeant Stial said. "Did we find everyone?"

"All except the one we need to catch," Seventeen said with a sigh, and took a long sip of the cold brew. "The commander keeps telling us that one has a real knack for slipping away." He shook his head and took another quick sip. "Colonel Mooren and his mate were there trying to follow him, but he said when we showed ourselves and closed in for the grab, it was like he evaporated."

"Evaporated? How?"

Seventeen shook his head again. "I sure wish I knew. Captain Mooren—Franni—has an uncanny sense of *feel*, just like Captain Casi. She's always been able to lock onto a *feeling* and stay on it. But somehow, this Nikle fella keeps slipping away. As you know, we had him in our hands last Friday and he got away. Did any of your guys get a glimpse of him?"

Sergeant Stial shook his head. "We don't have anyone that can *sense* someone. We can only go on what someone tells us."

"Would it have helped if we asked any of those that helped us in the tunnels?"

"Maybe," the Sergeant said, a smile quickly crossing his face—and just as quickly, he replaced it with a somber expression. "They probably wouldn't have been any more helpful than Captain Mooren was."

"Did you hear?" Seventeen asked. "That Cadet Lupis was the one that saw the gathering and contacted the commander through his ship?"

"No," Sergeant Stial said, "but after the tunnel incident, that doesn't surprise me. She seems to hear a lot of things when you least expect it."

Seventeen took a long sip of his beer and looked curiously at the sergeant. "What are you referring to?"

"Nothing," Sergeant Stial said, and took another sip, emptying his mug. He set it down and pondered it a moment, then looked at Seventeen. "Can I get you another?"

Seventeen looked at his mug, downed the last gulp, and handed it to the Sergeant. "Sure, thanks."

"You know you warned me," Sergeant Stial said as he set the two mugs on the table and sat back down.

"I did?"

"About Cadet Lupis," Sergeant Stial continued. "I've seen her twice now—in the library and then at dinner—but both times I feel we didn't really hit it off. When I'm around her, my mind seems to go numb, turns into jelly. I suddenly forget that I am a decorated marine squad leader and that I've faced enemy fire and led my men in conflict. I find myself unsure, fumbling like a schoolboy talking to a girl for the first time. I can't figure this out. I've known women and I've never been at a loss for words before. But this woman...this Cadet Lupis...seems to unhinge me."

Sergeant Stial looked at Seventeen and took a sip of his beer.

"So why do you say she hears things when you don't expect her to?" Seventeen asked. "Other than hearing the intruders and yesterday's gathering."

"Earlier this evening," Sergeant Stial said, "when the cadets were having their Solo Celebration, I passed in the corridor outside of the briefing room and I stopped to listen. I felt happy for them and their accomplishments, but I didn't interrupt. I wasn't invited and I think I might have been hearing Blaire's excitement. Anyway, as they got close to the end of the ceremony, two of my one-year direct reports stopped and started talking about what they figured went on in those ceremonies. I told them to be quiet, but one of them launched into comments about cadets getting their clothes cut off in public and the other made mention of Cadet Lupis and made suggestive, lewd comments about my intentions toward her. I was about to stomp on them for their deplorable conduct, drunk or not, when Blaire told me in no uncertain terms that she was not a trophy for me to put on a shelf and handle as I please or to discuss in such rude and vulgar manners. Before I could respond to her, she cut me off and I unloaded on the reports. They will think long and hard before they speak that way in front of their superiors again, and maybe even before they speak that way to anyone."

"Brig?"

"Twenty-four hours and possibly one stripe. I haven't decided on the stripes yet," he said, and took a long sip of his beer. "Sorry. They really pissed me off, and worse, Blaire heard them. And now she won't answer when I try to speak with her. She probably thinks I was part of that hallway conversation or that I was okay with them talking that way about her. It was maddening that they aimed their comments at me, but I don't like Blaire thinking I was okay with their inappropriate comments and innuendoes about her."

"Ouch," Seventeen said.

⚑ ⚑ ⚑ ⚑ ⚑

Blaire walked behind the girls as Keely led the way, dressed in a pretty, printed smock and colorful leggings. Caiti and Coli followed her, each wearing identical slacks and tops, hairbands, and accessories. Blaire smiled as Caiti and Coli induced the normal smiles, greetings, and questions when they entered the room.

'Can they tell which of you is which?' Blaire asked.

'Most. If they pay attention,' Coli said, and Blaire chuckled with them.

'If they don't, it can be fun, in a way,' Caiti added.

'What's so difficult about telling them apart?' Keely asked, and shrugged.

'I don't know. It isn't hard,' Blaire said, and chuckled again.

When Keely stopped in front of the refreshment table with its array of finger foods and filled cups, she looked up at Blaire, questioning. Blaire quickly looked around the room, but did not see Casi. *'Casi? They are offering Champagne. What do you want the girls to have?'*

'One cup,' Casi said, surprising Blaire. *'Then it's teas, 'ades, or soft drinks.'*

'Okay,' Blaire said, and looked at Keely and saw Caiti and Coli's smiles. "One cup. You've earned the privilege to be older and to celebrate for the moment."

Keely reached for a cup and slowly handed it to Caiti and then repeated the gesture, handing one to Coli. Blaire picked one up as Keely got one for herself.

"Have you had Champagne before?" Blaire asked, and they all shook their heads. "Then let me help. Take a very small sip and swish it around in your mouth," she said, and slowly explained the best way to acclimate their taste buds to the new, sometimes bitter, introduction to wine.

"Okay," Keely said, and took a sip as Nick stopped, staring down at her.

She looked up at his stern look, afraid he did not agree with her having Champagne. But Nick slowly relaxed his expression and smiled as he knelt down beside her.

"It's okay, love," he said with a huge smile, his eyes filling with moisture as he looked at her. "I was unfairly teasing you. You are the biggest little girl I know!"

"Boy," Blaire said in a rush. "I thought you were mad for a moment. Casi said—"

"I know. It's okay, Blaire." Nick smiled up at her as he slipped an arm around Keely's waist.

"You know...?" Blaire asked softly. "I didn't think you—"

"I don't, Blaire." He smiled and glanced at her. "Casi and I talked about this before tonight." He looked at Keely as she tried her second sip. "The girls, this one especially, have earned tonight."

"Of course. Thank you, Captain," Blaire said. "May I take

the cadets around and introduce them to the cadets I live with? They haven't spent much time here with the rest of us Wannabes."

Nick slowly stood up and smiled. "Certainly. I think they would like that, Blaire."

C.3486.744

"Ematl Approach Control," Cheral hailed as she and Keli prepared STSX12 for the morning descent to Nevar's surface. "Galactic Peace Force Apache Flight is in Nevar orbit and requests descent and approach to Space Port Ematl. Apache Flight has four heavy fighters, two patrol fighters, and two marine transports to assist in the recovery from the recent attack."

Cheral looked at Keli from the aft-facing pilot's chair.

"Are you sure we've got the right Approach Charts?" Cheral asked.

"Can't be sure, Major," Keli said, and glanced around at her monitors. "It's the most recent the Force has on file."

Cheral sighed and composed her thoughts.

"Ematl Approach Control," she said again. "This is Major Haak-Beeli, commander of QSTSX12, Apache Flight Leader. Apache Flight is requesting permission to descend to Space Port Ematl. Please confirm."

Cheral turned to Keli and let her shoulders drop. "We've been at his for half an hour and all I get is static. Are we using the correct communications channel?" She glanced at Kiile in the jump seat and tried to smile as he shrugged.

"Apache Four," Cera's voice said from the coms speaker. "There's a change in Ematl's Guardian."

"What?" Cheral asked, and she joined Kiile, looking over the canopy sill, knowing they would not see anything without visual enhancement. "What do you see?"

Keli started an optical scan.

"Color change," Cera said. "The red-purple is fading...Looks like it's...it's turning...green."

"Keli," Cheral said, and turned the pilot's chair to forward facing. "Is there anything in the procedures that says 'how' the Guardians communicate? Colors instead of words?"

"I'm checking."

"Thank you, Ematl Approach Control," Cheral said into the coms. "Apache Flight, flight of six is descending. Two Galactic Peace Force heavy fighters will remain in lunar orbit as sentries. We are bringing troops to help with clean up and we have medical assistance if necessary."

"Ematl's Guardian is definitely green," Cera's voice said with a hint of a girlish giggle. "The other Guardians are still the red-purple color."

⚓

Transport MT-6643M hovered near the Ematl Guardian's base and scanned the area as Apache Ten and Fifteen drifted over the cleared sectors of the city, looking for any signs that something had changed.

"ST12," Cera said into her helmet mic. "Ask Ematl Control if there are any survivors in the storm shelters. Ask if the shelters can be unlocked, opened. We're not seeing anything different than we saw last night."

"Request sent," Keli replied as Cera watched Ani settle and hover close to a large mound of debris half a Terran mile from the Guardian base.

"Apache Flight," Keli said. "I have a text response from the Guardian. Two percent of Ematl's population are in three of the shelters. Beacons will illuminate. Shelters unlocked. The rest of the city's population was either killed or removed in the attack."

"I think we now have a good idea who's responsible," Cera said. "There's a light! South of the Guardian."

"6643 sees it," the heavy voice of the nav-com announced.

"We're moving to check it out."

"Ani," Cera said. "I'm going to hover at a higher altitude and see if I can see the other beacons." Apache Fifteen was drifting up before Cera had finished stating her message.

▲

"The shelter's hatch is opening," 6643's nav-com's voice said. "We're setting down and will dispatch a squad to bring out all we can find."

"Thanks, 6643," Cheral said, and then turned her head to see Keli. "Ematl Control. Are there survivors in the other towns or cities?"

"It says yes," Keli said, and started to chuckle as she realized there were at least some survivors. "There are twenty-three shelters in twenty cities. Current status of sheltered population unknown. The Ematl Guardian says communications with the other Guardians is still interrupted."

"ST," Cheral said. "Please prepare a status report for the director and the marines' major general. Provide the details of our investigation and our communications with the Ematl Guardian. Explain the protocol and the use of colors. When compiled, Keli will review and transmit with an urgent request for more explosives handlers, rescue teams, and food supplies."

"COMPILING."

"Apache Ten, 4386," Cera's voice came through the coms. "Two more beacons. Northeast of the Guardian about a Terran mile and another west northwest, halfway to the port basin."

"4386 will drop a squad at each," came the reply. "Thank you, Apache Fifteen."

"DIRECTOR'S STATUS COMPLETE."

"Thanks, ST," Keli said, and immediately scanned the report. She made a couple of minor changes and reinforced the urgency of getting rescue support as quickly as possible. She glanced at the back of Cheral's chair and decided against the question she was going to ask. She made her own decision and sent the status. "Status sent."

"Thanks, Keli," Cheral said as she swung STSX12 around to survey the activity on the ground.

For the next Terran hour, slightly more than a galactic par, Apache Flight watched the marines as they slowly brought people to the surface and out of the three shelters. It saddened Cheral to see how few made it into the shelters compared to the numbers that had lived and worked in the city. The Guardian confirmed they had only a three-decipar warning, and Keli quickly computed the Terran equivalent: seventeen and a quarter minutes.

"Apache Leader," 6643's nav-com hailed. "We have found two hundred and ninety persons so far in the first shelter. They seem to be in reasonable health, with adequate food supplies, but terribly inadequate hygienic facilities."

"Thank you, 6643," Cheral replied.

"Message coming in," Keli said, and started reading the words floating in front of the matte-faced monitor. "Ten transports will arrive tomorrow, ETA one full turn from now. Four additional heavy fighters and two medical transports will accompany the marine transports."

"That's wonderful, Keli," Cheral said. "Pass the information to all of the ships and to the Guardian"

"Major Glean," Cheral hailed as she watched.

"Major?" Neel's strong voice answered.

"Can you and Debira take over from here?" Cheral asked.

"Yes, Major," Neel said.

"It looks like everything is under control now," Cheral continued. "Our marines will help all of the locals they can find, finish clearing the mines around Ematl, and with the help tomorrow, maybe they can have all of the shelters opened over the next two or three turns. We're in a surveillance and defense role now."

"Are you off, then," Debira asked, "for Belimoor?"

"Yes. I think it's time," Cheral admitted. "We'll pick up Ani and depart. Let us know if you need us for anything. We'll be *listening* for any call."

"Thank you," Neel said. "Give Neila our deepest sympathies for her loss and our greatest hopes for her future."

"We will. Thank you," Cheral said, and switched coms to the Guardian. "Ematl Departure Control. Q-STSX12 and Apache Ten are departing for a join-up in orbit. Then Q-STSX12 and Apache Ten will depart for Belimoor on Somstri. Q-LTVC21 will take over as Apache Flight Leader."

Cheral turned STSX12 and watched the Guardian's column.

"Text message. It reads: Safe trip, Q-STSX12. Thank you for your assistance, Apache Flight Leader," Keli said.

"The column flashed blue twice in rapid succession," Kiile said, still watching the Guardian. "Interesting system. I wish I remembered more. We could have been here much sooner."

"I know," Cheral said softly. "But we did get here and we were able to help those that were left. I think helping, even a little, is worth the effort."

Kiile smiled and leaned over and kissed her. "I think so too, Mrs. Beeli."

"Apache Ten," Cheral said, forcing herself to stay in character. "Ascend with me to orbit and join up."

Cheral smiled at Kiile as she pushed the thrust levers forward and pulled ST12's nose up.

▲ ▲ ▲ ▲ ▲

"Keli?" Cheral asked as she turned the pilot's chair to aft facing and unbuckled the straps. "Are you up to a turn?"

"Sure," Keli said, and smiled. "I can sleep up there as well as I can back here."

They passed in the central compartment and Cheral descended to the galley.

"Kiile? Keli? Ani? Tea?"

She took four containers from the storage drawer when they agreed. She pressed the first into the warmer and watched the warm orange light around the aperture indicating the warmer was in operation. When the aperture turned green, she snapped the container out and inserted the second. She repeated the process for the third.

She inserted the last container and turned to look up through the ceiling portal. "Two coming your way," she said, and when Kiile's face appeared she gently tossed the containers to him. "I'm going to stretch out for a minute or two."

She passed a container to Ani where she sat in one of the double-wide cushion chairs and then took her container and straw and lay out on the right-hand medical couch and pulled the retention net over her. "Hope I'm not bothering you, Ani," she said.

"No, you're fine," Ani said. "I'm just catching up on a little reading. We're what, nine pars en route?"

"About that," Cheral said, and settled, taking a sip of her tea. She thought about the morning's events and the previous night's discoveries and organized her thoughts to get the order and the content right. "ST, what time is it at home?"

"IT IS 1030 HOURS ON FRIDAY MORNING, EIGHT DECEMBER."

"Thank you," she said, and closed her eyes. '*STSX1, Casi, Stran. STSX12 has sent a complete mission report. Approximately four hundred survivors found in Ematl storm shelters. The Ematl Guardian claims only two percent of Ematl's population made it to safety—something like a thousand people. The Rings mounted a major rescue mission and marine transports and Q-Ships will arrive on Nevar before midmorning tomorrow, Ematl time. Major and Captain Glean are overseeing the operations with Apache Fifteen as their support. Lieutenant Cera unlocked the protocol key to open conversation with the Guardian and finally to open the shelters to let the people out.*'

'*Thank you, Cheral,*' Stran's voice replied. '*Casi is reviewing*

the report you sent. Very well done, Major. Are you on your way
to Somstri?'

'Yes,' Cheral said, and drank more of her tea. *'We are still
over seven pars out. Running a little late. We lost a little time this
morning getting to know the Guardian and learning part of the
language. It's all in the report. How was the ceremony last night?'*

*'The ceremony was nicely done, and Major Iims mentioned
Keli was supposed to be there and explained why she was missing.
He will include her in the first ceremony after you get back. Or
even a special ceremony, if need be.'*

'That's nice,' Cheral agreed. *'I'm sure the girls and Tayn did
okay.'*

*'We were very proud of them and Blaire. And we now have
Billie, Alyssa, Ridan, Kayli, and Kail in self-defense training.'*

'A lot has happened in a short week.'

'I guess it has,' Stran said.

'I'll let you go,' Cheral said, and yawned. *'I'm going to nap for
a few minutes before I go back up and man the coms. I'll let you
know how things go with Neila.'*

Friday, December 8

"Did you hear Cousin Cheral, Chy?" Sedona asked softly as
they got their trays at the lunch counter in the school cafeteria.

"Yeah," Cheyenne said, and started down the serving line
between Sedona and Sierra. "Sounds like they found a lot of
survivors."

"I heard Mom," Sedona started to say, but stopped when
a boy reached in front of them and grabbed a dessert plate.
Sedona watched as he cut in at the front of the line and slipped
his card into the cashiering machine. "Anyway, she said they
had just started and found out only about one or two percent of
the people in that town made it to shelter."

"Wow," Cheyenne said. "That's not many."

They collected their main course plates and drinks, swiped their cards, and found a table near the windows overlooking the playgrounds. Sierra absently looked at the blowing snow streaking past the windows as they sat down and huddled to talk.

When they finished eating and had sent their trays of dirty dishes down the conveyor to the kitchen, they went back to their table and passed the time with idle talk and conversation for the rest of the lunch period.

"There's another one," Cheyenne whispered, and turned to the window. She peered through the snow to the southeast and the corner of the high school classroom wing near the east parking lot. "It's a man in a light green coupe at the end of the parking lot."

"I *see* him," Sedona and Sierra said together.

"He has that same *feeling* the others had," Sierra said, and reached out to *feel* the area around the school and the woods just south of Webb and Walnut.

'Six,' Sedona said. *'Get the numbers off of the car we're feeling. Give them to Wally and tell him where the car is. Wally or his deputies need to visit this car and the man inside it.'*

The period bell rang and the girls slowly walked to their classrooms.

"Wally will take care of him, Chy," Sierra said. "Don't worry. We'll tell Tayn and Billie. See you after class."

"Right," Cheyenne said, and hurried down a different hallway to her classroom.

Sedona and Sierra continued to their classroom and took their seats. Classes started as usual, and they were in the middle of a math test when Sierra looked up, glanced at Sedona and she turned and looked at the blackboard wall just as the sound of a deputy's patrol car siren burped twice. Sierra looked back at her test page and *felt* Wally and Thom get out of their cars and approach the light green car. Wally tapped on the window of the car and asked the man to get out. He stepped back and Sierra jumped when the man pushed the door open and pointed a pistol at Wally. She felt like he was pointing it at her.

A sudden brilliant flash filled her mind and she realized she was holding her breath. Their teacher had noticed her twitch and her ashen expression. When Sierra shook her head, she saw their teacher bent over Sedona's desk, talking to her.

Sierra inhaled quickly and saw Sedona do the same, looking as pale as she felt. She tried to smile and shrug it off, but their teacher was concerned and asked them to follow her to the school nurse.

"We're really all right," Sedona said as their teacher pulled her up and was urging Sierra to follow her.

Suddenly the bell in the hallway began ringing and people scurried past the doorway. Their teacher hurried to the hall and asked someone what happened. She turned back to the class and told everyone to get down and to get under their desks. Sierra looked at Sedona as they complied.

'Wally's all right,' Sedona said. 'It's over now. The man in the green car is dead.'

One Twenty-Six

"Peace Force Somstri Watch," Keli hailed on the guarded com channel. "Apache Four, QSTSX12, inbound Somstri from Nevar."

"Apache Four, Somstri Watch, Q-KVCC6, receiving you," the feminine nav-com's voice responded. "Please activate IFF and authorization."

Keli switched IFF on and sent the requested code.

"Apache Four, state your purpose," the woman asked.

"Special Mission at the request of the director. The authorization is all I am at liberty to discuss," Keli said in a level tone. "Apache Four is a requested unit of Apache Squadron, under the command of Commander Stran Geaardt, and our mission is under the explicit orders of the director."

A long silence ensued and finally the woman answered. "Authorization accepted, Apache Four. You may descend into Somstri's planetary space."

"Thank you, KVCC6," Keli said in a more pleasant tone.

"Do you have our meeting spot mapped?" Cheral asked. Keli saw her glance over her shoulder.

"Display coming forward," Keli said as the three-dimensional translucent globe appeared in the space between Cheral and the forward panel of the cockpit.

Kiile studied the map from his place on the jump seat as a green line spiraled around the globe from their location in space to a spot on the surface.

"Thirty Terran minutes," Keli announced. "Our communications indicate Neila and her grandfather will be arriving at the meeting place a few minutes before us. We should be able to get a physical confirmation before we land."

"Very good, Keli," Cheral said. "Let's continue to keep the details of our mission under wraps. IFF off."

"IFF off," Keli confirmed with a chuckle. "We are still sensor blocked and fully cloaked. Shields are on."

"Ani," Cheral said. "We'll hold in a low orbit so we can release Apache Ten. Follow us down and land after we do."

"Okay, Major," Ani said. "I'll get suited up."

▲

Cheral slowly swung STSX12 around the adequately large clearing amidst the heavy stand of sage green and lavender trees that covered the area behind a large stone dwelling in the rolling hills just beyond the southeast edge of Belimoor proper. The grounds and wooded area had the appearance of an estate with numerous small, well-kept gardens, each bordered with hedges of blue-green and foliage with purple bushes at obvious corners, precisely arranged around the main house and two additional smaller houses.

"There's an elderly man and a young girl sitting on a stone bench," Cheral said, mostly to let Keli and Kiile know what she was sensing. She knew Ani also sensed them. "The bench is at the edge of the clearing where a wide, grassy path leads from the house. I don't *see* anyone else—no groundskeepers, no gardeners, no one in the other buildings. Pre-landing checks."

"Checks are complete," Keli said as she configured STSX12 for landing. "Apache Ten. Apache Four is preparing to land."

"I don't see any threats, Apache Four," Ani replied. "There are no others around the buildings or the grounds besides the two on the bench."

"We're 'go' for landing," Keli said to Ani and Cheral.

▲

"Gpada?" the girl in baggy pants and a white tunic top asked her grandfather.

"Speak in Galactic Standard, Neila," he said, and squeezed her hand.

"Yes. Do you know what they are like?" the blond-haired girl asked, and looked up at his aged, parchment face. "My father? Is he nice?"

"I do not know your father, the man," he said with a weak smile. "Only as a boy. The man I know only of him, from his father when we used to visit you in Turell. He always had very nice things to say about Kiile."

"I know he is very honored in the Peace Force Marines," Neila said, and kicked her foot absently. "But what is he like? He's a stranger and I do not want to go with strangers. I wish I could stay here. You are the last one I know."

"I know this is very hard for you," he said, and smiled down at her. "We will see how long they can stay and visit so you can get to know them. If they did not care, they would not have come such a great distance for you."

Neila snapped her head around and looked at the clearing. "Did you hear that?" Neila asked.

"I missed it," he said. "What did it sound like?"

"I don't know," she said, staring at the emptiness. "Like someone very big stomped on the ground. Now, there is a whisper, a very soft sound of wind." She glanced at him and then back at the clearing. "Someone is coming, but I do not see them."

Startled, Neila jumped, nearly falling off of the bench when a man in a mottled khaki and white uniform, and two women in tight-fitting blue-black uniforms suddenly coalesced out of the seemingly vacant clearing.

Neila looked at her grandfather's smile and turned back to the three in time to see a fourth, another woman in another blue-black uniform materialize in another part of the clearing.

"My apologies for startling you," Cheral said. She quickly introduced Lieutenant Quil and Captain Tigs and then turned to Kiile. "I am Galactic Peace Force Major Cheral Haak-Beeli of the Apache Squadron, and this is the man of most interest to you, Peace Force Marine Captain Kiile Beeli."

Kiile stepped forward and extended his arm to the elderly man. "Greetings, Anthor of Marit. It has been a very long time since we have had time to speak or drink tea. Not since I was just a boy."

"Kiile of Beeli," Anthor said with a wide smile. "It has been a long time indeed. You were not yet in the Peace Force at that when. But now, I must introduce you to the reason for your visit."

Anthor turned and gestured to Neila.

"This is Neila of Kiile," Anthor said, and Neila made a bowing-like gesture of greeting.

"It is nice to meet you, sir," she said as she straightened and stood close beside Anthor. "Grandfather Anthor tells me you are my father."

"It is wonderful to meet you as well," Kiile said with a bow of his own. "And yes. I am told you are my daughter."

She stepped forward, nearly as tall as his shoulders, and looked at him very closely. She looked at one side of him and then at the other, then stood in front of him and looked up again. "May I touch you, sir?"

"Certainly," he said, and extended his hand.

She took it gently and smiled. "I was not certain you were real."

"Not real?" Kiile asked, surprised. "Because we've never met before?"

"No." She smiled. "Because you appeared out of nowhere, walking across our clearing, suddenly there."

"Neila?" Cheral asked, and smiled at Anthor. "Would you and Anthor walk with me into the clearing?"

"Not I," Anthor said with a wave of his hand, and then looked at Neila. "Go with the major. She has something very surprising to show you. I have already seen what she will show you. Many years ago. I will wait on our bench."

He turned back to the bench and Kiile helped him sit down so he could watch as Cheral led Neila out into the clearing.

"We are part of a fighting squadron, Neila," Cheral started explaining. "And so it is necessary that we keep others from seeing everything we do or where we go." Cheral stopped and looked at Neila. "This is where we were when you saw us appear. Another couple of steps and you will see my fighter. He is hidden under an invisible veil—we call it simply 'cloaking.' Captain Tigs has another fighter, different from mine, just a little farther back and off to our right. Captain Tigs flies cover for us, to be sure no one is following or seeing what we're doing." She smiled at Neila. "Are you ready to see my ship?"

Neila slowly nodded and Cheral took her hand. Together they stepped forward and Neila about stumbled when STSX12 suddenly appeared, his long nose looming above them.

Neila's mouth moved, but no words came out as Cheral led her under the left pylon to the aft portal.

"We will show you the insides another time," Cheral said as they proceeded around and back to the nose along the right side. "You can see everyone by the bench from here, but they cannot see us. Not until we walk back through the veil and become visible to them again."

"This is very surprising," Neila said in a soft, astonished voice. "I do not know what words to use."

"We call it pretty amazing," Cheral said. "Essential, but definitely amazing."

As they walked back to the group, Neila kept turning around and looking at the apparent emptiness.

"You have seen that before?" Neila asked Anthor when they reached the bench. "It is very surprising." She glanced at Cheral. "The major says they call it amazing. When did you see it, Grandfather?"

"When Kiile left Turell to join the marines," Anthor said. "He was about your age then. The recruiters left using the disappearing method, so no one could follow them home. Only the special ones know where the Peace Force is." Anthor looked at them and asked. "Would you like to come inside? It will be getting hot in a little while, and I am not up to spending my time out in the heat."

Kiile bent to help Anthor, and Cheral caught his other hand as he stood up. Neila picked up Anthor's sitting pad and followed them to the stone dwelling. Keli and Ani turned and *felt* the area around them again, and then joined the group as they walked to the house.

'ST12 *is closed up. Secured,*' Keli said to Cheral as they entered and Neila closed the door to the outside.

⬥

"You have a very pleasant home, Anthor," Kiile said as he helped Anthor through the door into a nicely furnished sitting room. "Neila, where does Anthor like to sit?"

Neila showed Kiile and helped maneuver Anthor to his favorite overstuffed chair in front of the entertainment unit. She fluffed his pillows and raised his feet onto a low footstool, thanked Kiile, and then asked if she could get them something to drink. Kiile watched as Cheral, Keli, and Ani followed her into the food-preparation portion of the room and Neila pointed out the things they could do.

"I must say, Anthor," Kiile said softly as he sat down on a low stool beside him. "You are looking very well for a statesman your age."

"Thank you for the lie, Kiile," Anthor chuckled, "but we both know I'm ready to join my mate. I've been waiting for you to come so Neila can move on in her life. She cannot stay here any longer."

"I am sorry we didn't come sooner," Kiile said. "Apparently it took a little time for your message to reach me, and I must admit it was a big surprise. I had no idea."

"I knew it would take time," Anthor said, "but I had to find you. The date for me to leave the estate was set during our last winter, and this was to be Neila's and my last, wonderful summer adventure together. But then Nevar was attacked and she had nowhere to go, no home to go back to. Of course I extended, but my time is running out. Our adventure has not been as happy as we planned. The estate was going to transfer to Milna so they could move here to live, away from the daily hardships of working their farm. But now, it will transfer to Neila when she is of age."

Kiile leaned forward and set his elbows on his knees. "Thank goodness she was here, Anthor," Kiile said softly, and Anthor nodded. "And I am very grateful that you sent for me."

Kiile straightened as Neila came back into the room with a tray of ornate cups and various serving utensils. Cheral, Keli, and Ani followed with other trays of pitchers, carafes, and various add-in ingredients.

Neila set her tray on the oval table in front of Anthor and gestured to where she wanted the others placed.

"Please continue, Gpada—sorry, Grandfather. I've been listening," Neila said as she fixed Anthor a cup of a juice he liked.

"Very keen hearing, this one," Anthor said with a wide smile. "Very little gets past her. She even heard you land and walking in the clearing. The veil had her confused, though."

"Yes," Neila admitted as she watched Cheral fix Kiile a cup of tea with appropriate add-ins. "Living on the farm, good hearing is sometimes a benefit." She sighed and Kiile saw the moisture collect in her eyes.

"I am so very sorry you cannot go back to Turell, Neila," Kiile said, and handed her a hand wipe from the tray beside him. "We just came from Nevar, and..."

"It is bad, is it not?" she asked, and held his eyes.

"It is very bad," Kiile said softly. "Turell does not exist anymore. All of the farms across the planet are gone. Crops, villages, towns, homes, all are gone. Above ground, the cities are just scattered rubble. Very little identifies the places as population, business, or industrial centers."

"The Guardian at Ematl says the people had a three-decipar warning," Cheral said softly. "Maybe a little more in some areas, but not enough time for any of the villagers to get to a town or a storm shelter."

"Is everyone gone?" Neila whispered.

"No, but almost," Kiile answered. "In Ematl, less than two percent of the city reached the shelters before the Guardians had to close them. Cheral's other two fighters and two marine transports are continuing the search for survivors. A larger rescue group will arrive in a few pars, and by this time tomorrow, we hope to know how many were not killed or taken."

"Taken?" Neila asked, and Kiile saw her startled expression.

"Yes, Neila," Kiile said, and started explaining the key points of the Peace Force's efforts to stop the business of trafficking slaves. "If you would like, we have some history files on board ST12. You can learn some about Terra and about what we have done in the past years to try and stop the slavers."

"Thank you, Kiile," Neila said, and straightened her shoulders. He saw her eyes were still wet, but her manner was poised and respectful. "You must know that I do not want to leave the places I have known all my life. I am given no choice, but I do not want to go with you."

"I know, Neila," Kiile said. "It is horribly unfair that you must leave, but I am hoping you will trust us—me. I will do everything I can to protect you, keep you safe and well, and help you learn. You can teach me about your family and we can teach you about ours. Unfortunately our lives have changed, and I can only hope you will give me the chance to make the best of this situation and to see that I do care about you."

She inhaled deeply and looked at him as she let her breath out. Kiile knew she had a lot of fear and worry on her mind.

"I have studied Terra some," Neila finally said. "It does look like a nice place, geographically. But it seems to have its share of personal, people-on-people problems."

"It does," Kiile admitted. "And we live in the secret background to those problems, trying to fix and correct the problems that we can."

"Grandfather has some letters," Neila said, glancing at Anthor, "he received from his son that moved to Terra. He let me read them."

"Gpada has a son on Terra?" Kiile asked in surprise, turning to look at Anthor's smile and nod.

"When Tor was in the University in Zeupa," Anthor said, "on the other side of Somstri, he met a local girl, Canri, and after they graduated, they mated and then immigrated to Terra as part of a research team. They liked it so much, they petitioned to stay."

"Cousin Tor's letters said they live in someplace called Colorado," Neila said. "It has farms and grasslands in one part and beautiful mountains, canyons, and dashing rivers in the other part. They have a son and a daughter, much older than me, grown up and moved away."

"That is very close to where we live," Kiile said as Cheral took his cup and refilled it. Kiile noticed Neila watching Cheral.

"I checked my age," Neila said, "with one of Gpada's programs. Here, today, I am five Galactic Standard years and two hundred and forty-six turns. It said I'm fourteen Terran years, four Terran months, and twelve Terran days old. I was born on 3481.499."

"That makes you about the same age as Carrie Anne," Cheral said with a smile as she set back in her chair. "Her mother and she are moving back to the valley next month. She might help teach you about the Terran culture from a younger person's perspective."

Saturday, December 9

"What have you got in mind?" Hench asked Greg as they sat across from each other, finishing their morning meal. "You look like you've gotten one of Annie's summer cherry pies all for yourself."

"Something good," Greg admitted, and glanced at Leeana. "Maybe not that good, but good." He set his cup down and split another biscuit open, spread butter and jelly on a half, and then slowly took a bite.

Shara chuckled at his dramatics. "Just tell them, love."

"Okay," Greg said, and then finished his bite and washed the remnants down with his coffee. "I nosed around, a little behind your back, Hench, to be sure everything is ready."

"Go on," Shara urged as everyone around the table waited.

"All right," he said. "Today, I want our four—Tayn, Sedona, Sierra, and Cheyenne—to cross-train in the patrol fighters. Iims has four Class 2's available for the next four days. Then, tomorrow or the next day, I want to expose them to live combat training with generated targets."

Tayn and the girls' faces danced with the news as they waited to hear more.

"I'm glad you've made arrangements," Hench said, "so I can work this out for you." His expression slowly turned to a smile. "We can use the usual practice area."

Greg nodded. "Iims asked that when we take our cadets out, we allow him to bring his four newly soloed cadets. I told him I thought that would be acceptable, but that I would ask you before giving him an answer."

"Oh? You did, did you?" Hench laughed.

"I knew you wouldn't mind, Hench," Greg smiled. "They need to have live fire training also. It's the next logical step."

Hench raised his cup and took a long sip of his coffee. He smiled at the children, Meara, and then at Shara and Leeana. "I presume we are picking Cheyenne up on the way to Obscure."

"Certainly." Shara smiled. "She's already anxiously pacing

on her balcony."

⋏

"Have you heard from Cheral and Kiile?" Hench asked as he followed Leeana and the children out the back door. Greg walked with him as they turned toward KKLC14 waiting in the pasture beyond the rail fence.

"As I mentioned the other night," Greg said, "they have found some survivors. It appears that their Guardian System has been in full working order since the attack. One exception is a single city system that failed under siege. When our patrols began searching Nevar after the attack, no one followed protocol and Nevar's Approach Control was never addressed. They just barged into Nevar's planetary space and the Guardians interpreted them as part of the attackers, more of the threat. They also saw the acoustical mines as a threat, and between the two, kept the survivors locked away from our help."

"How many survivors have been found?" Hench asked, nodding at Greg's explanation.

"Cheral said less than two percent in Ematl, the space port city," Greg said with a sigh. "Kiile's home village is completely gone, as are all of the other villages. She said that without the geographical coordinates, they wouldn't have suspected Turell ever existed. They brought in a number of transports to expand the search and their efficiency, but she hasn't reported yet today."

"They went on and met his daughter?"

"That went well, I think," Greg said. "Very bittersweet, as you would expect. I don't have any real details, but they plan on staying on Somstri a few days before they consider starting back."

Hench nodded and smiled at Greg.

"I guess I better get these eager cadets back to work," Hench said. "Are you coming out later?"

"Yes," Greg said. "We need to get into town and talk with Wally about yesterday first. Then we need to talk with Franni about Thursday."

C.3486.745

"Will I be living with you, Kiile?" Neila asked as they walked through the gardens behind Anthor's dwelling. She walked beside him and he saw her glance often at Cheral and the other two.

The afternoon was not too hot for Kiile's taste, and he knew Cheral was enjoying the time among the different gardens and plantings.

"Yes," Kiile said. "On Terra, Earth, it is normal for families to live together until the younger ones, the children, are old enough to be on their own."

"Does the major live with you?" Neila asked, and looked up at him.

"Not yet, but she will be. Cheral and I are recently mated," Kiile explained.

"That was not hard to figure out." Neila smiled and nodded. "Even though the major did say her name was 'Haak-Beeli' instead of 'with Kiile.' I suppose the Force has done something with the names."

"They have," Kiile said, and explained how he ended up with Beeli as his last name and how the cultural norm was for the mate and their children to take the man's last name. "I would like for you to be known as Neila Beeli, so everyone will know I am your father and that they should come to me if you need anything. Will that be all right with you?"

"I am 'of Kiile,'" she said. "So I suppose that would be truthful in your system. Yes, that will be all right with me."

"Thank you, Neila," Kiile said, and smiled hugely. "Now, back to your question on where you will live. We decided to wait and arrange for us to have a single, private apartment for all of us to live in together," Kiile said. "It will have two separate bedrooms, one for you and one for us. A living space, similar to Anthor's living area, or parlor, a bathing facility that we can each use, honoring each other's privacy, of course." He stopped at the strange expression that came across her face.

"A whole sleeping room just for me? And a room just for bathing?" Neila asked. "Don't you mean a place in your room?"

"No, Neila," Cheral said. "You are certainly old enough to have a space just for you. Our room would be right beside yours, but separate. You'll be able to come into our room almost anytime you want to. Is that okay?"

"I...I guess so," she said.

"Didn't you have a room at home?" Kiile asked.

"There was only one room at home. We all slept, bathed, and ate in the same room," she admitted. "Me, my two brothers, mother, and sometimes, her friend Bdor. My duty was first meal and last meal. And farm work."

"Well, we can prepare our meals in the apartment if we wish," Kiile said, moving the conversation along, "but the facility has some of the best cooks—ah, food preparers—in the entire Peace Force. They prepare food of all specialties in a dining hall we call a Mess."

"It's a mess? Why would you eat there if it is a mess?" Neila asked.

"No. No, Neila," Cheral chuckled. "It isn't in a mess, like untidy or unfit. In the services they have always called the dining hall by the name 'Mess.'"

"Oh. Very strange." She looked at Kiile, her expression still uncertain.

"Yes, it is strange." Kiile chuckled. "Strange indeed. The facility is a military facility, Neila," Kiile said, and looked down at her, "and that means it will be a little different than what you are used to. But we will try to show you everything you need to know, and who to talk to if you need something when we're both on duty."

"Will I have duties to perform each day?" Neila asked.

"Food preparation? Washing clothes? Bedclothes?"

"No. Not like you are thinking," Kiile said. "You will have to help us keep your room and the apartment tidy, but duties are something we need to figure out. Were you still in schooling in Turell?" When she nodded, he continued. "Then we will need to see where you are level-wise so we can continue your education from where you are now. It will be different from what you're used to, but a lot of it will be similar, I think. School might be your duties. We'll see."

"Is there something you would want to be doing each day?" Cheral asked softly.

"Farming," Neila said in soft reply, "is all I know how to do. Is there something for a farmer to do in this place you live?"

"We will strive to use the talents you learned farming," Kiile said with a smile, "and see if we can put them to use in new things for you to learn."

"Have you ever ridden runners?" Cheral asked.

"Runners?" Neila asked, uncertain of the term.

"On Terra, they are called horses," Cheral said with a smile. "We can look them up in your information on Terra. My cousin, the commander's wife, teaches riding. She was a champion rider until she joined the Force, and now her daughters are collecting the prizes. They are twins, almost eleven and a half Terran years old. And the commander's sister, who is right now flying cover with my flight over Nevar, has a ten-and-a-half-year-old daughter."

"I truly think you'll make good friends where we live, Neila," Kiile said as they started back toward Anthor's main dwelling. "Everyone is anxious to meet you."

"They want to meet a farm girl?" Neila asked, and he saw the puzzlement on her face.

"Be proud of who you are, Neila," Kiile said firmly. "You and your family worked farms that fed many, many people. That is very honorable."

"You did not want to be a farmer," Neila said. "You wanted

to leave and become a marine."

"Not because I didn't like farming." Kiile grinned. "I joined the Force so I could help others differently than providing food. I think it was the right calling for me."

Neila pondered Kiile's explanation and comments until they reached the main dwelling and she opened the door for them. She went straight to the living area and stopped beside Anthor.

"Did you have a nice walk, Neila?" Anthor asked, his voice weaker than it had been earlier in the day.

"Yes, Gpada," Neila said and knelt down beside his chair. "Are you all right?"

"Right enough," Anthor said softly, and patted her hand.

She turned to Kiile. "I think his Sustenance is running out. Stay with him so I can make a call. Please."

"Of course, Neila," Kiile said, and took the stool beside Anthor's chair.

Neila got up and hurried into the next room—a study or office, Kiile surmised by the bookcases he saw as she opened the door.

"Can I get you some juice or something else?" Kiile asked as Cheral sat down on another stool. Keli and Ani settled on chairs nearby.

"No, no. But thank you, Kiile," Anthor said calmly, and smiled at the four of them. "Is there any way Neila can take some of her *Gpama's* things with her to Terra?"

"What things would she take?" Cheral asked softly, and Kiile knew they all felt the seriousness of Anthor's condition.

"I would like her to take the sleeping room furniture," he said. "The bed was not used much before her grandmother passed. And the clothes press, and the Memories Chest." He sighed. "Anything of her grandmother's. Neila should have that part of her dowry to enjoy now."

"May I see how large the items are?" Cheral asked. "So I can arrange for shipping."

"Aah. Here she is," Anthor said as Neila came back into the room.

"A three-gillot package will be here in a decipar," Neila said. "How long will this one last, Gpada?"

"Two turns, child," Anthor said. "That will be long enough, I think." He smiled at her and then told her what he had asked of Kiile. "Will you take the major—"

"It's Cheral, Anthor," Cheral interrupted. "Just call me Cheral, please."

He smiled and nodded. "Take Cheral up to our room so she can see how many and how large the items are. Be certain she sees everything you would like to take with you. Kiile says you will have your own space and we want you to have proper things to put in it."

"Yes, Gpada," Neila said, and led Cheral to the stairs. "Do I call you Major or—"

"When we are together informally or as a family," Cheral said, "even if you do not feel like we are a family yet, please call me Cheral. I have to be the major when I am on duty and with the other pilots and such. Sometimes I bend the rules a little, though."

"Thank you," Neila said, and turned the corner at the top of the stairs. "It is this room." She pushed the door open. "I did not expect him to ask me to take anything. I thought it would be secured until I have reached the age to inherit."

"Neila." Cheral smiled and stopped in the doorway, surveying the communal chamber. Three separate sleeping areas were set against different walls, and each had the necessary furnishings. "He wants you to have what is important to you, so you will always remember this part of your life. The memories of your grandparents should be with you forever, just like memories of your mother and your life before all of this." She took a deep breath and looked around the room. "Can you show me what you want to take so I can arrange for it to be shipped?"

"Shipped?" Neila asked, looking at Cheral in surprise.

"Yes," Cheral said. "I have ways. I will have a proper-size container here by morning and I will have it packed and loaded so it will arrive safe and undamaged at Shadow Base in four turns on the supply transport. Is that okay?"

Neila's head bobbed in disbelief. "You'd have what I want to take shipped? To wherever they need to go? No matter what it costs?"

Cheral smiled. "Neila. Just show me what you are taking and let me get it home."

▲ ▲ ▲ ▲ ▲

The low overcast gave the already cold and windy day a gloomy feel. Greg parked their truck in the lot behind the marshals' office and they barely noticed the snow had stopped sometime midmorning as he helped Shara out and guided her up the back steps.

"Morning, Greg, Shar," Wally greeted, crossing the room from the coffee urn, extending his hand as they stepped in and quickly closed the door.

"Morning, Wally," Greg said, and waved at Thom and Deputy Day sitting at their respective desks. "Do you and Thom have a few minutes?"

Wally glanced at Thom's smile. "Sure. Want to use the conference room?"

"Why not?" Greg asked rhetorically, and turned Shara to the room in the corner of the office.

"Catch the phones for us, Bill," Wally said, and followed them into the room.

"I suppose you want to talk about yesterday," Wally said as he and Thom took seats across the round table from Greg and Shara.

"Yeah," Greg said. "Mostly wondering if you have an ID."

"Name is Joseph Reeds," Thom said, laying a thin folder on the table. "An older son of a Robert Reeds, related to the Niles Reeds namesake of the Niles Reeds Ranch. His father, Robert, was in the group Kiile's men picked up on Thursday."

"Does that play into why he was at the school?" Shara asked.

Greg did not have to see Shara's expression to know how much this incident was bothering her.

"No to the why," Wally said. "But I have to think his dad's capture had something to do with his attitude, his reactions when we inquired."

"Sure," Greg said, and looked at Shara, knowing he had to ask the question that sat heavy on Shara's mind. "But since he died at the scene, we have to ask."

"Do you think," Shara asked, quickly, "he was planning to use force against the children? To make them come with him? Greg is sure he wasn't trying to injure them or worse. Since they are valuable to the slavers."

"I'm sorry, Shar," Wally said softly. "I can see this has unsettled you. But you know as much as we do. I have to agree with Greg in that I don't think he was out to shoot any of the kids. Obviously he was armed, and that helps me with the locals when it comes to justifying the need for deadly force, but why he was at the school, armed, we cannot be sure."

"I'm glad the girls realized he was there," Thom said, "and let us know. Billie said Cheyenne contacted her and Sierra told her that Sedona had contacted Tayn. Your girls were on top of it and made sure no one got hurt or confronted."

"Is this going to make a big news splash?" Greg asked, changing the subject.

"I'm not sure," Wally said. "The locals are handling it okay and I've made a statement to our bi-weekly paper, trying to reduce the speculation. Whether they will leak it or send it to a wider audience, I don't know."

"At least none of the kids were out on the playground when

it happened," Shara said. "That will help some."

"Yeah," Wally agreed. "The school locked down for about a half an hour, but it was all over before they knew there was an issue. We've started running background checks on him and the ones picked up on Thursday. Maybe we can find something we can use."

"How is Pat Brownly doing?" Shara asked.

"Abe says she can almost sleep through the night," Thom said.

"Abe said?" Shara looked at him, surprised.

"Yeah." Thom smiled. "He comes by every day to let us know how she's doing. Eddie's dropped in on her a couple of times and offered for her to come up to our place during the day, if she wants to. Mary at the Boutique sends a new flower arrangement each morning, and Connie sends coffee and a sweet roll."

"So Abe's taken an interest again?" Shara asked, trying to understand.

"Abe's always been interested, Shar," Wally said. "They divorced over an argument because she couldn't have kids. Abe has supported her, and gave her the cabin and land it's on. Pat was the one that felt like she betrayed him, if that's the word, for marrying him and not telling him she couldn't bear children."

"I sure didn't know," Shara said, and folded her arms. "Ask Abe if she likes cherry pie. Annie makes the best in the valley."

One Twenty-Seven

"We just received an update from Apache Five," Keli said as Cheral climbed the rungs into ST12's central compartment. "Is Kiile with you?"

"No," Cheral said. "He's still visiting with Neila and Anthor. Ani's been talking about how she felt when she arrived at Obscure. Maybe that will help ease some of Neila's concerns." Cheral pulled out a jump seat, sat down beside Keli, and turned to the illuminated monitor. "What does Debira have to say?" she asked.

"A total of eight hundred and seven survived in Ematl," Keli started. "Less than hoped. Many died in the shelters. 6643 assigned the more significant cities to the ten transports when they arrived, and LTVC21 gave the heavy fighters sweep details in different cities to mark the mines and to look for anything new since communications with the Guardians began."

"Have they found anything in the other cities?" Cheral asked, trying to read ahead.

"They have adequately cleared the mines in four cities," Keli said, "two east of Ematl and two southwest. A total of three hundred and twelve from all four." Keli looked at Cheral, her expression discouraging. "It does not look very good."

Keli turned back to the report. "LTVC21 moved to Wiibsa and one of the transports dropped a squad to handle the mines there. Thirty-five mines and only ten were recovered from the shelter."

"Kiile said that shelter could hold twice the town's population," Cheral said, disbelief apparent in her whisper. "Where are all of them?"

"Debira said," Keli continued, "that knowing this was the only safe place for Kiile's family and Neila's family, she went down and personally talked with some of the people they found."

"And?" Cheral asked when Keli hesitated.

Keli took a deep breath. "They said that the first thing they knew of the attack was when a large group of huge, wing-like ships swept over the area just as the alarms sounded. They sprayed the plains as far as they could see, with a wispy gas, like they were spraying the fields for pests or weed control or crop fertilization. The survivors said they were in town and ran for the shelters when the alarm sounded, but around them, people collapsed in midstride or where they stood. The few that survived barely made it inside the shelter before the Guardian closed the doors and sealed them. They were surprised at how little time they had—maybe a half or a quarter of a decipar."

"The villages essentially had no warning," Cheral said, and Keli saw her shoulders fall. "Then all they would have to do is come back and pick up all of the captives they wanted. No resistance, no fights, no losses, except for the victims."

Keli shuddered, thinking of the slavers quietly, effortlessly picking and sorting their unconscious booty.

"Did any of the farmers or villagers make it to any of the other towns?" Cheral asked softly.

Keli forced herself to look at the monitor and push away the thoughts that threatened to overwhelm her.

"None...reported yet. Wiibsa was the closest for Turell, but maybe others heard the alarms sooner and maybe..." Keli let her words drop. "If any made it to a town, it will be only a few. Only ten made it in Wiibsa, a town of around four hundred estimated, including the children. Pretty well confirms Kiile's family and Neila's family were taken."

⋀ ⋀ ⋀ ⋀ ⋀

Like all of the cadets in the combat strategies class, Blaire watched as Major Iims opened the classroom door and listened to the messenger. With a nod, he closed the door and turned back to the class.

"Cadet Lupis," he said. "You are requested to join the commanders in the Flight Ops briefing room. Please continue this study this evening. I will test everyone's retention of the details tomorrow."

"Thank you, sir," Blaire said as she switched her station's monitor off, closed her digital pad, and slipped it into the pocket of her loose-fitting khakis.

Curious about the summons, she hurried without concern. She was slowly getting used to sudden and unannounced meetings with those in authority.

She pushed the briefing room door open slowly and slipped inside and quietly closed the door to wait, but Shara immediately waved her to the table. Colonel and Captain Kooich, Commander and Captain Geaardt, and Colonel and Captain Mooren sat around a table, and Shara pulled a chair out between herself and Franni.

"Come and sit, Blaire," Shara said. "We've been discussing your alert last Thursday."

Blaire relaxed at Shara's informal manner and hurried to take the proffered seat.

"Thank you," she said, and glanced at each of them.

"Please give us an accounting of when and what you felt," Greg said. "We'll explain what's going on in a minute."

"Yes, sir," Blaire said, and began. "I was on my outbound leg of my solo flight when I first felt the same feeling I got when the intruders came up the tunnels. It was a weak feeling, and stationary, and I was concentrating on my mission so I didn't take time to investigate it.

"I followed Major Iims' Flip-File, and after completing the requirements for the mission, I focused on the unchanged sensation. It was south of Obscure, in the valley, so I swung out and came up the valley, slowly and in the clouds. I contacted STSX1 and told him to not reply because I wasn't allowed to have a conversation during the solo mission. I told him that if he could confirm the ID of the sensation, to contact you. I figured I would ask about it after I finished, but you were coming and everything was in fast motion when I landed. I debriefed with Major Iims, but everything had calmed down by the time I finished and I figured it would be inappropriate to contact you and ask."

"Did you feel the presence of Don Nikle among the group?" Franni asked.

"Yes, ma'am. Just like I have before," Blaire said. "He was talking to the group. When I first entered the valley, he was upset over a woman that was supposed to be killed, or should have died. I'm not sure which, but whatever was supposed to happen didn't, and he said the men he sent had not come back, just like the others. I'm not sure what others."

Greg smiled. "Every time Don has sent men to attack or do one of his villainous deeds, we have been able to stop them and capture his men. Thus, none of them have come back. When he set up the ambush last week for Deputy Reeds near Community, we almost caught him as well."

"Twice since then," Franni said, "I have followed him only to have his sensation break up and quickly drift apart and disappear. I can't follow him after that." She twisted her smile. "Have you had that happen to you?"

"No. Not exactly," Blaire said. "When I flew up from the south on Thursday, his sensation seemed to waver a lot, you know, stronger and then weaker and then stronger again. It wasn't strong and forceful like it was when he watched his men attack the commander's ranch and the Jordans' ranch."

"That's right," Shara said softly. "You did say you *felt* that night."

"Yes, intensely," Blaire admitted.

"Have you thought about why his sensation changes?" Franni asked.

"I have, but I don't have any answers." Blaire shrugged with a weak smile.

"When you're on patrol or when you have idle time," Shara said, "I'd like for you to concentrate on Nikle's *feeling* and see if you can *see* him. Obviously, he is doing something that is making it hard for us to *feel* him. Maybe on purpose."

"Yes, ma'am," Blaire said. "I'll keep an ear out for him—in a manner of speaking, of course."

"Thank you, Blaire," Shara said. "With Cheral, Ani, and Jill away, I feel like we're shorthanded when it comes to *sensing* our enemies."

"How's their mission coming?" Blaire asked, and realized they might not want her to know. "I mean, if it's all right to ask."

"It's all right to ask, Blaire," Greg said. "I don't know how much you know, but in June the planet Nevar was attacked and all of the population seemed to have disappeared. Early investigations showed no signs of life, and rovers that we deployed exploded. The attackers mined the surface of the planet so no one could investigate.

"I sent a flight of four, with Cheral in command, to investigate." Greg explained how the operation developed, and that as of noon Obscure time, they had recovered just over eight hundred people. "So far, only a few city dwellers made it to safety. No signs of Kiile's family or of Neila's family have been found."

"Neila? Who's Neila?" Blaire asked.

Sunday, December 10

Blaire finished an early breakfast with Cadets Milik and
Ilistr and knew she had to hurry for Major Iims' pre-mission
briefing. She excused herself from her friends, took her
tray and dishes to the kitchen conveyor, and dropped the
recyclables in the appropriate bins. Quickly checking to be sure
she had her digital pad, she hurried out into the corridor and
turned left. Almost not recognizing him, she passed Sergeant
Stial without the least of gestures.

"Cadet Lupis!" Sergeant Stial said in a stern and official
voice.

She stopped in reflex and slowly turned, snapping a salute
to his uniform.

"Sorry, sir. I'm in a bit of a hurry," she said as he returned
her salute, knowing that being in a hurry was no excuse for not
saluting a senior officer.

"One moment, Cadet," he said formally. "I must apologize
for the disgraceful conduct of two of my reports last Thursday.
I was appalled by their behavior and am indeed sorry that you
had the misfortune to overhear them, especially during your
time of celebration. They were disorderly and foulmouthed,
and their conduct was exceedingly unbecoming a marine." His
voice softened. "I must further apologize for their personal
slurs and innuendoes against your person. Against myself was
one thing, but you've done nothing to warrant such behavior
from a marine—especially a marine from this facility and
command. I beg you, please. Accept my sincerest apologies for
their unacceptable conduct." He nodded. "Thank you, Cadet.
You may go."

She watched his back in startled amazement as he spun on
his heels and marched away from her. Then she remembered
her own obligations, turned, and hurried to the briefing room.

C.3486.746

'*Major,*' Keli said. '*A marine transport is approaching with the shipping container you requested.*'

'*Very good. Thanks,*' Cheral said. '*We will be out front. Have them place the container in front of the dwelling where we are.*' Then Cheral looked over her juice glass at Neila. "It's here."

Cheral got up and went to the front door, opened it, and Neila followed her out onto the hard pack used for a drive. She looked up and pointed for Neila.

"Can you hear the ship?" Cheral asked.

"Yes, now," Neila smiled. "How did you know it was coming? It is still a long distance."

"Keli told me," Cheral said, and smiled as she pressed the button on the signaling device she held in her hand. "She has been talking with them so they know where to come."

Cheral watched Neila's awe and attention as the transport slowed and hovered over them. The aft portal opened and a gantry pole extended.

"Is that it?" Neila asked with a tinge of excitement in her voice as she saw two marines pushing a large box out.

"Yes, Neila," Cheral said. "Once the cargo container is out, they will lower it to the drive."

Neila was surprised when four marines jumped on top of the container as it started down. "Are they going to load it for us?"

"They sure are. All we need to do is point out what we want them to put in it."

Cheral and Neila watched as the soft commotion brought Kiile and Ani out to watch. Kiile said he had tried to get Anthor to come, at least to a window, but the old man had politely refused. He preferred the comfort of his overstuffed recliner, as he said he did most of the days and nights.

Its emphatic *thud* announced the container's arrival on the drive near the front door, and each of the marines bent to disconnect the lifting cables. Cheral saluted the squad leader as he jumped down and approached her.

"Major Haak-Beeli?" he asked, returning the salute.

"Yes, Corporal," Cheral said. "Are you our packing assistance for today?"

"Yes, ma'am," he said with a smile, and handed her a small packet. "These are orange dots"—he made a circle with his thumb and first finger—"about this size. If you will place a dot on each item you wish us to pack and load, we can get started."

"Neila," Cheral said, and turned to the girl. "Please lead the way."

They all followed Neila through the front doorway and up the stairs to the sleeping room. Cheral leaned close to Neila. "I'm glad we straightened up last night. We wouldn't want them to think we are messy people, would we?"

Neila smiled and Cheral handed her a package of dots and set her to the task of marking the bed, the sleeping pads, the clothespress, and the armoire along one wall, the Memories Chest at the foot of the bed, the two night tables beside the bed, and the matching ornate chair and footstool. Neila affixed her dots to a number of accessories and then set them aside for individual packing and loading.

Cheral looked around the room for Neila's personal effects while the marines tended to the furniture pieces.

"Neila? Did you have a travel bag or chest when you came?"

"Only a small one," she said, and crossed the room. She grabbed a rumpled blanket that had slipped off her sleeping pad, quickly folded it, and laid it across the foot. Then she pointed to a medium-sized travel case at the end of the bed. "This one. My clothes are in it and some are hung behind the door."

"Maybe this afternoon," Cheral said as she looked at the limited assortment Neila had, "we can pick out what you want to wear for the trip and we can pack the rest in your case. Would that be all right?"

"Yes," she said, looking a little dejected. "It won't take long. I do not have much."

"That's fine," Cheral said, and smiled. "What you don't have we will get when we get back. There's a wonderful little clothing store in town, and I bet they have a number of things that will fit you perfectly."

"You mean we can go to town and buy clothes?" Her eyes were wide with disbelief.

"Certainly," Cheral confirmed. "Either the three of us can go or we can take one of the cadets with us. Sometimes men don't like to go clothes shopping."

"I have never been to town to get clothes," Neila said softly. "*Pama*—sorry, Mother always got my things from the other families when their kids outgrew them and they had things that would fit me."

"That pretty tunic top you wore yesterday, with the pretty stitched design?" Cheral asked. "Was that a castoff that your mother got?"

"Oh, not that one." Neila smiled. "Mother made that one and did the handwork herself. She made it large so it would still fit when I began to grow." She plucked the front of her tunic as if to emphasize where. "And it still does."

"Well, young lady," Cheral said, and turned to look at Neila as she put her hands on her hips. "The base commandant's daughter is going to have some new, nice-looking, store-bought clothes. Hand-me-downs are all right sometimes, but they will only be nice ones if we get you anymore."

Neila stared at Cheral and slowly smiled. "That sounds very nice, Cheral. Thank you."

"I don't see any cold-weather clothes," Cheral said, a little concerned. "Being summer here, you wouldn't have any with you."

"No, I did not bring any."

"That's okay. I'll have Shara meet us with some boots, heavy pants, and a suitable coat," Cheral said half out loud. "It is full winter at home. And we do live in the mountains."

"Mountains sound so beautiful. Are they as pretty as the pictures we looked at?"

"Yes, Neila, they certainly are. And now, being winter, we have lots and lots of snow. It makes our valley look like a wonderland."

"I've never seen a 'wonderland' before." Neila grinned, then remembered Cheral's words. "You said I was the base commandant's daughter. Is Kiile a base commandant? Like in charge of this place you live?"

"Yes, Neila, he is." Cheral smiled back at her.

"Oh my."

"Oh. Another thing I was curious about," she said as she checked on the marines' progress and diligence. "I know you can research Anthor's computer files."

"Yes," Neila admitted. "We do not have a very big library, but I showed you last night that I know how to use the equipment and access the files."

"How much computer training have you had?" Cheral asked, remembering Neila's familiarity with the system.

"I...used to program all of our farming equipment," she said sheepishly, and then explained. "Mother made the boys do the heavy work and they never learned how to run the systems. She always thought I was weaker than my brothers, so I got the programming and troubleshooting duties."

"Aah, I see. But you weren't weaker than your brothers?"

"No." Neila smiled. "I could take almost any of the boys in our village in a fair wrestle or fight. I could even lift heavier bales and throw things farther."

"Impressive. I like that." Cheral smiled. "And I don't mean so I can make you do more work. Programming? What sort of equipment did you program?"

"The plowers, the tillers, the levelers, the planters, the fertilizers, and the harvesters," Neila said proudly. "They all followed routes, guided from the satellites' positions, and they needed to have their routes set up for the seasons, what we were planting, fertilizing, and harvesting. Maintenance schedules and software updates and upgrades and other routine things."

"Very nice, Neila," Cheral said. "Please give me a list of program types you have worked with. We'll get a computer system that you can use at home and we'll show you how our systems work as well."

Cheral turned to the door when Kiile called up the stairs to see if anyone was interested in a tea or juice break. She asked the marines, and when they admitted they would welcome a short break, Cheral had Neila lead them downstairs for refreshments.

"Neila," Kiile said as he took a seat beside her. "Your grandfather said he wanted you to have any of the books from the library that you think you would like to take."

Neila's eyes lit up and she got up and went to Anthor and hugged him in thanks. When she came back and sat down, she said she had some favorites and would set them out.

"Corporal," Kiile said, and set his cup down. "Do you happen to have any containers that would accommodate books?"

"Yes, sir. Some," the corporal said. "We have two medium-sized ammo crates that should pack and seal books adequately."

"Very good." Kiile smiled at Neila. "Pick out your trove when you can, and we'll see how much we can pack."

⋏

"Looks like we have everything in," Cheral said as she came back in through the front door. "The transport is almost here, and I'll go with it to be sure the shipping orders are correct and understood."

"May I come with you?" Neila asked as she peeked around the doorframe and looked at the sealed container.

"Neila," Kiile said softly from his stool near Anthor. "Please stay with your grandfather and me. Cheral will only be gone for a short while, and it's all official business stuff. Probably not very interesting, anyway."

Cheral nodded. "Your father's right, Neila. I won't take any more time than I need to and you only have a little more time with your grandfather. Enjoy his company. Kiile, the lieutenant and...Where's Ani?"

'Apache Ten is powering up. We are your cover, Major. Where you go, we go.'

Cheral chuckled. "I should've known. Okay. Lieutenant Keli and ST12 will be here with Kiile. I'll ride with the marines and Ani will bring me back." Then she looked at Neila with a conspiratorial look. "Maybe you can get them to give you a tour of ST12."

⋀ ⋀ ⋀ ⋀ ⋀

"Major Iims," Stran said into the coms. "May I address the cadets?"

"Certainly, Commander," the major's voice replied through the cockpit speakers. "Cadets. Please pay attention."

"Major Iims will select a cadet for his or her turn in the arena," Stran explained. Caiti, Coli, and Keely stood around him in STSX's cockpit and listened. They knew Tayn was listening aboard KKLC14. "This is the first time you will experience return fire from your targets, so remember your strategies. I have set a remote to generate the scenarios and you will have to react to your scanners, to your *feelings*, and to use your ingenuity and training. Each target will act and react like its true counterpart. Each scenario will generate a different target type, specific for that engagement, so you will have to think on the fly. Today will be solo engagements, and as training progresses and the targets become more powerful, you will eventually fly multi-ship engagements. One word of caution. Hits from the targets are real! Real damage can occur, and real injuries sustained. Good luck to each of you. Colonel Kooich."

"Thank you, Commander," Hench said. "I have but one piece of advice. And most of you have heard me give it, repeatedly. Be calm and think! Act and move! Quickly! Then, calmly, set up for your next move. As your experience grows, your agility will also improve. Good luck, cadets. Major Iims, the session is yours."

"Thank you, Colonel," Major Iims said, followed by a short silence. "The exercise arena is defined by highlighted marker remotes forming a spherical volume you must stay within. Exiting the sphere before a winner is declared will stop the session, and points will be deducted for an early withdrawal. The session will start with a flash on your scanner and finish with the announcement of a winner. Bring the boundaries up on your scanners. Cadet Ilistr. Move into the arena."

The anxious cadets watched as Apache Patrol Four moved forward and into the vast arena, quickly diminishing in the distance. They turned to their scanners to follow the action as the blue dot moved toward the center of the sphere.

Caiti, Coli, and Keely stood behind Stran's chair and watched the three-dimensional display and saw the transparent globe pulse, announcing the beginning of the session. They watched and waited, feeling Cadet Ilistr's growing anxiety, but nothing seemed to be happening.

⋏

Caiti looked at her dad's seriousness as he watched the display, and how his lips moved in anxious anticipation as he compared his thoughts to what he saw. She forced herself to not eavesdrop, even though she knew it would be an extremely beneficial lesson to know.

Suddenly a flash in the center of the sphere caught her attention and the dot moved. She waited, and again the dot flashed and moved. Then it went out.

"Was she hit twice?" Coli asked, and saw Stran's slow nod.

"And she doesn't know where the target—sorry—the enemy is."

Finally, a new, red dot appeared in the arena and Keely smiled. "She lit it up. Now she has a chance."

▲

Stran smiled and looked at Keely over his shoulder, then without saying anything, turned back to watch.

The session lasted almost five decipars, half a Terran hour, before Cadet Ilistr destroyed the enemy light fighter, after much exchanged fire and being hit a third time.

As Cadet Ilistr settled in formation with the other cadets, Major Iims congratulated her on a successful session.

"Cadet Dnar," Major Iims announced. "Into the arena."

"Step back," Stran said, and quickly spun the chair to aft facing and stood up. "Show them how it's done, Cadet Keely."

Keely took the chair and swiveled it to forward facing as it adjusted to her. Stran drifted back to the nav-com compartment and settled to watch the display there. Caiti and Coli joined him.

▲

"STSX," Keely said as she eased him forward. "Cloaking on, sensor blocked, shields full. Secondary shields on standby. Please put a private marker on the display so I don't slip out of the arena."

"CLOAKING ON, SENSOR BLOCKING ON, PRIMARY SHIELDS ARE FULL AND SECONDARY SHIELDS ARE STANDBY. PRIVATE TRACKING MARKER DISPLAYED."

"Thanks. Light up the target, please," Keely said as she guided STSX along an arc just inside the spherical boundary.

Across the sphere and above the plane of her arc, the red dot appeared, also circling just inside the boundary.

"*Feels* like a Kyddellan heavy fighter. Shielded, two turrets and one forward-firing fixed cannon. Do you have a solution?"

"FIRING SOLUTION CALCULATED AND LOCKED."

"Okay. Let's wake it up."

Keely fired a full volley and jinked a degree of arc and then closed on the red dot's position. She swung STSX a quarter turn as the red dot moved toward her firing position, keeping STSX broadside to the target as it closed.

"Full volley, all turrets," she said, and squeezed the trigger.

The red dot winked twice and disappeared.

Keely was still watching the display when Major Iims' voice rumbled through the speakers.

"Looks like someone was paying attention in class. Congratulations, Cadet Dnar. Well done. Cadet Lupis. Into the arena."

Keely repositioned STSX in his original formation slot as Blaire's patrol fighter vanished from view and slipped forward into the arena.

"I should've just done him with one shot," Keely said as Stran drifted forward and stopped behind the pilot's chair.

"Yes, you could've. But this way you've set the bar high without shutting out the competition. You've forced everyone else to do it in one or two shots. And without getting hit. Very good thinking, Keely."

She snapped her head around to see Stran's wide smile.

"I bet Blaire does it in one volley," Keely said, and turned back to watch the display. "Hey! There are two red dots."

▲

Blaire studied the two dots as she drifted closer, watching their motions. Slowly she saw a pattern in their movements and pushed Apache Patrol Five closer. She entered a firing solution for one dot into the upper turret and the solution for the second into the lower turret. She knew they were both heavy fighters and well shielded and that her turrets only had two cannons. She toggled the firing frequency to four volleys, one hundred milliseconds apart, hoping to emulate the Q-ship's quad-cannon turrets.

As she leveled on a rolling plane between the two dots, she

admitted she was being vain, wanting to show off a little, to show everyone a local newbie was as good as anyone else. Then she quickly shook her head and chided herself, focusing on the real importance of the moment. A miscalculation and these mere *targets* could destroy her ship and leave her drifting in space. Or possibly worse.

She focused, watching the display, and then sent the diagnostic codes. The two fighters suddenly materialized and she pushed the thrust levers forward. Apache Patrol Five darted forward between them and she toggled the trigger. Patrol Five shook slightly, silently, as the turrets unleashed their volleys, and she spun the fighter around and shoved the thrust levers to full, ready to make a second pass.

She saw the images wink and flutter and slowly disperse, the red dots disappearing from the display. Her mouth dropped open; something looked familiar.

⅄

"Whoa! Did you see that?" Keely shouted, and bounced between the straps and the chair.

"Calm down, Keely," Stran said firmly. "Yes, we certainly did."

"That was beautifully done," Caiti and Coli said together.

"That it was. Almost as nicely as your win, Keely," Stran said, and winked at Caiti and Coli as Major Iims announced the next cadet.

"Cadet Coli Geaardt. Into the arena."

⅄

Veiled and sensor blocked, STSX slipped into the arena without leaving a trace of their existence.

"Okay," Coli said softly, almost to herself, hushed as if talking would give her position away. "Stay cloaked, sensor blocked, and shields full."

"COMPLYING."

Coli closed her eyes and *felt* the arena, and slowly the

sensations seemed to congeal into the essence of the ships.

"I have three heavy fighters. Can you *see* them in my mind?"

"YES."

"They're staying a little spread out. If we were between them do you have the range to get all three at the same time?"

"YES. ONE IS CLOSE TO MAXIMUM NORMAL RANGE. IT WOULD BE UNFAIR TO GO TO LONG-RANGE MODE. THE PATROL FIGHTERS DO NOT HAVE THAT CAPABILITY."

"Good point," Coli said, and moved inward, circling on a smaller sphere inside the paths of the targets.

She glanced at the empty display between her and the front panel, empty except for her Private Tracking dot.

She turned her attention back to her sensations. "All three are Kyddellan signatures, therefore all three are enemy targets."

"CORRECT."

"Wouldn't surprise me if they mixed enemy and friendly targets in these sessions. Do you have a solution on the three targets?"

"YES. YOU VISUALIZE VERY CLEARLY."

Coli turned into the targets, aiming for the point in space that gave the shortest range to each target. She toggled the trigger and the three turrets fired double volleys, and the sensations fluttered and slowly dispersed.

⅄ ⅄ ⅄ ⅄ ⅄

Don Nikle settled back into the cushions of the overstuffed chair in his sister's living room and waited for the arranged time. It was a long shot that they would even want to talk to him, but he had to try. No longer for Bernice's memory, his reasons were now personal; he stared at his gauze-and-bandage-wrapped leg and the bandages hiding the charred, functionless stump that used to be his right hand.

173

Ahaar's old communicator buzzed at precisely five o'clock local time and he took a deep breath as he awkwardly toggled the 'answer' button with his left hand.

"Nikle here," he said in an official tone, pleased that it was a voice-only connection.

"Mr. Nikle," the slightly metallic voice said. "I am Chimr, an aide to Prince Lukré, and he bade me to contact you concerning your plans to rebuild Terran support for his, shall I say, endeavors."

"Thank you for making contact," Don said. "It has been a long time since a shipment has been made from here and I thought—"

"Prince Lukré knows how long it has been and how difficult the last year of your missed shipments must have been," the aide's voice said. "Have the previous obstacles been neutralized?"

Don took another deep breath. "Not completely, but I need an outside attempt to confirm or disprove whether our changes can restart the supply operations."

"What sort of an outside attempt?"

"We think the small ships that are left to lift captives have been here on Terra long enough to be recognized as belonging here," Don explained. "We have flown one on regular trips to the back side of the Terran moon with no interference. We speculated there was a detection system placed here that identified freighters and cruisers of outside origin that intended to land on the planet. And since our flights to the moon have not been challenged, we think the detection system is no longer operative or our ships are no longer perceived as foreign."

"Encouraging, though not conclusive."

"Correct," Don said, feeling uneasy. "We have made two trips with captives aboard and returned with the same results."

"And now you would like the prince to authorize one of his valuable ships to come to your planet and see if it is detected and if so, possibly destroyed. Am I correct?"

"Basically, yes. My intent is to meet your ship, and if the insertion is successful, transfer one or two shiploads of captives to your ship. That would be in the interest of reestablishing business connections."

"I wonder myself, Mr. Nikle," the aide mused, "why the prince would even consider your meager offering when he has shown the galaxy that he has the capability of collecting captives, one whole planet at a time."

"I understand if he chooses otherwise," Don said.

He knew his options were smaller markets for his smaller offerings, assuming he could deliver. That was the crux of the matter: delivery. If not, he was stuck with the already overused local planet-side markets and the possible consequences that went with them.

"I will advise the prince of our conversation, Mr. Nikle. If he has any continued interest, someone will contact you via this medium. Good day."

Nikle stared at the silent communications device and slowly reached out and pushed the 'disconnect' button. *Maybe there's a chance,* he told himself encouragingly. *Maybe.*

One Twenty-Eight

Blaire was surprised when she filed in with the other seven cadets and saw Colonel and Captain Mooren sitting at one end of the head table. Major Iims, Colonel and Captain Kooich, and Commander and Captain Geaardt also sat at the table as she expected, since they were all part of the day's exercise.

"Please take a seat," Major Iims said without standing, and gestured to the chairs arranged in an arc before the table. "I must congratulate each of you on your efforts in today's engagements. I know it can be very unnerving the first time one thinks about being shot at. Unfortunately, 'return fire' doesn't always mean you get to take the first shot. But as a learning experience, I want to discuss the engagements and how we can improve our capabilities. I have also asked Colonel and Captain Mooren to join us, since you are now assigned to his command whenever he has need or when he sees fit to include you in an engagement or even a surveillance operation. Plan to be available to support him in whatever capacity he chooses to use you when you are not engaged in studies or mandatory rest times. The only exceptions will be for our younger cadets that still have non-cadet education to accomplish and some parental restrictions to abide with."

All of the cadets smiled.

"With the commencing of Live Fire Training, we have started a tally board for this class. The board will show your points for each session and a running total up to graduation. In addition to the points, the board will show the number of targets 'killed' and a running total up to graduation. Since we are not at the same level of combat encounters as we were when the director established the school twelve years ago, the tally board is a little different, and we hope it will still encourage your improvement. The competition should be with yourselves, for improvement, and not with your colleagues for highest score. Not everyone can be a number one. Colonel Kooich, would you like to convey the honors?"

"Good afternoon, cadets," Colonel Kooich said, and the cadets responded with the repeated greeting. "My intention was to have Colonel Mooren announce the standings of today's exercise, but I find that for the first time since we instituted the Generated Target System, in all of its glorious wonder, today we were shown that our scoring system is seriously flawed. Our system gives you ten points for a perfectly executed engagement, detecting the enemy, illuminating the enemy for the scanners, and eliminating the enemy when exposed visually. Not since Captain Casi's presence on the battlefield have we seen a *Dance in the Dark,* and today we witnessed two exquisitely performed *Dances.* Because they have not been seen in the last ten or more years, the Dances were not factored into a perfect engagement score. But that said, our dilemma is that detecting, illuminating, and eliminating the enemy is also a perfect engagement. The key is for you to accomplish your mission, your attack, without the enemy detecting you. Therefore, with the commander's approval and until we revise our points system, I will consider today's scores a learning exercise and will only award each of you your 'kills' for the board.

"Cadet Ilistr scored one kill. For the next engagement, please review your tactics and *always* be prepared for battle. As an esteemed colleague of mine once told a student of his, 'hostilities can come from the most unexpected places,' so *never* approach a hot zone without cloaking, sensors blocked, and shields full, unless your ship is damaged such that these essentials are not possible. Even a cloaked, sensor-blocked, and completely disabled ship can let the enemy drift past without incurring further damage.

"Cadet Dnar scored one kill. I am wondering, Cadet, why

you fired a non-lethal wake-up shot."

"Stupidity, sir?" Keely asked as she stood up and endured a few snickers. "For a moment, I did not take the exercise as seriously as I should have. It will not happen again. Sir."

"I see. Thank you, Cadet Dnar, for your candor." He cleared his throat and continued.

"Cadet Lupis scored two simultaneous kills. Taking them both out at the same time was well conceived, Cadet. Efficient and clean. Good instincts, Cadet Lupis."

"Sir," Blaire said, and stood. "If I may. The conception was not mine. I copied the maneuver from many of the encounters in the history files on Captain Casi's engagements. The patrol fighter does not have the firepower necessary to bring down two battlecruisers, but I figured I could emulate a Q-Ship close enough to handle two heavy fighters with that tactic. Sir."

"Thank you, Cadet Lupis," Colonel Kooich said, and smiled at her. "I see history files are good for something after all.

"Cadet Caiti Geaardt scored three simultaneous kills in her *Dance in the Dark*. Was that choice from studying Captain Casi's history also?"

"No, sir," Caiti said as she stood up. "When Mr. Don Nikle's men attacked Headquarters the week after Labor Day, I was with the commander as we faced the oncoming intruders, in the open, in front of the main house. Cloaked and silent, the Indian instinct of surprise suddenly made sense to me. The commander explained we should let them move to a place to our advantage and then launch our attack, on our terms. That seemed appropriate for today's engagement. Actually, for any engagement. You just have to be certain of your enemy, and that he's actually your enemy."

"Thank you, Cadet Caiti. Very profound thinking." He smiled at her and then continued. "Cadet Coli Geaardt scored three simultaneous kills in her *Dance in the Dark*. Since everyone has an explanation they are willing to share, does Cadet Coli have one?"

"No, sir," Coli said as she stood up. "What can I say? We're twins. We think alike and sometimes we act alike."

"Hmm. Did you two discuss tactics during the exercise?"

"No, sir. Our da—excuse me, the commander is very strict on that subject. He monitors us, all of us, during our training to be sure we do not violate that rule. We each have to do the exercises ourselves. Afterwards, after the briefing, it's a different matter and we discuss them in detail. Sir."

Colonel Kooich looked at Coli as she sat down, and then said, "Cadet Kooich scored three kills. Two simultaneous and one in cleanup. Do you have an explanation you wish to offer?"

"Not really, sir," Tayn said. "I simply rushed the first shot and had to regain a firing solution on the third fighter."

"I see. Cadet Huml scored two kills. Anything to add, Cadet Huml?"

"No, sir." He started to say something else, but closed his mouth, smiled, and said nothing.

"Thank you. Discretion is often the wisest choice. Cadet Milik scored two simultaneous kills, but there is a note here that you did not fire a shot? Please explain. I have to hear this."

"Sir," Cadet Milik said as he stood up. "A fortuitous error? I had a firing solution on the two fighters and I was going to follow the example of Cadet Lupis. I dove for the space between them, but just as I passed directly between them, I caught the cloaking and sensor-blocking master switch with my wrist strap. It was loose, you see sir, and...well, I reinstated them as quickly as I could and turned for a second pass only to realize the fighters had both shot at me in that moment when I was visible, missing me and taking each other out. Sir."

Colonel Kooich stared at Cadet Milik and finally gestured for him to sit down. Hench turned, looked at Stran and Crem, and slowly shook his head before returning his attention to the cadets.

"Thank you, cadets. Today has been enlightening. I hope it has been as enlightening for you as it has been for us. Thank you."

"Colonel," Stran said, and stood. "Before you excuse the class, I would like to extend an invitation to each of you involved in today's exercises, staff included, to the ranch this evening for a celebration of your 'victories,' no matter how they were attained. Seven o'clock, casual dress. The drinking lamp will be on."

⋏ ⋏ ⋏ ⋏ ⋏

"I expected you to think of doing a Dance, Blaire," Cadet Milik said, and looked at Caiti and Coli as they walked through the dining room in the ranch's main house.

"I almost did," Blaire admitted, "but I had the same kind of vanity stroke Keely had. It seemed like our instructors wanted us to 'show' them the kill. Once I saw Caiti surprise everyone with her flawless sneak attack, it was obvious that was the ultimate victory."

Caiti and Coli both blushed. "Not ultimate, Blaire," Caiti said. "I know there are tactics we haven't even thought about or heard of yet. But I did think about them mixing the targets up a little. Maybe in future exercises, they will."

"What do you mean?" Cadet Milik asked.

"You know, to slip in a friendly," Caiti said. "The problem with a Dance is the risk that you don't sense everything about the target, and maybe miss something. It's like Keely, on her solo flight, sensing that enemy fighter following the space station. Everything said it should be okay for the station to evaporate him, but then she felt a familiarity, like she should know him. She didn't know it, but she was sensing the pilot's Peace Force tag."

"The enemy fighter was one of ours?" Cadet Huml asked. He had stopped to hear the explanation and sat down when Caiti finished.

"Not the fighter," Caiti replied, "but the pilot was a marine pilot given the task to evaluate a fighter they captured. That's the risk, the test, if you're going to do a Dance."

"So, in many respects," Cadet Huml said, "lighting up the enemy is a safer way to go."

"I don't know," Blaire added. "It's still risky. The sensor can analyze the ships when we light them up and we can verify what it is when we drop their veils, but our systems don't tell us if the pilot is friend or foe. That's something you have to figure out yourself."

"Man. What if you don't have the Talent to sense the presence of things?" Cadet Huml looked from one cadet to the others.

"It's the same as feeling someone's tag," Coli said. "If you can do that, I think the rest should be just training yourself to *hear* what you're feeling."

"Maybe that's a Talent that can be enhanced," Caiti offered.

"Maybe," Blaire said absently as she digressed and looked around the great room. She spotted Franni pouring herself a white wine, talking with Keely. She turned to the group, excused herself under the pretense of needing a refill, and crossed the room to wait for a turn to speak with Franni.

She stopped behind Keely, smiled at Franni, and reached for the decanter of red wine.

"Oh, hi, Blaire," Keely said brightly. "Wasn't it nice of Uncl—the commander to invite us all tonight?"

"Yes, yes it was," Blaire said. "Sorry, Keely. I didn't mean to interrupt."

"That's all right. I suppose Captain Mooren is tired of listening to me ramble on so much."

Blaire looked at Keely's glass. "Are you getting a little giggly? Sneaking wine when Dad's not looking?"

Keely smiled at Blaire and then at Franni. "Just a little, watered down. I'd like to say I'm sneaking it, but Dad knows."

Franni smiled. "I wanted to congratulate you on your

tactics today. It doesn't matter if you copy someone successfully or not, but you executed everything very well today." Franni raised her glass to Blaire.

"Thank you, Captain," Blaire said. "I did want to mention that now I understand what you meant by Nikle's sensation sort of fluttering and dispersing."

"You do?" Franni asked.

Keely watched Blaire with deep interest.

"Yes, ma'am," Blaire said. "I felt it today, with the generated targets. When I hit them for the kill, their sensations winked and fluttered and slowly dispersed, like eddies of energy spinning off in many different directions and evaporating."

Franni's mouth fell open. "Blaire! That's it!" she said softly, emphatically. "Nikle's using some kind of an image generator, like we're doing to generate targets. That has to be it. We're feeling him just like we feel the targets. And when he deactivates, we're feeling the energy dispel." Franni suddenly looked around the room. "Come on, you two. We're going to talk with the commander and Colonel Kooich."

C.3486.747

"I know you cannot obey," Anthor said softly, holding Neila's hand as she sat on the stool beside his recliner, "but you must not feel sad. Once they seal the dwelling and the sheds, I will go with the Handlers. I will be all right and I will see your *gpama* again."

"But Gpada," Neila said, dabbing the tears from her eyes once more. "I don't want you to go. I don't want to leave you."

"I am sorry, Neila. I hoped you would like your father and like what he can offer you."

"I do like him, Gpada. I did not think I would, but I do. And I like Cheral and Lieutenant Keli and Captain Ani," Neila said. "I think they truly like me and I am glad, because I have no choice other than to make this work. And now I have to lose you too."

"I know this is very hard for you," Anthor said, and patted her hand. "But I must go. I have been living on Sustenance too long, waiting for you to be cared for. Now, I can rest and you can have new chapters in your life. You will even have a new family to learn to love and enjoy. I doubt they will make you work too hard to pay for your room and keep."

Against her will, Neila had to laugh softly. "Cheral says I won't have duties like that anymore, but that I can choose things I want to do. She likes that I know computers, and that I have things Mother gave me and that I will have things of yours and *Gpama's* for the memories. And she says we are to go shopping, I think that is what she called it, to buy new clothes. Just for me. Not used by someone else first, 'unless they are suitable,' she said."

"That is very nice, Neila," Anthor said. "I know this is the right thing for you. You will meet many new friends and will have a grand adventure."

Neila rose up, put her arms around his neck, and hugged him as tightly as she dared. "I love you, Gpada, and I will miss you terribly."

"I will miss you also, Neila," he said, patted her back, and ran his fingers through her long, blond hair. "And I will be waiting with Gpama to see you when your time does come. We will not have forgotten you, either. Now stand up and dry your eyes. The people have come to seal the dwelling. Do you have everything you want to take?"

"Yes, Gpada. Everything except you."

He laughed, a soft laugh that he knew she would always remember.

"Please let the men in so I can take care of the signings." Anthor gently pushed her toward the front door. "Then go and ask Kiile and the others to come so I can say goodbye."

"You don't want me to stay and help?" Neila asked, stopping

before she opened the door.

"This is one thing I have to do, child," Anthor said softly. "The Handlers are only a few decipars behind the Sealers. Let them in and then go and get Kiile, Cheral, and the others. Please, Neila."

Resigned, she opened the door and let the two men in. They went to Anthor and began their discussions, and feeling strangely alone, Neila stepped out and hurried around the stone dwelling and down the wide path to the clearing in the sage green and lavender trees.

⅄

"All twenty cities have been scanned, and most of the mines have been disarmed and removed," Debira said.

Keli was bent over the nav-com consoles, busy listening to the update from Nevar while she entered the navigational waypoints and essential data for the trip home.

"Survivors?" Cheral asked.

"I've sent you a list by city, but the results are poor for a whole planet." Debira sounded dejected. "Grand total is about two thousand, a little less. The marines started immediately evacuating them to a Peace Force medical facility, and we understand the major-general has started collecting private and commercial donations to start rebuilding the planet and the eco-structure. There is also talk about revising the Guardians and to add planetary defensive systems and even a marine base to provide a second space port for the non-agricultural needs of the planet."

"Casi would say this is like closing a gate after the horses ran away, but it will be good," Cheral said as Neila's head popped up through the floor portal. She motioned Neila to come up and continued. "What are your plans?"

"We seem to be running out of things we can do to be helpful," Debira said, with a little more spirit in her tone. "The marines have everything under control and the Force has assigned some additional Watchers on a rotating basis. So for now, we're about finished."

"Very well." Cheral smiled at Debira's words and at Neila as she looked over Keli's shoulder. "Regroup for a rest cycle as soon as you feel it is appropriate. Then, after a good rest with no demands, come home. We are leaving within the hour, I think."

"Thank you, Major. Neel will be pleased to hear," Debira said with a sigh. "And Cera is definitely ready to be home with her mate and Keely. I understand Tayn, the girls, and Blaire tipped the class scoring up on edge yesterday. Caiti and Coli each got three simultaneous kills *Dancing in the Dark.*"

"You don't say," Cheral said with a huge grin. "We haven't seen that done since their mother did it, before they were born."

"Nope, but we have now," Debira said. "Safe trip. I will pass the orders and see you back at Shadow Base. You'll beat us by a day, I suspect."

"We'll be looking for you and will plan a private reunion. We have someone very special for you to meet. Safe trip. Apache Four out," Cheral said, and watched Neila as Keli explained what she was doing.

"Apache Five out."

Cheral stepped off the dais and stopped beside Keli and Neila. Neila looked up and smiled.

"It is very detailed, is it not?" Neila asked.

"Very." Cheral smiled and looked toward the dwelling. "I see the men are here to seal up the house."

"Yes," Neila said. "Anthor asked me to come and get you so he can say goodbye. The Handlers are coming in a few decipars, and he will have to go."

"I see," Cheral said as she put her arm around Neila's shoulders and pulled her to her side. "Then we should do as our elder has asked. Keli? Are you near a break point?"

Keli made a few more keystrokes and looked up. "Yes.

Everything entered is good and everything else will wait until I get back. Shall we find Kiile and Ani?"

"He's outside," Neila said. "He told me he was doing a 'walk-around' inspection to be sure everything looked okay for the flight home. Ani's below reading."

"Then we'll get them on our way," Cheral said, and gently pushed Neila to lead the way.

⋏⋏⋏⋏⋏

Kiile drifted down into the central chamber and stopped between the galley and the sleeping area. He could see Neila sitting quietly in the forward-facing, double-wide cushion chair, hands folded in her lap, eyes closed, and an unhappy expression on her face. He decided a canister of tea could wait and he turned and drifted into the seating area.

"Are you all right, Neila?"

"Yes," she said, but did not open her eyes.

"I can see that is not quite true," Kiile said softly, and moved to her seat. "Nor should it be. May I sit with you?" he asked as he unfastened her lap strap and settled himself beside her. He quickly rebuckled the strap so they wouldn't drift away.

"I know this is hard for you," he said. "Probably harder than I think it is. Leaving Nevar and Somstri was always hard for me too."

"I guess it would be," she said, still not opening her eyes. "But now, I have nothing to come back for."

"You will own your Gpada's estate one of these days, and if you decide you want to go back and live there when you've grown, you will be able to." He waited and then slowly put his arm around her shoulders and held her gently to him. "You know, I don't have anything to go back for anymore, either. My parents, my brothers, aunts and uncles were all at home, just like your mother and your brothers were. They are all gone too."

"Do you miss them, Kiile?" Neila asked, slowly opening her eyes and looking up at him.

"Certainly," Kiile said. "Now that they are gone and I cannot ever see them again, I miss them more than I ever have."

"You don't act like it. Did you not cry for them?"

"Yes, Neila. Many months ago, and again when we got to Nevar and saw what had happened. I cried a lot and Cheral was there to help me—just like I am and she is here to help you too." He inhaled and slowly let his breath out. "In front of the people that work for me or with me, they expect me to be strong and always in control for them. I cannot show my feelings until I am alone, or now, with my family."

He took a tissue from the wall dispenser and wiped her eyes. "No one expects you to ignore your feelings, Neila. And I certainly understand how you feel. Now you know how I know. We both have lost our families and our place on Nevar."

She leaned against him for a long while and Kiile wanted her to hold him as well, but he knew he had to be patient. He was hers, heart and soul, from the first moment that he saw her, but he knew she was not his.

"What shall I call you?" she asked without moving away from him.

"What would you like to call me?"

She shrugged gently under his arm.

"Well, the children—young men and women that you will meet—call their fathers 'Father,' or 'Dad.' Some others call their fathers 'Pop,' but seldom call them by their given names. If it makes you more comfortable, I will understand if you still want to call me Kiile. If you ever feel like calling me your father, you may choose."

"Thank you, Kiile," Neila said. "Is Cheral my new mother?"

"In a way, I suppose. You will hear people at home call her your stepmother, which simply means that she is married, mated, to your father. She is not taking the place of your mother, but she will be your friend and help you all that she can. She will help me make our life together the best we can make it."

"She told me I could call her Cheral."

"That's nice," Kiile said.

"Cheral said we can go and buy me new clothes and some winter clothes," Neila continued. "Will you go with us? She said you might not want to because men don't like to shop—I think that is what she called it."

"Yes, it's called shopping." Kiile smiled. "And yes, I will learn to go shopping with you. Cheral is right, though—shopping is not something men look forward to doing like women do."

"What do men like to do instead?"

"Everyone is different, but I like working with the men on the transports, the remotes, the facility operation and equipment, weapons stations, the control and guidance systems. I like—"

"I like to program guidance systems," Neila said, and Kiile stopped and looked down at her.

"You program guidance systems?"

"Yes. I told Cheral that one of my duties on the farm was to program all of the farm equipment to follow the routes we chose for the seasons and the crops we planted. They had to do the heavy work and stay on course."

For the next hour or more, they sat together and talked about the things each other liked and disliked, what Obscure was like, what was there, what was around it, and the need to keep its existence secret. They talked about the people in the valley, the geography, the topography, and the way the towns and population were distributed.

"You know," Kiile said, suddenly realizing he had overlooked a very important thing. "We're going to have to teach you to speak like the rest of us that live on earth."

"Oh," Neila said, and stiffened. "I did not think about that. They would not know Galactic Standard, would they?"

"No," Kiile admitted. "The peoples of earth speak many different languages and many different dialects of each."

"Many?" She looked up with wide eyes.

"Yes, but no one speaks them all." Kiile chuckled. "In our part of Earth, they speak a dialect of Western English."

"Do I have to go to a school to learn it?"

"No, Neila," Kiile said. "We have a training module that STSX12 will implant and your mind will access while you sleep. The first sleep cycle will set your standard and grammar so you can speak normal, non-technical conversations. The second and the third will fill out the basics of the language in the local dialect. If you have a long sleep cycle on the trip, you will probably absorb two of the sections."

"Will the people be pleased to see me?"

"Very much, Neila," Kiile said. "Especially Cheral's cousin and their daughters, her husband's sister and their daughter, and Colonel Kooich and their son. Many know you are coming, and some do not know yet. I have only shared our details with those that report directly to me—my staff, if you will—and those I work for. But rest assured, everyone will like you once they've met you."

▲

Keli flew the first leg of the trip home and Cheral watched for search signatures in the nav-com compartment. Once Keli had them out of the Somstri Watch area and out of the scanners' normal range, they collected Apache Ten and Ani transferred aboard.

Ani joined Keli in the cockpit and they chatted amiably as the first leg progressed. Cheral thought about Kiile and Neila, and *listened* when Kiile settled to talk with her. It was what she needed, and Cheral supposed it was something Kiile needed as well.

Proud of how well Neila publicly accepted the situation and bore up to the Sealers closing up the house and buildings and to the Handlers taking Anthor away, Cheral keenly felt

Neila's anguish when she sat down, crying in the double-wide chair. She was relieved when Kiile went to check on her without urging, knowing he thought about Neila a lot, concerned that she would not be able to settle into the new customs, culture, or her new family, easily.

Rechecking the scanner, she asked ST12 to watch for any probes and sat back to *feel* for Shara.

'*Shar, are you busy?*' Cheral asked when she did not feel any specific activity around Shara.

'*Hey, Cousin. Nothing going on right now. I decided to take advantage of the quiet time to get some book work caught up. The ranch still needs me to check on it every now and then. How's your trip? I got the Nevar reports and wish you had better luck.*'

'*You know all we know about Nevar and the survivors,*' Cheral said. '*But I wanted to talk to you about two things. First, to tell you we are on our way with a wonderful, gorgeous, blue-eyed, blond-haired girl in our keeping. We should be back in the valley tomorrow, estimated arrival at seventeen twenty hours.*'

'*From your aura, she must be wonderful. Has she accepted the situation at all?*'

'*Mostly. She knows we don't have a lot of choices, and I think the two days we spent with her and her grandfather helped a lot. Kiile was instantly taken with her, and I think she'll have him wrapped around her little finger in no time at all.*'

'*And you?*"

'*Probably just as quick.*'

'*You sound like it. You said you had two things to tell me.*'

'*Yes,*' Cheral said. '*I need a big favor.*'

'*Sure. What do you need?*'

'*Winter clothes,*' Cheral admitted. '*Pants, shirts, boots, and a nice coat. Like the girls have.*'

'*I can see if I have anything around here—*'

'*No. That's the big part of the favor. I need new, nice ones. All Neila has ever had are hand-me-downs, and I want her to start* with new, just-for-her new, clothes. She only had a few changes with her at her grandfather's—all but one tunic top are hand-me-downs. Everything else was at her home in Turell. I'd shop for them myself, but she'll need them as soon as we land. It's summer on Somstri.'

'You know this is not a problem,' Shara said. 'Give me sizes, favorite colors, and any particulars, and I'll stop at the store after I pick up the girls. Do you mind if they help shop for their new cousin?'

'Not at all. I'll have ST12 send you a list of her sizes and any particulars he has. She needs everything from unders to outers. Thanks, Cousin.'

'You're very welcome, Cuz. Anything else?'

'Yeah,' Cheral admitted. 'Can you meet us at Obscure and come aboard when we land? She'll be riding jump seat as we land, and I would like her to change into her new clothes before we take her into the facility.'

'Want to land at the ranch?'

'Yes,' Cheral said, 'but I think it's better if we start at home and let her see where she's going to call home. Then we can visit the ranch, maybe after a light dinner. The furniture her grandfather gave her will be in on the supply transport Wednesday. I think Kiile and I will have to shop for ourselves so we'll have stuff as nice as hers.'

'We'll be there to meet you and I'll bring supplies aboard as soon as you let me in.'

'Thanks, Shar. ST12 sent Neila's size file to STSX. I'll let you go and get myself back to work. Talk to you tomorrow unless you need something more.'

'Talk to you tomorrow.'

▲ ▲ ▲ ▲ ▲

Captain Mooren pushed the chime of Cadet Lupis'

apartment and waited. Blaire opened the panel, and in surprise, greeted the captain.

"Blaire, are you available?" Franni asked as Blaire asked her in. "If you are, I have a mission that I would like you to accompany me on."

"Yes, ma'am. I was just studying tactics."

"Tactics? After your example yesterday, I would have thought you had tactics mastered."

"No, ma'am," Blaire countered. "One can't ever know all of the best tactics without constant study."

"Well, this is not the topic I wanted to discuss, Blaire," Franni said. "Study the subject, learn what worked, but use your ideas to improve wherever necessary. That's what Casi taught me."

"Thank you," Blaire said. "You said you have a mission."

"Yes," Franni said. "Can you come with me now?"

"Yes, ma'am," Blaire said. "What do I need to bring?"

"Put your Blues on and then meet me at TTYF8 in about ten minutes. You and I are taking the 'family' fighter for a ride."

"Yes, ma'am. I'll be there."

⋏

"Take the jump seat, Blaire," Franni said as they entered TTYF8's aft portal and she stopped to secure the airlock panel. Then she followed Blaire to the central compartment. "I was thinking about your sense of the dissipating energy as it might apply to our Mr. Nikle."

Franni slipped into the pilot's chair and swiveled to forward facing.

"TTYF, cloaking on, sensor blocking on, shields full, please."

"AS REQUESTED. SYSTEMS ARE MISSION READY."

"Thank you. Hover at three hundred feet," Franni said as she toggled the arrays of switches on the armrests.

TTYF8 rose gently and drifted up through the shield dome,

leveling as commanded.

"Ignition."

"IGNITION READY."

Franni slowly pushed the thrust levers forward and hand-flew TTYF to an altitude just above the atmosphere. She drifted toward the center of the continent and slowed to a geosynchronous hover somewhere over Missouri.

"Do you *feel* him?" Franni asked softly. "After your description of the generated targets, I decided to see if we could pick out his sensation elsewhere."

Blaire closed her eyes and concentrated. "He's north. Much stronger with our altitude."

"Are you sure?" Franni asked. "He still feels unsteady, mottled, to me."

"Stay high and move north," Blaire said softly. "You know, you really should have asked Keely to come."

"Keely?" Franni asked, surprised. "Why Keely?"

"She felt Nikle from the start," Blaire explained. "Before his men attacked the ranches, she and Shar's girls knew they were there. Keely *heard* Nikle waiting in the tunnels. The commander confirmed that she was sensing him, and not someone else."

Franni shook her head. "I didn't know that, Blaire."

"All three of the girls seem to be sensitive to his *feel*," Blaire added. "My dad told me that Nikle sent men to the school to watch them and the girls knew. They knew after school when the men were waiting for them and tried to take them, and they knew the man with the gun was waiting in the school parking lot last Friday. Does he *feel* stronger, more coherent to you?"

"Yes, seems to be clearer," Franni said. "You think he's underground somewhere?"

"That's my guess," Blaire said. "What I don't understand is why he was 'mottled' to you and he wasn't to me."

"I guess I made the right choice," Franni said, and smiled at

Blaire, "and brought the right person with me after all."

"He's between Skokie and Evanston," Blaire said, trying to ignore Franni's compliment. "Just east of the channel. I wonder if we have an address on Nikle's widowed sister's house."

"What?"

"Dad said that Abe Brownly told Wally, when they talked after Nikle tried to have Abe's ex-wife killed last week," Blaire explained, "that Nikle had been staying at his widowed sister's place. I am wondering if we got an address."

"TTYF, contact STSX1 and see if anyone has an address on Don Nikle's sister's place." Franni looked at Blaire. "You keep up on all of the local police work too?"

Blaire smiled. "What can I say? I grew up as a deputy's daughter and I keep an ear to the ground. I stay in touch with my folks and I have to admit, since I joined the Force, my dad has been very supportive and helpful. We actually talk cases now. I'm not his overly curious, meddling child anymore." Blaire suddenly refocused. "He's in one of the houses in the block between Glenwood Street and Pond Street, and between Bowling Avenue and Lone Pine Avenue."

Blaire leaned forward against the jump seat straps, closed her eyes, and focused on the ground moving slowly under them. "Large house...fourth from the northeast corner, Lone Pine and Pond...big, rundown garage or shop building in the backyard... has two basements...lots of odd equipment..." Blaire took a deep breath and straightened up, suddenly feeling disoriented. She grabbed the armrest.

"Are you all right, Blaire? You're pale."

Blaire nodded slowly. *'STSX? Can you take these images I have and analyze them? I haven't done that before, and I don't know if I did it right.'*

'CADET LUPIS, YOUR IMAGES ARE VERY GOOD. THE COMMANDER WILL REVIEW THEM, BUT YOU HAVE PUSHED YOURSELF TOO FAR THIS DAY. TTYF HAS COMBASSA BEANS AND YARROW FRUIT YOU SHOULD

EAT TO REDUCE THE TENSION AND REGAIN YOUR
STRENGTH. ADD SWEETENER FOR THE TARTNESS.'

"Franni," Blaire said softly, "STSX says you have combassa
beans and yarrow fruit that I should eat. One of them needs a
sweetener."

Franni swiveled her chair to aft facing and guided Blaire,
suddenly lethargic, down to the galley. She sat Blaire on a pull-
out and mixed the sweetener into the yarrow fruit tube, opened
the combassa bean paste, and handed them to her.

"Eat the beans first," Franni said, and Blaire ate the paste
without a second thought. "Now let's get you stretched out so
you can relax."

Franni guided Blaire to the right medical couch and pulled
the retention web over her.

"Mind if I ask what you did?" Franni asked as she passed
the medical scanner over Blaire.

"I gave STSX a complete set of images for both floors of the
house and all three levels of the out-building and basements,"
Blaire said absently, and sucked a small amount of the fruit
out of the tube. "I also gave him a list of the odd devices and
equipment Nikle has in the lower basement and in the house.
Some look like strange communications equipment. No one
else is in the house. It doesn't look like his sister lives there
anymore."

"Take some more fruit," Franni urged as Blaire's voice
softened and she seemed to drift from one thought to another.
"Finish it, Blaire. We'll head back now. Finish the fruit and
sleep."

One Twenty-Nine
Tuesday, December 12

"Thanks again for coming yesterday," Franni said as she took her cup from the dispensing machine in the Mess and followed Casi to the table. "I'm still a little shaken by her reaction. Does that sort of thing always take such a toll?"

Casi glanced around the Mess and picked seats away from the normal breakfast traffic.

"Always? No," Casi said, and sat down. She took a bite of the coffee roll, shook her head, and smiled. "I keep forgetting these are not like Annie's rolls and cakes. Anyway, STSX thinks that somehow, Blaire collected all of the data all at once, like taking a picture. Normally, one goes through the buildings in a slow progression, giving the information time to be stored or sent to storage."

"She told me she had never done that before," Franni said.

"She probably didn't know she could," Casi admitted. "And therefore, we haven't given her any instructions on what she should have done. I think I need to spend more time with her and see what she can and can't do."

"Did someone show you how?" Franni sipped her coffee and took a bite of her breakfast wrap.

"Stran did," Casi said, and smiled. "He guided me through my first in-depth study, Ahaar's complex. Even then, I was exhausted, searching for too long at a time. When I finished, it was like someone cut the power cord. I woke up seven hours later cradled on Stran's lap."

"I think Blaire slept from the time I put her on the medical couch until this morning," Franni said. "She looked okay when she came through for breakfast about an hour ago."

"Good," Casi said. "I hope she doesn't push it too much today, even if it is her day."

"Her day?"

"Nineteenth birthday," Casi said, and sipped her coffee. "I wanted to have a party for her, but with Kiile and Cheral coming home today, I'm not sure if I should. I asked Cheral to bring everyone out to the ranch after they get settled. And speaking of settled, I have to check on the apartment's progress."

"Did Crem have it right, that Kiile has a daughter?"

"He sure does." Casi smiled. "She is very pretty. Fourteen and a half of our years. I brought her a passel of new clothes and had them put in her room. Cheral says her grandfather gave her a bedroom full of furniture, and it'll arrive on the supply ship tomorrow."

"So they're going to live together here in the facility," Franni mused.

"That's the plan at this time," Casi said. "After Neila gets settled and accustomed to our culture, or mixed culture, they may try to move outside, into a normal house or cabin."

"Neila? That's a pretty name," Franni said. "Well, I'm certain Neila will be a frequent guest at Headquarters and that will help her adjust. When do they get in?"

"ETA seventeen-twenty," Casi said, and stuffed her napkin into her empty cup. "Do you have time to check out their apartment with me?"

"Sure," Franni said, and stood up. She pushed the chair under the table and tossed her trash into the recycling bin. "You know, a birthday party for Blaire might be a good thing for Neila to see and help her lose some of the fears and anxiousness she must be feeling."

"You just might be right," Casi said, and Franni followed her out into the corridor and they turned right.

⋏

"I knew they weren't making room for them in Billeting," Franni said, "but I didn't know there was another wing with enough room for apartments."

Casi smiled and slid the main entrance panel open.

"Stran, Seventeen, and Kiile agreed this wing would be adequate for the commandant's residence," Casi chuckled as she led the way in. "It allows for a very spacious dwelling. The living and entertaining area is large enough to handle twenty or more"—she continued to the kitchen area—"and plenty of food-preparation area if they decide to use it, or need space for the Mess to cater any gatherings they might have."

Casi stopped at the hallway entrance and turned to look back across the main room. "Tall ceilings in every room, a full bath here in the main hallway for guests, just off the kitchen, and each bedroom with its own bath."

They stepped into the large master bedroom and Casi was pleased that all of Cheral and Kiile's things were there. She smiled. "At least someone was thinking and found a queen-sized bed and didn't move the two single cots."

"A single cot might be enough for a while," Franni laughed as Casi checked the bathroom for their personals and an adequate supply of towels and bed linens.

"This looks serviceable," Casi said. "Now for Neila's room."

She stopped in the doorway and, shaking her head, looked at the large, nearly empty room with simple cadet furnishings, a single cot, nightstand, lamp, a straight-back chair, and a clothes press.

"I sure hope Neila's furniture comes on that supply ship," Casi sighed. "Otherwise, she's going to be a very disappointed girl. Excuse me a minute." Casi focused her thoughts. *'STSX, contact Seventeen and tell him we need some kind of temporary wall and floor coverings and decorations for Neila's room in Kiile's new quarters. Thanks.'*

Casi led them back to the kitchen area and began looking in

the cabinets. "I don't do much cooking, Franni," Casi said, "so give me your opinion. Does it look like they have the right stuff here for food preparations?"

Franni went from cabinet to cabinet and finally said, "They look pretty well stocked, but I think I'd ask the cooks in the Mess to come and see what they think."

"Good idea," Casi said, and started to the front door.

She stopped at the sound of running feet and the squeaks of a wheeled cart. She was about to say something when the panel slid open and a corporal pushed a cart through the door with some framed pictures and rolls of rugs and tapestries on it.

"Sorry, Captain," the corporal said between deep breaths. "I had these collected but had not brought them yet. It's good that you're here to pick what you think will be appropriate."

"Thank you, Corporal." Casi smiled. "Please take them into the second bedroom."

Casi and Franni followed the corporal and stopped in the center of Neila's room.

"Let's see what you have brought," Casi said, and the corporal bent to the task of laying the rolls on the floor and unrolling them for her inspection.

⋀ ⋀ ⋀ ⋀ ⋀

"Congratulations," Seventeen said as he stopped beside Blaire's table. She was finishing her cake and coffee. "I heard something special was happening today."

"Yes, sir. Captain Kiile and Cheral are coming home today," Blaire said, intentionally misconstruing his meaning. She smiled. "Thank you, sir."

"May I?" he asked, and gestured to a chair.

"Certainly," Blaire said. "I have a few minutes before I need to get back to the lessons."

"I have to admit," he said as he sat down, "somehow, you

200

have beguiled everyone—even the cooks. I can only think of one other time when they've been talked into doing cakes for a celebration. Well, maybe twice before."

"I'm sure I'm no one special," Blaire said, and finished her coffee.

"Do you have anything special planned for the day?" Seventeen asked. "Meaning personal plans and not just more study and practice."

"Not really. I've already talked to my folks," Blaire admitted, and shrugged. "So I guess I've about done it all. And with Kiile and his new addition arriving today, I think there'll be a lot going on without me adding to the agenda."

"Very well," Seventeen said, and then his expression turned serious. "Have you talked to Sergeant Stial recently?"

Blaire's smile slowly faded. "Why would you ask me that?"

"There are things about Thursday that you don't know," Seventeen said, "and I think you're being a little hard on the sergeant."

"What? You think he can—"

Seventeen held up his hand and Blaire stopped.

"Did you know, Blaire, that he was just as taken aback as you were?" Seventeen said, speaking soft and level. "I saw him here in the Mess that night after your ceremony. He looked as devastated as he said he thought you felt. He said you wouldn't talk to him after that."

"No. I wouldn't," she said, a challenge in her eyes and in her tone. "I didn't want to hear any more of his—"

"Those were not his remarks, Blaire. You were hearing two disorderly marines."

Blaire cooled a minute. "He did catch me Sunday and apologized for the men's behavior and the things they had said, the implications and the innuendoes. But he didn't apologize for his actions."

"His actions? What? Apologize for putting two of his men

in the brig for twenty-four hours for conduct unbecoming a marine? Apologize for demoting them one stripe for fifty days with the stipulation that they can only get them back if they are shining examples of marine conduct, order, and discipline during that time?" Seventeen watched her and waited a minute before continuing in a calm voice. "You have a right to be angry, Blaire. But I would hope you direct your anger at the right individuals, and for the right reasons."

"I didn't know..." Blaire finally said.

"No, you didn't. Sergeant Stial would not boast or tout his actions in the situation. He simply did what a squad leader had to do, as unpleasant as it may be," Seventeen explained. "And he would apologize for any misconduct and try to keep it from happening again, to you or to anyone."

"At first, when I knew he was listening to the ceremony, I felt flattered," Blaire said softly. "He felt like he was proud that I had succeeded."

"He was, Blaire. And I've said all I'm going to," Seventeen said, and smiled. "I felt I needed to say something because I am not happy when someone thinks badly of one of my marines, especially when it's due to a misunderstanding. I want you to be happy that you are here and to not have misgivings about the character of your fellow officers and enlisted men. Whichever way you and Sergeant Stial decide to get along is your business, but you should at least try to clear the air and be on speaking terms. You both are going to be working here—and with your skills and talents, possibly together on occasion—and there should not be ill feelings. Not in this case, for these reasons."

"Thanks, Seventeen," Blaire said. "I'll think about it."

Seventeen watched her as she got up, tossed her trash in the recycling bin, and left the Mess. He wondered if there was something else bothering her, but then quickly dismissed his concern. She had experienced so much change in the past two weeks; there was no way she could feel calm or at home yet.

⋀ ⋀ ⋀ ⋀ ⋀

'Hey, Cuz,' Shara called to Cheral, waving to Billie as she hurried onto Thom and Eddie's porch, up the steps, and in through the kitchen door of their house. *Are you still going to be on time?'*

'*We'll be early,'* Cheral answered. *'About seventeen-oh-five. Is that going to be a problem for you?'*

'*I don't think so,'* Shara said. *'We just dropped Billie off and I'm heading out to the ranch with Tayn and the girls. It's been snowing, so it'll take us a little more than a half an hour to get there. A quick cleanup and we should be able to get there ahead of you. Land outside and I'll bring Neila's things on board. Then you can move ST12 inside. There are a lot of folks that want to say hello when you exit the ship.'*

'*How many are a lot of people?'*

'*Everyone that's not on duty.'* Shara smiled to herself and chuckled. '*How does Neila like space travel?'*

'*I think she's an old hand, but she really likes the view from the jump seat. I gather the trip from Ematl to Belimoor and back was like riding in a barrel.'*

'*Are you going to eat in the Mess? Or would you like a home-cooked meal?'*

'*We have a choice?'*

'*Yes, unless you don't like birthday parties. It's Blaire's nineteenth and we thought attending a party might be something Neila might like as well.'*

'*I sure don't mind, and I think she might like some of Annie's sweets,'* Cheral said. *'I'll contact you when we're in the atmosphere.'*

'Okay, Cuz. Talk to you then.'

Shara glanced at Sedona riding shotgun and looked back at Tayn on the passenger side back seat and Cheyenne in the middle. "Everyone okay? Cousin Cheral says they'll be here at about five after five." She figured they might have been listening, but said it out loud anyway.

"We're fine, Mom," Sierra said from behind her. "Do you think Neila will like the stuff you bought?"

"I sure hope she will," Shara answered. "If not, we'll exchange them when we come back into town tomorrow. Cheral wants to take her shopping so she can pick out things she likes. You can show her some of your things tonight if you like."

"We can do that," Sedona agreed. "Are Chy and Uncle Nick coming?"

"They're invited. I just need to make sure Blaire can make it."

"You think, Mom?" Sedona asked. "Haven't you talked to her yet?"

Shara gave her a "you've gotta be kidding" look and focused. *'Blaire, are you busy?'*

'No, Shar. What's up?'

'Just checking about tonight. You haven't pulled any unexpected patrol flights or anything, have you?'

'No. Still planning on coming. You said I should bring a couple of friends. Is that still okay?'

'Yes. I've asked Wally and Carole and your mom and dad.'

'Thanks. That's very nice of you.'

'You're very welcome, Blaire. We'll talk after Kiile and Cheral get down and settled.'

'Okay. Talk to you then.'

"Anyone have an idea how much snow we've got this season?" Shara asked to help pass the time.

⁥⁥⁥⁥⁥

"Major," Keli said in English from the cockpit, "we are approaching our moon. You said you wanted to take the last leg and the landing."

Cheral was sitting in the double-wide cushioned chair across from Kiile and Neila when Keli called. She looked at Neila. "My turn. Do you still want to watch from the jump seat?"

"Yes. I certainly do," she said, taking her time to say the words correctly.

"You're getting the hang of it," Cheral said, and unbuckled her straps. "Let's go."

Cheral got up and drifted to the central compartment and up through the ceiling portal. As she turned forward and slipped into the pilot's chair, she watched Neila swing onto the jump seat and deftly buckle the harness. With a wide smile at the girl, Cheral swiveled the seat to forward facing and pointed to the large globe drifting past on their left.

"That's our moon, Neila," Cheral said. "And we will be about one lunar diameter away at our closest point as we pass. Once we get past, we will see our planet ahead of us."

A few minutes passed and Neila's eyes grew wide and her face broke into a wide smile as the blue, cloud-mottled Pacific Ocean stared back at them under a full afternoon sun.

"That is so pretty," Neila said in a whisper. "Is that all water? The blue?"

"Yes, love. That is our largest ocean," Cheral said, "and where we are going is along the right edge, north of the maximum, the equator. It's slipping into night there and we'll land just after our local sunset."

Mesmerized by the view through the canopy, Neila inhaled the long minutes as the planet slowly grew and grew in front of them. At about one Earth's diameter out, Cheral rolled STSX12 to place the planet above them and leveled.

"We need to transfer Ani so she can land," Cheral explained, and swiveled the chair to aft facing. "Keli, please take the chair while I get Ani transferred."

The process took the routine five minutes and when Cheral was back in the pilot's chair, she smiled at Neila, who was waving enthusiastically at Ani as Apache Ten drifted up beside them on the right. Then Ani cloaked.

Cheral resumed their approach and started to graze the atmosphere just west of the North American west coast. She watched Neila's bright expression as they crossed the coastline, and she remembered to hail Shara and let her know they were getting close.

Cheral pointed out the valley, hidden in deep shadows behind the brightly lit Rim Mountains as they approached from the northwest. The fresh snow was brilliant with the yellow hue of the setting sun.

"Shara said it was snowing most of the day," Cheral said, "but it looks like the clouds are breaking up and blowing out."

Cheral drifted down north of the north spire and across the Rockin' H, its lights brilliant in the early dark. Cheral pointing to the Flying M's and the lights of Riggin and then she slowly turned them south. She heard Keli call Approach and get their clearance to land outside briefly.

"Now remember how we cloaked ST12 in Gpada's clearing?" Cheral asked, and when Neila nodded, she continued. "Where we are landing and where we live is cloaked just like that. As we get closer to the ground, it will look like we are going to hit the trees, but when we pass through the veil, you'll see all of our base and the launch facility."

Cheral watched Neila tense as they settled closer and closer to the apparent trees, comforting Neila by reassuring her that Apache Ten was still there, off their right wing. "We're almost there, Neila."

Suddenly, ST12 and Apache Ten settled through the veil and the clearing south of the portal became clear, filled with Q-Ships and the smaller fighters. Neila looked quickly from one to another.

"They're just like ST12, almost. No, that one with the two stripes is just like ST12. And some of the others are like Captain Ani's."

"Very good, Neila," Cheral said as she swung ST12 around so the aft portal faced the portal hatchway near the west side of the launch bay. "Set systems to standby," Cheral said to ST12 and to Keli. "We'll move inside in a few minutes."

"Ship's secure, Major," Keli said as she toggled various switches on the nav-com consoles.

Cheral unbuckled and said, "ST, open the outer airlock for Captain Casi." Then she turned to Neila. "She's bringing you some warm clothes so you can dress before we move inside."

Cheral took Neila's hand and helped her get her feet under her. Then down the rungs to the lower deck with Neila close behind.

Neila stopped and stared as the aft portal opened and three raven-haired women in blue-black uniforms stepped in. "I brought the official welcoming committee," Shara said as she led the girls in and the inner panel closed behind them.

"Shara," Cheral said, and gently slipped her arm around Neila and urged her forward a step. "This is Neila. Neila, this is my cousin and her two daughters."

Shara quickly took Neila's hand and clasped it between hers. "We are very pleased to meet you, Neila." Then Shara stood back and introduced the girls. "My daughters Sedona and Sierra."

Sedona stepped forward and gave an uncertain Neila a tight hug, followed quickly by Sierra. "Glad you're here, Cousin," they said together.

"Oh," Sedona said, and handed Neila a sack. "Some lined jeans, a floral print flannel blouse, heavy socks, and boots."

"And I have a coat, gloves, and a cap," Sierra said, "but if you're moving ST12 inside, you won't need them right away."

Cheral herded a quiet Neila to the central compartment and helped her look through the clothes. Neila slipped into the shower chamber and changed into pants and the blouse, smiling hugely at the fit and the softness of the shirt and lined pants.

"How do those fit?" Cheral asked and turned Neila around to see all sides.

"Very well," Neila said. "They are so soft and fresh smelling, and I like the flowered print. The colors are so nice, like our crops."

"I'm so glad you like them," Cheral said, and laughed softly. "They really do look nice on you. Here, socks. Put these on. They will keep your feet warmer than mine do. See if the boots fit."

In a short moment, the new-looking Neila stepped into the central compartment and Shara smiled. "I think we did all right, girls."

Neila stepped into the aisle and stopped at the foot of the medical couches. "Kiile, what do you think?"

Kiile, silently watching the activities, smiled hugely. "I think you're the prettiest thing I've ever seen. Well, maybe both you and Cheral are the prettiest things, but you look wonderful."

"Thank you, Kiile," Neila said, and smiled at him and then at Cheral.

Sierra stepped forward and handed Neila the coat. "Try this for fit. You'll need it when you come to dinner at the ranch later. If it isn't right, Mom and Cheral can take you to exchange it tomorrow."

Neila took the coat and slipped it on, smiling as she pulled it tight around her and pushed the soft collar up around her neck with her shoulders. "This is very nice. Thank you. Thank you all."

"Okay," Cheral said. "We have standing room only, but if you want to hang onto something while I reposition ST, you can."

"That's okay, Cheral," Shara said. "We'll go back down the stairs and greet you along with the rest of the facility that came out to see you." Then she smiled at Neila. "We're so very glad you're here, Neila. See you inside."

Shara and the girls turned and ST opened the airlock panel. Sedona and Sierra waved back to her as the panel closed behind them and Cheral, with Neila right behind her, headed back to the cockpit.

"I've never met twins before," Neila said as she buckled the jump seat straps. "Do twins always look like they could be the same persons?"

"Sedona and Sierra are identical twins, which means they are genetically the same," Cheral said as ST12 started to lift and turn to face the section of the launch portal as it opened. "Doug and Rose, friends of ours, also have twins, but they are not identical. One is a boy and the other is a girl. You'll meet them soon."

As Cheral maneuvered ST over the opening and slowly let him drift down inside, Neila looked at the immense launch bay half filled with people.

"Do all of these people work for Kiile?" Neila asked softly.

"Most of them," Cheral said. "We're down, so let's go meet a few."

⚓

Greg stood at the base of STSX12's ramp with Shara, Sedona, and Sierra. Paul Hawkins, Major Kooich with Leeana, and Tayn stood beside them, and Colonel Mooren and Franni stood beside them. Somehow—Nick was not sure how—he found himself and Cheyenne standing beside Greg and Shara, opposite the Kooiches. Seventeen and Forty-two stood behind the group.

The aft portal opened and Kiile led Cheral, Neila, and Keli down the ramp. He introduced Neila to Greg and then looked at Cheral. "I think you need to make this introduction."

Paul stepped forward and hugged Cheral enthusiastically.

"Neila," Cheral said, and slipped her arm around Neila's shoulder. "I'd like you to meet *my* grandfather, Paal Haak, also known as Paul Hawkins."

Neila stepped forward and took his hand and looked up into his smiling eyes. "I am very glad to meet you, sir."

"Neila," Paul said softly. "I am glad to meet you too. May I have a hug?"

"Yes, sir. You may." And she stepped forward and hugged him. "Thank you, sir."

Kiile smiled and turned Neila and began introducing her to each of the others, but Neila stared at Cheyenne when she was introduced to her and Nick.

"Cheral?" Neila asked softly, leaning close to her. "What has she done to her hair?"

Cheral chuckled and smiled. "Nothing, Neila. Every now and then, we have children with red hair. It is actually considered rather rare and beautiful."

Neila turned back to Cheyenne. "I am sorry to stare, Cheyenne, but I've never seen red hair before. We only had brown and yellow on Nevar and Somstri."

"That's okay, Neila," Cheyenne said, and smiled. "Mom and I and Blaire are the only redheads in the valley. At least the only ones we know about."

"Your mom is not here?" Neila asked.

"No. She flies Apache Fifteen and will be back tomorrow. She was helping on Nevar."

"That's right. Your mom is Key-ray?"

"That's her Mission Name. Family calls her Jill. She's the commander's sister."

"So if Cheral is my stepmother, then I'm a step-cousin to Shara which means I am a step-cousin to you?"

"Sorta complicated, I know," Cheyenne smiled. "We'll talk about it over dinner, but you're family. Not a 'step' anything.

You're my cousin and you're Sedona and Sierra's cousin." Cheyenne stepped back and glanced at Greg. "I think they want to go and show you your new home. I haven't seen it yet."

"Captain," Greg said when Cheyenne and Neila stopped talking. "Your reports would like a word from you." Greg handed Kiile a wireless mic.

"Thank you, Commander," Kiile said, and turned to the group. "I'm sorry if all of you cannot see us. I thank you for your support while we were away. I will make a mission briefing available on the information network so you can see what happened to Nevar. It's obvious that Prince Kiese's replacement, Prince Lukré, has devised methods of stealing whole planets' populations. The commander's mission to Nevar allowed us to find unexpected survivors and to learn what actually happened. My thanks to the commander for letting us try. Secondly, my part of the mission was to find and bring home a very special person from my home town on Nevar." Kiile turned to Neila and asked without the microphone. "May I have your hand?"

She slipped hers into his and he held it gently. Together, they turned to the assemblage. "Fellow marines, Shadows, and pilots, I would like to present to you my daughter, Neila Beeli."

The bay burst into cheering and applause and Kiile, smiling hugely, looked down at Neila. He caught Cheral's hand and lifted both of his arms to show off the two women in his new life.

⚲

"Where are we going?" Cheral asked as Seventeen led them away from Billeting, down a wide, well-lit corridor.

"To the commandant's quarters, sir," Seventeen said, smiling with more mirth than he should have at his commander's expense. "We didn't think it was suitable for the commandant and his family to be annoyed by the nightly rituals of the working class."

Seventeen stopped at a corner and looked at Kiile with a sincere smile. "Sir, the men and I, with the help of the commander and his wife and daughters, are extremely pleased to present you with the new commandant's residence. We hope you will like it in the same vein it was created." He turned and gestured to the wide patio in front of a double-panel front door. "The commandant's residence, sir."

Kiile gently pushed Cheral and Neila forward, and he followed. Forty-two led the rest of the entourage behind them, into their quarters.

After they had surveyed and admired the living room, the dining area, and the kitchen area, Seventeen stopped them at the entrance to the hallway. He looked at Neila.

"Miss Neila," he said. "I know your belongings are coming on the supply transport tomorrow, but the commander's wife took special care to decorate your room the best we could until then. If you will follow me, I would like to show you your room, your personal space." He straightened and gestured to the hallway.

He followed Neila to the doorway and into her room. She stopped and stared at the colorful rugs and wall hangings and smiled at the pictures of farms and mountains and one of a planet late in the day, half in the afternoon sun and half in the deepening shadows of night. Many city lights dotted the surface among wide expanses of greens and darkness.

"Somstri," she whispered. "How...?"

Cheral stepped up and stopped beside her. "Your dad took that image out of the video we took during our approach to Somstri, when we came to meet you. He had it enlarged and Shara had it framed and hung for you."

Neila looked at Cheral and smiled through wet eyes. Then she turned to Kiile, walked to him, and hugged him tight. "Thank you, Kiile. Thank you."

"You are very welcome, love. Very welcome indeed." Kiile had to wipe his eyes before he could release her.

⋏ ⋏ ⋏ ⋏ ⋏

Sam stopped on Oak in front of Deputy Lupis' home, got out, and was halfway up the driveway when Dan escorted Mandy out of the house.

"Well, hello, Sam," Dan said, and extended his hand. "I didn't hear you pull up." Dan absently looked up and down the street and quickly glanced at the clearing sky with brilliant patches of bright stars.

"Evening Dan, Mandy," Sam said, catching Dan's quick glance. "It's going to be a cold one tonight, with the cloud blanket gone." Then he looked at Dan. "I'm sorry for just dropping by, but this is Blaire's birthday and I was hoping you might have heard from her."

"Yes, Sam," Mandy said. "She talks to us pretty regularly."

"I hope she's doing okay," he said, hesitant to say what was really on his mind.

"She seems to be fine," Mandy said.

"I don't know when I'll see her again, but I thought, well, I wanted to ask you to give this to her when you do see her." Sam handed her a small, gaily wrapped package. "It's her day and I wanted to drop it off for her. It's nothing important, but I thought of her when I saw it and just had to get it. Please tell her I wish her a very happy birthday. I miss seeing her, especially on her birthday."

"We'll be sure she gets it, Sam," Mandy said, taking the gift.

"Thank you," Sam said, and slowly walked back to his jeep, got in, and then drove around the corner at Kelly.

⋏

Mandy looked at Dan as he helped her in and closed the door to their hard-topped jeep with the deputy's star on the hood and doors.

"I don't think Blaire has any idea how much her sudden

213

disappearance and silence are hurting Sam."

"No," Dan said as he started the engine. "From my talks with Sam, I know she doesn't."

▲ ▲ ▲ ▲ ▲

Greg was standing to one side of the dining room, watching everyone huddle around Blaire sitting in the central part of the living room, as she opened her presents. The mood was happy, with lots of giggles and laughter. Two of Blaire's friends and fellow cadets sat close, Dan and Mandy stood looking over her shoulder, Kiile with Neila and Cheral, Alyssa and Ridan to one side, and the Kooiches and Nick, Cheyenne, Sedona, and Sierra closed the ring of attention surrounding her.

Greg smiled at Carole and Shara standing across the room from him, talking with Meara. He knew they were talking about Blaire's quick assimilation into the training and the routines of a cadet, but the topic of Neila and her adjustment kept coming back into their conversation.

Wally leaned over the dining room table and slid another piece of Blaire's birthday cake onto his plate, then turned and resumed his place beside Greg to watch the happy group.

"Sorry, Greg," Wally said, and took another bite. "Annie makes the best cakes." He smiled and followed the bite with a sip of his coffee, then his tone turned more serious. "I wanted to tell you we found out who that fellow was at the school Friday. He was waiting to pick up his son in defiance of a restraining order his ex-wife had against him. When Thom and I arrived, he must have thought we knew about the order and came up with a gun when I asked him to step out of the car. He was a threat, but not to your kids. He wasn't part of the Don Nikle issue."

"That's good to know," Greg said. "Though I don't think it helps the man's wife and son much."

"Of course not," Wally agreed. "I just wanted you to know I

don't think Nikle was involved in that one."

"Thanks, Wally," Greg said, and finished his cup.

"It looks like Kiile's daughter is taking all of this in," Wally said, changing the subject.

"I hope so. Everything is so new to her, and yet she's old enough to have developed interests and maybe relationships before the attack. It's when the laughter has quieted and they are together in their new home that concerns me. This will be the first night for just the three of them, and I hope Neila can see that she's not alone."

◢ ◢ ◢ ◢ ◢

Blaire was about to palm her room door open when Sergeant Stial entered Billeting and stopped at the corridor branching to the marines' section. He nodded when he saw Blaire standing at her door.

She turned to face him and he slowly walked to her.

"You look like you're on duty, Sergeant," Blaire said softly.

"Just off, Cadet Lupis," Luc said. "It was a long day outside and it seems I missed Captain Kiile's return."

"I'm sorry to hear that," Blaire said. "They made quite a stir among the troops."

"I hear his daughter is very pretty and almost grown," Luc said, and shook his head. "I'll have to tighten the reins on some of my men."

"Most likely." Blaire smiled. "She *is* very pretty, and has no experience with men or a situation like this. She's a bit vulnerable and we need to be sure she isn't exploited or led astray."

Luc smiled. "I see you've already taken her under your wing."

"All of us that have met her have," Blaire said proudly.

Luc noticed the bag she had set beside her door and

the still-wrapped gift she was holding. "This morning I remembered this was your day, and I must apologize that I remembered late and did not get you anything."

"Thanks, but why would you think you should get me anything?"

"Because that is what friends do. And even though I made you angry and you haven't wanted to speak to me, I still consider you a friend."

"About that," Blaire said, and took a deep breath. "I think I jumped to a wrong conclusion. I think I was too wrapped up in the whole soloing thing and I obviously didn't listen closely enough to realize that you weren't thinking or saying those unkind things. For that, I have to offer my apology."

"Thank you, Blaire," Luc said softly. "That means a lot."

"I heard what you did to your men over that, and I'm sorry I caused a situation that led you there."

"That is just it, Blaire. You haven't caused anything. I've only been in your company twice, and was a little bumbling both times. You seem to have that affect on me, but nothing you have said or done would remotely justify the crass behavior of those two men. So let's just say I've started them on an overdue rehabilitation program for their own good and for the good of the Corps."

"Okay."

"Thank you, Blaire," Luc said. "I have kept you too long and I see you still have gifts to unwrap. Possibly I can see you another day."

"I'd like that, Luc," Blaire said.

Luc smiled, turned, and went back to the corridor leading to his room, and Blaire palmed her door open.

C.3486.748

Knobaal's Prince Regent Wilmet Kiese Lukré sat straight

in the high-backed cushion chair behind his semi-circular conference table in his private conference room adjoining his private suite. Before him, his directors of his Intelligence and of his Information Security Departments sat rigid across the table.

"As I explained earlier," Prince Lukré continued, "I have been thinking about the rumored secret communications those within the Peace Force seem to possess. My late uncle, Prince Kiese, seemed to believe the rumors were true to the point that he even tried to arrange a marriage with one expected to be strong in the capability of *hearing* those of the Traders blood and those of the Peace Force blood."

The director of intelligence nodded without speaking.

"When the humanoid woman was reported as having been accidentally terminated, I understand another woman, maybe slightly less desirable than the first, was found and substituted." The prince ran his fingers over his bearded chin. "Which means, there are likely others that possess the talents he was seeking." He held them with a fixed stare, his expression hard. "I want those talents! You have three turns to bring me a plan and a schedule to locate and collect the rest of that talent pool."

Shara and her extended family's journey continues in
Paladin Shadows Series Book 12:
Garda Nua Part 3: Right Does Not Ask Permission.

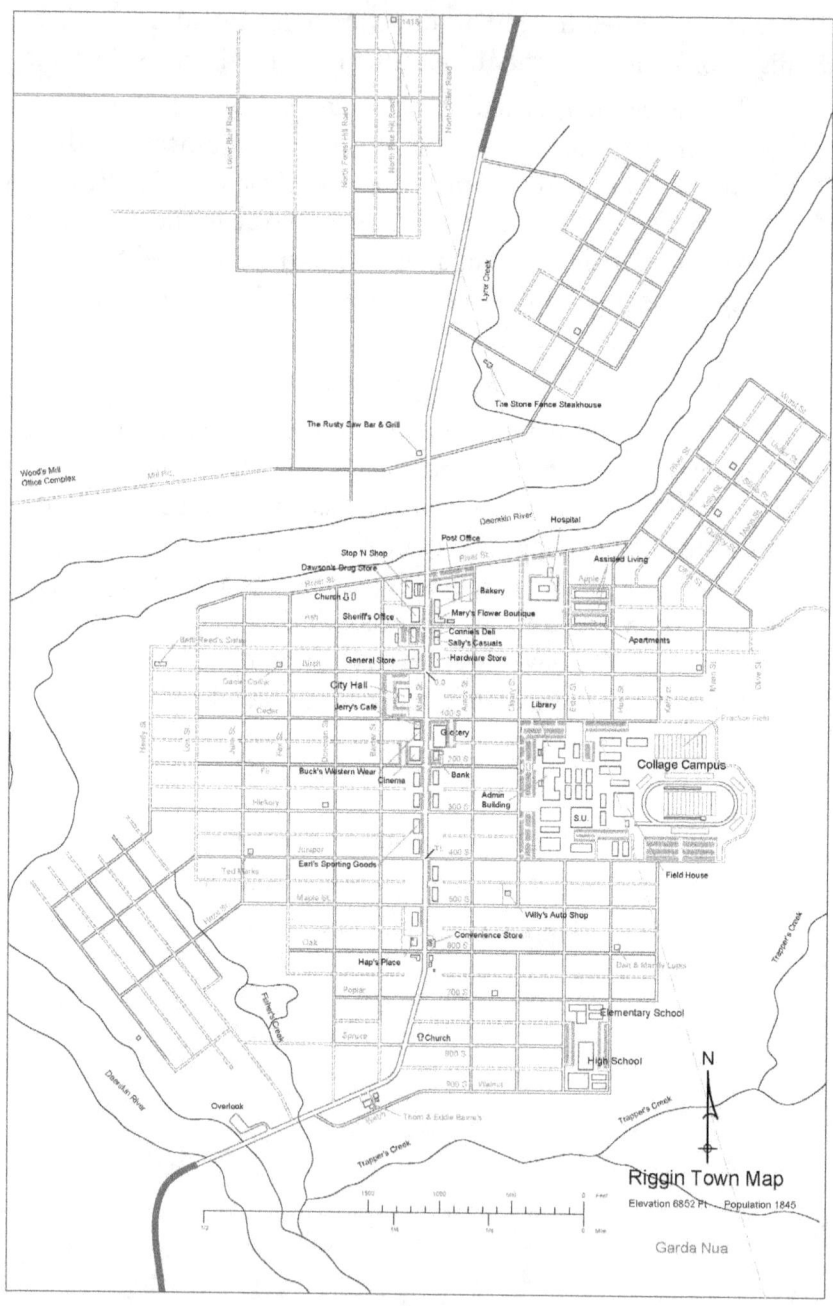

Riggin Town Map
Elevation 6852 Ft — Population 1845

Garda Nua

Riggs Valley Map

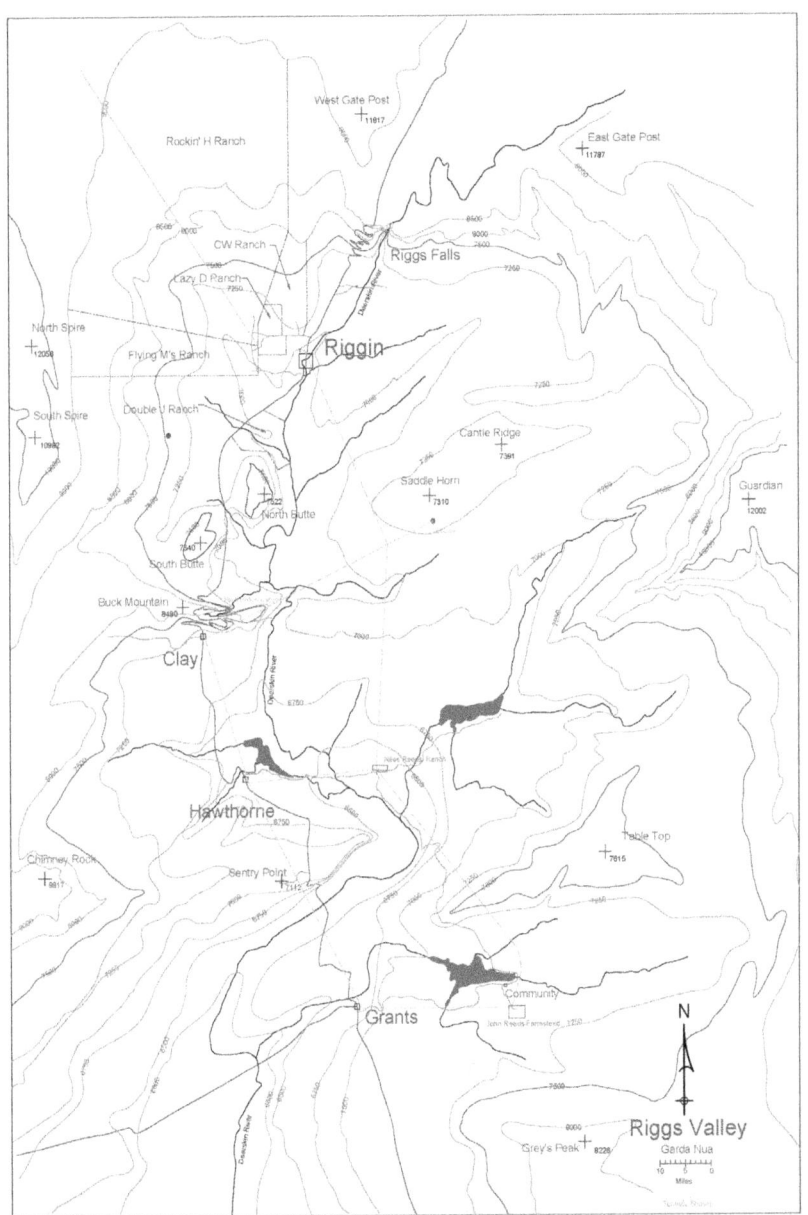

Glossary

Characters:

-A-

Annie — Cook at the Malone's Flying-M Ranch.

Anthor of Marit — Neila's grandfather. Living in Belimoor on Somstri.

-B-

Baine, Thom — State Deputy assigned to Riggin under Marshall Wally Lima. Father of Billie.

Baine, Eddie — Thom Baine's wife. Maiden name: Eddie Collier. Married on Dec 31, C.3482.750, age 35 yrs. Mother of Billie.

Baine, Billie — Daughter of Thom and Eddie Baine. Born on November 10, C.3483.429. Age 8 yrs old.

Beeli, Kiile — Captain, a Marine Squad Leader in the services of the Galactic Peace Force. Commandant of Marine base at Point Obscure. GPF Terran ID: USL15-EFM. (Kiile pronounced quickly Kī-īle.) ¬

Bren — Short version of Greg's nickname, 'BrenCara,' for Shara. Meaning: "Special Raven Haired Friend."

Brickle — Sedona's favorite horse. Named for her mottled caramel coloring.

Bucky — Cheyenne's favorite horse. Named for his buckskin coloring.

-C-

Cadet Pilots	Cadet students training in the art of space combat.

Apache Patrol Two:	Cadet Huml
Apache Patrol Three:	Cadet Milik
Apache Patrol Four:	Cadet Ilistr
Apache Patrol Five:	Cadet Lupis, Class 2 Fighter
Apache Patrol Six:	

Camerso	Gentleman's Gentleman to Prince Lukré. Previously the Gentleman's Gentleman to the late Prince Kiese.
Cara	Second house girl at the Malone's Flying-M's Ranch.
Cassel, Brendan	Coleen Malone's second husband, mate. (GPF Terran ID: IAL01 SS3)
Cassel, Coleen	Husband/mate to Brendan Cassel, second marriage. Previous marriage: Coleen Reese. Maiden name: Coleen Malone.
Chairman Sorgat	Principal Officer in the Trader's Union
Coleen Malone	See Malone, Coleen
Coleen Reese	See Reese, Coleen
Collier, Eddie	Floral Arranger at Mary's Flower Boutique. 24 yrs old when she married Thomas Baine. Daughter of Daniel Collier. No siblings.
Collier, Daniel	Eddie's missing father. Non-terran family name is Calr.

-D-

Dnar, Cera	Jill Jordan's GPF name (Pronounced: Key + ¬¬ray; Means: Fiery Red). A Captain and pilot in the GPF.

Dnar, Jadn	Bob Jordan's non-terran name.
Dnar, Jesi	Nick Jordan's GPF name. A Captain and pilot in the GPF.
Dnar, Keely	Cheyenne Jordan's GPF name.
Danny	Shara's 15 yr old black stallion. Retired from competition.
Davis, Carole	Waitress at Hap's Place. Shelly's younger sister by one year. 23 yrs of age when Wally was assigned to Riggin.
Davis, Marty	Husband of Rusty Davis. Father of Shelly, Carole and Todd Davis.
Davis, Rusty	Wife of Marty Davis. Mother of Shelly, Carole and Todd Davis.
Davis, Shelly	Raised in Riggin, wife of Lt. Jim Woods. 36 yrs of age. Mother of Carrie Anne Woods.
Deputies, Special	

In Riggin:

Thom Baine.　　See Baine, Thom.

William (Bill) Day See Day, William

Dan Lupis. See Lupis, Dan.

Ted Marks. See Marks, Ted.

Scott Plumen　　See Plumen, Scott

Harvey Saulter　　See Saulter, Harvey

In Hawthorne:

Bill Trent

In Grants:

Thad Reeds　　Rural Support

Willy Carle

Dílis	Shara's 15 yr old black-faced roan. Greg's favorite and named by him. (Pronounced Jee + lus)

Director, Peace Force	Identification AGL36Q

-E-

Elders, The Family	Brian Woods	(deceased)
	Harry Woods	(deceased)
	Harold Danley	(captured)
	Malcolm Clotter	(captured)
	Charley Clotter	(captured)
	Dave Barns	
	Don Nikle	

-F-

Family Council   Support council for the Council of Elders, the nearly extinct governing body of the southern Riggs Valley. Normally ten members, only remaining members:

William (Bill) Copper

Jack Wilton

Fighters, Apache Squadron

Apache One:	Q-STSX1
Apache Two:	Q-KKLC14
Apache Three:	Q-TTYF8
Apache Four:	Q-STSX12
Apache Five:	Q-LTVC21
Apache Six:	Q-MKCC5
Apache Seven:	Q-KVWC33
Apache Eight:	Q-LLRT12
Apache Nine:	Q-KCMM9
Apache Ten:	Class 2 Patrol Fighter – Ani Tigs
Apache Eleven:	Class 2 Patrol Fighter – Emli
Apache Twelve:	Class 2 Patrol Fighter - Barba
Apache Thirteen:	Class 2 Patrol Fighter – Rose

McIntire

Apache Fourteen: McIntire	Class 2 Patrol Fighter – Doug
Apache Fifteen: Dnar	Class 2 Patrol Fighter – Cera
Apache Sixteen:	Class 2 Patrol Fighter – Jesi Dnar
Apache Seventeen: Lupis	Class 2 Patrol Fighter – Blaire
Apache Eighteen:	(Unassigned)
Apache Nineteen:	(Unassigned)
Apache Twenty:	Q-QRTT7
Apache Twenty-One:	Q-JCCV4

-G-

Geaardt, Stran	A Shadow. An undercover agent. A Commander in the Galactic Peace Force. Pilot of Q-STSX1. GPF ID: HQZL09-ES. Pronounced "Gee (as in Geese) + art."
Geaardt, Casi (Casey)	A Shadow. An undercover agent. Stran Geaardt's partner, wife. A Captain in the Galactic Peace Force. Pilot of Q-STSX1. GPF ID: HQZL09-ES2.
Geaardt, Caiti	Registered name of Sedona Malone. GPF ID: HQZL09-ES2.1 assigned on her eleventh birthday.
Geaardt, Coli	Registered name of Sierra Malone. GPF ID: HQZL09-ES2.2 assigned on her eleventh birthday.
Geaardt, Moira	Registered name of Coleen Malone
Gpada	Means Grandfather, in the cultural language of Nevar.
Gpama	Means Grandmother in the cultural language of Nevar.

Greg Malone	See Malone, Greg

-H-

Haak, Cheral	Captain/Major in the Galactic Peace Force. Pilot of Apache Patrol Ten, Class 2 Patrol Fighter as a flight student. Advanced to Major and assigned Q STSX12 with Nav-Com Lieutenant Keli Quil. Granddaughter of Paal Haak. Mated with Kiile Beeli on C.3486.738 (Cheral Haak-Beeli).
Haak, Paal	Commander, Galactic Peace Force Academy, Tactical Strategies Instructor, Retired. Grandfather of Cheral Haak.
Hank	Forman at the Smallwood Ranch.
Hawkins, Paul	Brother of Andrew and Nancy Hawkins. Grand Uncle to Shara Smallwood. (aka Paal Haak.)
Hawkins, Clea	Unplanned daughter of Andrew Hawkins and Katherine (Reeds). Married to Henry Smallwood. Mother of Shara, and surrogate to two other daughters. (Deceased.)

-J-

Jordan, Robert (Bob)	Owner of the Jordan Double-J Ranch. Nick's father.
Jordan, Darcy	Nick's Mother. Darcy Reeds married to Ben Jordan. (Deceased.)
Jordan, Nicholas	Aka, Nick. Husband of Jill Thomas. Father of Cheyenne Darcy Jordan. A Captain and Fighter Pilot in the Galactic Peace Force. Pilot of Apache Sixteen, Class 2 Patrol fighter. GPF Terran ID: IAL36 SS.
Jordan, Jill	Nick Jordan's wife (Jill Thomas) for

11 yrs. Age 34 yrs. Married May 17; C.3482.522. Red Headed mother of Cheyenne Darcy Jordan. A Captain and Fighter Pilot in the Galactic Peace Force. Pilot of Apache Fifteen, Class 2 Patrol Fighter. GPF Terran ID: IAL36-SS2.

Jordan, Cheyenne Darcy — Red headed daughter of Jill and Nick Jordan. Age 10 yrs. Born July 10, C.3482.941. Favorite horse is Bucky. GPF Terran ID: IAL36-SS2.1. Familiar Nickname: Chy (Pronounced Shy)

-K-

Kiese, Prince — Warlord Prince of Knobaal (deceased).

Kiile — See Beeli, Kiile.

Kooich, Hench; Major — Colonel in the GPF, Commander of Q-KKLC14. GPF ID: RWKR17-SC.

Kooich, Leeana — Major Kooich's mate (wife). Captain in the GPF, Nav-Com officer and pilot on Q KKLC14. GPF ID: RWKR17-SC2.

Kooich, Tayn — Son of Hench and Leeana Kooich. Age 11 yrs old. Born September 30; C.3482.658. GPF ID: RWKR17-SC2.1.

Kym — Third house girl at the Malone's Flying-M's Ranch.

-L-

Lima, Wally — State Marshall, 37 yrs old, permanently assigned to Riggin. GPF Terran ID: IAL05-SS.

Lima, Carole — Wally Lima's wife, 34 yrs old. (Carole Davis.) Married January 29;

	C.3482.413. GPF Terran ID: IAL05-SS2.
Lima, Alyssa	Daughter of Wally and Carole Lima. 9 yrs old, born April 22; C.3483.227. GPF Terran ID: IAL05-SS2.1.
Lima, Ridan	Son of Wally and Carole Lima. 8 yrs of age, born May 16; C.3483.616. GPF Terran ID: IAL05-SS2.2.
Lukré, Prince	Replacement for Prince Kiese.
Lupis, Blaire	Daughter of Dan and Mandy Lupis. 18 yrs of age. Redhead. Joins the Force through Greg and Shara and begins training to be a Shadow and to fly Fighters.
Lupis, Dan; Deputy	State Deputy assigned to Riggin under Wally Lima. Wife Mandy. Daughter Blaire. (Registered Family name: Lomr.)

-M-

Malone, Coleen	Married to Tom Reese (1), and to Brendan Cassel (2). GPF Planet-side ID: IAL01-SS. Registered Moira Geaardt.
Malone, Greg	Husband of Shara Malone. 40 yrs old. Born March 17, C.3471.868, married to Shara Smallwood Nov 13, C.3482.336. Married for 12 yrs. GPF Terran ID: IAL02-SS. Father of Sedona and Sierra Malone. Great Nephew to Gary Woods. Son of Coleen Reese (Malone).
Malone, Shara (Shar)	Wife of Greg Malone. 40 yrs old. Born June 20, C.3471.963, in the same year as Greg Malone. Mother of Sedona and Sierra. GPF Terran ID: IAL02 SS2.

228

Malone, Sedona	dentical twin daughter of Greg and Shara Malone. Age 11 yrs, born August 18, C.3482.615. Favorite horse is Brickle. GPF Terran ID: IAL02-SS2.1.
Malone, Sierra	Identical twin daughter of Greg and Shara Malone. Age 11 yrs, born August 18, C.3482.615. Favorite horse is Strawberry. GPF Terran ID: IAL02-SS2.2.
Marks, Ted; Deputy	State Deputy assigned to Riggin under Wally Lima.
Matti	Head house girl at the Malone's Flying-M Ranch.
Meara Wrth	See Wrth, Meara.
McIntire, Doug	Husband of Rosalee (Mitchell) McIntire. Married June 6, C.3483.272. Married for 9 yrs. A Captain and Fighter Pilot in the Galactic Peace Force. Pilot of Apache Fourteen, Class 2 Patrol fighter. Father is Tom, aka Tor of Anthor, mother is Karyn, aka Canri of Lomsi; both from Somstri, living in Greely, CO.
McIntire, Rosalee (Rose)	Wife of Doug McIntire. A Captain and Fighter Pilot in the Galactic Peace Force. Pilot of Apache Thirteen, Class 2 Patrol fighter.
McIntire, Kaylie	Daughter of Doug and Rose McIntire. Age 8 yrs. Born Sept 2, C.3483.725.
McIntire, Kail	Son of Doug and Rose McIntire. Age 8 yrs. Born Sept 2, C.3483.725.
Mosl, Corporal	GPF Marine Squad Leader, Thirty-two. Assigned to Lieutenant Kiile's Battalion protecting Obscure and supporting the Terran Campaign. (Pronounced: Moh-sul)

-N-

Neila	Kiile's daughter, Neila of Kiile (Neila Beeli). Born and raised in Turell on Nevar. Grandfather lived in Belimoor on Somstri. Blonde haired, blue eyed. (Pronounced: Neil + ah)
Niki	Head house girl for Wally and Carole at the CW Ranch.

-P-

Pada	Means Father, in the cultural language of Nevar.
Pama	Means Mother, in the cultural language of Nevar.
Piper	House girl and cook at Jill and Nick Jordan's home on the Jordan Ranch.

-Q-

Q-STSX1	Commander Stran Geaardt & Nav-Com Captain Casi Geaardt. Campaign Commander for Terran Campaign and Apache Squadron's Flight Training School. (Apache One.)
Q-KKLC14	Colonel Hench Kooich & Nav-Com Captain Leeana Kooich. Campaign's lieutenant and Flight Operations Commander under Commander Geaardt. (Apache Two.)
Q-TTYF8	Colonel Crem Mooren & Nav-Com Captain Franni Mooren. Campaign Wing Commander under Colonel Kooich. (Apache Three.)
Q-MKCC5	Major Aillx Romaan & Captain Colbee Donnr. Wing Second under Major Mooren. (Apache Six.)
Q-KVWC33	Major Daaws Miiles & Nav-Com

	Captain Meecia Miiles. (Apache Seven.)
Q-LTVC21	Major Neel Glean & Captain Debira Glean.
	- (Apache Five)
Q-LLRT12	Major Deni Bradg & Nav-Com Captain Mri Bradg. (Apache Eight.)
Q-KCMM9	Major Pti Fila & Nav-Com Lieutenant Lori Tam (Apache Nine.)
Q-JCCV4	Major Ronl Bids and Nav-Com Captain Emly Bids. Joined Apache Squadron after supporting the attack of 4 January and getting repairs done at Obscure. (Apache Twenty-One.)
Q-QRTT7	Major Amel Clef and Nav-Com Captain Pela Clef. Apache Squadron B-Group Wing Leaders. (Apache Twenty.)
Q-STSX12	Major Cheral Haak and Nav-Com Lieutenant Keli Quil.
	(Apache Four)
Quil, Keli, Lieutenant	Major Cheral Haak's Nav-Com Officer on Q-STSX12.

-R-

Ranch Hands	At the Smallwood Ranch: Jimmy, Tom (Tommy), Billy and Dusty.
Reeds	Terran family name of the controlling Family in southern Riggs Valley.
Reeds, Glory	Daughter of Thad and Betti Reeds. 21yrs of age, living in Riggin, attending Riggin College.
Reeds, Sam	Son of Thad and Betti Reeds. 25 yrs of age, living in Riggin. Finished college studies at Riggin College. (Registered as: Donl Jst.)

Reeds, Thad & Betti	State Deputy out of Grants. Living in Grants with his wife and working for Marshall Wally Lima. Son Sam and daughter Glory.
Reese, Coleen	Married to Tom Reese (1), mother of Hew and (by an Affair) of Greg Malone. Maiden name: Coleen Malone.
Reese, Tom	First husband of Coleen (Malone). (Deceased.) Distant relation of Gary Woods.

-S-

Shara Malone	See Malone, Shara
Smallwood, Shara (Shar)	Unplanned daughter of Henry and Clea (Hawkins) Smallwood. Youngest of three. 40 yrs old. Born June 20 (solstice), same year as Greg Malone.
Smallwood, Henry	Full blooded Apache, American Indian. Married Clea Hawkins, father of Shara Smallwood.
Stial, Sergeant	GPF Marine Squad Leader, Forty-two. Assigned to Lieutenant Kiile's Battalion protecting Obscure and supporting the Terran Campaign. (Pronounced: Steel)
Strawberry	Sierra's favorite horse. Named after her pinkish coloring; a strawberry roan.
STSX	Q-STSX1 is a late generation, Shadow Class Corvette, nicknamed as a type as Q ships, operated under the command of Stran Geaardt. The latest in the long evolution of the GPF's Shadow ships. The name is

synonymous with the ship's central computer system ID.

-T-

Taam, Crl — Jack Thomas' non-terran name.

Thomas, Jack — Married Amy Woods, daughter of Gary Woods. Father of Jill. Financial Officer at the Woods Lumber Mill. (Father of Greg Malone by pre-marital affair with Coleen Reese.)

Thomas, Jill — Daughter of Jack Thomas and Amy Thomas (Woods). Six years younger than Shara Smallwood and Greg Malone.

Tigs, Ani; Cadet — Cadet Pilot of Apache Patrol Three, Class 2 Patrol Fighter.

Tmn, Officer — One of Prince Lukré's Intelligence Officers.

-W-

Wardly, Anne, Lt. — Staff Assistant and Aide to Admiral Baker, space station S.S. QuickSilver.

Woods, Harry — Son of Horace Woods. Longtime head of the Woods Lumber and Mill (Retired). Father of Gary, James and Brian.

Woods, Gary — Son of Harry Woods. Father of Bill Woods.

Woods, James — Son of Harry Woods. Father of Amy Woods.

Woods, Brian — Son of Harry Woods. Unmarried. Current head of the Woods Lumber and Mill.

Woods, Bill — Son of Gary Woods; no siblings. Father of Jim Woods, Lieutenant (USAF).

Woods, Jim, Lt.	Son of Bill Woods; no siblings. Married to Shelly Davis, father of Carrie Anne Woods.
Woods, Amy	Daughter of James Woods. Married to Jack Thomas, mother of Jill Thomas.
Wrth, Meara; Captain	Galactic Peace Force Marine Medic. Terran age 47. (Meara, pronounced: MYAR + ah). Attending Medic for Sedona and Sierra's birth, for Tayn Koovich's birth and for Cheyenne Jordan's birth. Retired from the Force on 3482.698 at the age of 35 Terran years. Hired by Shara and Greg on 3482.701 as their resident Nanny.

Places and Things:

-A-

Aleemill	A mining colony on Feranni, 30 degrees North of West from Daneubois.
Angrilat	A Principal commercial complex in the Kyddellan System
Antheria	Major Commercial Planet in the Tunst System. Known as a Heavy World with a gravity index of 2.02 times Galactic Standard.
Aridont	City on Listera, cite of water rioting.

-B-

Baile	Planetary system of the planet Rygon.
Belimoor	Major import and export city on Somstri. Home of Neila's maternal grandparents.
Betolle	Planet in the Daneets System. Home planet of Lieutenant Franni Kaal and her hometown of Casimir.

Botuni	Planetary System of agricultural plancts Nevar and Somstri.
Brekshiir	A wrist mounted laser weapon, consisting of one or multiple optics and fired by a unique sequence of mental commands. Specifically designed for the GPF Shadows.
	Brekshiir 170 Single Optic wrist Unit, 50 pulses with a range of 300 yds in air.
	Brekshiir 490 Wrist Clusters is the most common in the GPF, consisting of 4 laser units, 50 pulses each with a range of 300 yds in air. Individually fired or in combination.
	Brekshiir 710 Wrist Clusters, upgrade of the 490. 70 pulses with a range of 300 yds in air.
Brigstoan, Patrol Cruiser	GPF Patrol Cruiser designed for interception and boarding of suspect transports. Operated with a standard pilot crew, fifty aerial marines, a separate pilot crew and a Medical staff.

-C-

C.Date	A date referenced to the galactic calendar. A galactic year is comprised of one thousand galactic turns.
	Example: C.3482.329 is the 329th day of the galactic year 3284. It is also the 310th day of the current story year, November 6th.
Caldite Throwing Dart	A coveted and highly guarded GPF tool, used to inject a sedative or toxin upon impact.

Casimir	City on the planet Betolle, home town of Franni Kaal.
Cellystoan	Planetary system in which the Warlord Prince's home planet, Knobaal, orbits.
Centipar	One hundredth of a par. Similar to a terran minute.
Chain	A terran unit of measure. 66 ft. or 22 yds. or 100 links or 4 rods. There are 10 chains in a furlong and 80 chains n a statue mile. An acre is 10 square chains (that is an area of one chain by one furlong), (or 43560 sq. ft.).
Clay	Town in central Riggs Valley, 93 highway miles south of Riggin.
Colbr	Planetary System with three agricultural planets: Copus One, Two and Three.
Combassa Beans	A vegetable from the agricultural planet Somstri, usually prepared as a paste, high in fiber and nutrients. Prescribed to Casi by STSX to ease the tensions of their missions.
Corsecain	Planet in the Gashii system. Prominent for numerous bloody battles in the Moulit Wars.
CW Ranch	Carole's Ranch: Carole Davis' 65,000 Acre (101.5 sq. mi) ranch above her dad's Lazy D ranch. She named it 'CW Ranch' when she married Wally Lima.

-D-

Daneets System	Planetary system of the planets Betolle and Feranni.
Daneubois	City of Universities & Higher

	Learning on the planet Feranni in the Daneets System. Cheral Haak's Home Town.
Dangcee	Mining colony on the fourth planet of the Greel system.
Double J Ranch	A 43,138 Acre (67.4 sq. miles) horse ranch owned by Nick's father, Bob Jordan, situated between the North Butte and Riggin.
-E-	
Ematl	Space Port and major City on Nevar.
Envirocube	Shipping container with independent life-support systems for transporting personnel through space in the unpressurized holds of freight carriers.
EVA	Extra-Vehicular Activity. Working outside a satellite, space station or shuttle, in the vacuum of space.
-F-	
Flying M's Ranch	Horse ranch belonging to Shara Malone (Smallwood). 209,275 Acres (approx 327 sq miles) split off of Paul Hawkins' larger ranch to its north. Situated West of Riggin. (Previously known as the Smallwood-Hawkins Ranch, Shara renamed if after she married Greg and before the girls were born.)
-G-	
Galactic Peace Force	Galactic policing organization headquartered in the Gridelin Rings.
Galactic year	Equivalent to 1000 terran days, or 2.7397 standard terran years. See C.Date.

Gillot	A unit of measure roughly equivalent to a terran ounce.
Grants	Town at the south end of Riggs Valley, 186 highway miles south of Riggin.
Greel System	Planetary system in which the Pico Mining Company has established numerous mining colonies.
Greymn	Major Industrial complex on Omerai Two, renowned for its weapons manufacture. Model 40 is hand weapon most widely used by the Trader's Guild.
	Greymn Model 40: 40 destructive pulses with a range of 400 yds in air.
Gystrom	Manufacturing source of the GPF's Mark Series Cloaking Transmitters, based in a secret location in the Gridelin Rings.

-H-

Hawthorne	Town in central Riggs Valley, 128 highway miles south of Riggin.

-I-

IFF	Identification, Friend or Foe. An identification system to determine if an entity, craft or forces are friendly, and to determine their bearing and range from the interrogator. The system is capable of transmitting a hail to another system on command.
Issl	A root tuber, high in minerals and vitamins, from Copus Two in the Colbr System. Translated as Bread Root.
Istlar	Major City on Tanjera. Home city of

Thomas Baine's parents.

-K-

Kaaspr

The standard issue brand of hand laser weapon for the Galactic Peace Force. Model 106 is the current standard laser hand weapon used in the GPF. Replaced the previous standard, Model 88.

Kaaspr Model 106: 50 destructive pulses with a maximum range of 350 yds in air.

Knobaal

Home planet and seat of the Royal Throne of the Warlord Prince Kiese. Located in the Cellystoan planetary system.

Kyddel

System in which Angrilat's home planet resides.

-L-

Lazy D Ranch

Martin Davis' 15,455 acre ranch (24.15 sq miles).

-M-

Millipar

One one-thousandth of a par. Similar to in concept but equivalent to 3.456 terran seconds.

-N-

Navigationmate

A ship's crewman assigned the duties of navigation and Astronavigation.

Nevar

Farming Planet in the Botuni System. Home planet of Kiile.

Nuth

An icy planet in the Sadth System. Site of the Galactic Peace Force's Prison for Exiles and Prisoners of Importance.

-O-

Omerai Two — Industrialized planet in the Kyddel system, noted for its arms manufacturing.

-P-

Par — A fundamental galactic unit of time. Twenty-five pars in a Galactic Standard Turn (Day). Similar to a terran hour.

-Q-

QuickSilver — Planet Earth's multinational, manned orbital space station. (S.S. QuickSilver.)

Q-Ships — Nickname for the Galactic Peace Force's two man Recondite Corvettes. Specifically used by Shadows in their various roles of information gathering, defense and protection.

-R-

Riggin — A small college town in the northern point of Riggs Valley, western United States, planet Earth.

Rockin' H Ranch — A 1,263,950 Acre (1975 sq. mile) horse and cattle ranch belonging to Paul Hawkins and Nancy Hawkins (deceased), situated NW of Riggin.

Rygon — Home planet of the very old Geaardt family name, located in the Baile System.

-S-

Shadow — Undercover agent of the Galactic Peace Force with specialized training and abilities in clandestine operations and information collecting, generally thought to be able to hide in plain sight.

Somstri   Agricultural planet in the Botuni system.

Sora root   A plant grown on Nevar, Somstri and Copus One and Two. Used as a spice or herb. Side effect and primary use is to reduce female fertility, a natural contraceptive.

Smallwood-Hawkins Ranch   Horse ranch belonging to Shara Malone (Smallwood). 209,275 Acres (approx. 327 sq. miles) split off of Paul Hawkins' larger ranch to its north. Situated West of Riggin.

-T-

Tanjera   Planet in the Ambali System.

Teligrin   From or of the planet Teligr.

Teligr   Manufacturing site for many GPF used toxins and chemical weapons. Home planet of Eddie Collier's father, Daniel. Family name Calr.

Tissl   Mining colony on the third planet of the Greel system.

Trader's Union   The Stellar Merchant's Guild's black market and slave trading business arm.

Tunst   Planetary system of Antheria.

Turell   Kiile's home village on Nevar.

Turn   A Galactic Standard day, consisting of twenty-five pars. Essentially the same duration as a terran day of twenty-four hours.

-V-

Vidcom   A video communication device.

241

Vidscreen | A video display screen.

-W-

Wiibsa | A small town northwest of Turell on Nevar.

-Y-

Yarrol Fruit | A light flavored, tart fruit from the agricultural planet Somstri served warm, high in minerals and nutrients. Prescribed to Casi by STSX to ease the tensions of their missions.

-Z-

Zeupa | Renowned agricultural city on the planet Somstri in the Botuni System.

Books by Aidan Red

Paladin Shadow Series
Terran Assignment Triptych
Book 1: Things are not as they seem.
Book 2: When luck is not enough.
Book 3: Fate has a different idea.
Terran Recruits Triptych
Book 4: In the wake of chaos.
Book 5: Terran Talents join forces.
Book 6: New rules of engagement.
Operation Retribution Triptych
Book 7: The training phase.
Book 8: Taking the fight off-world.
Book 9: Luring the Prince into the open.
Garda Nua Triptych
Book 10: The proliferation of Talent.
Book 11: When a planet is stolen.
Book 12: Right does not ask permission.
Assignment: Casha-Six
Book 13: No Warning
Book 14: The Best Laid Plans
Book 14: A Change of Heart

Eight's Warning
Book 1: The Past Hunts.
Book 2: The Past Attacks.
Book 3: The Price of Escape.

More Books by Aidan Red

Keeper and His Tiger
Book 1: An Unexpected Complication.
Book 2: Deadly Undercurrents.
Book 3: The Trap.

Fearin' the Banshee

About the Author

Aidan Red's passion for aviation and aircraft design, engineering, and a deep interest in space and space travel go back many years. An avid reader from an early age, Aidan, with great trepidation, ventured into the world of writing during college. With real world experience in business aviation, Aidan's creative side led him to create an alternate world where the beautiful Riggs Valley was born and Shara's life became chronicled in his epic science fiction series, Paladin Shadows.

Paladin Shadows consists of the five triptychs (three-part works), *Terran Assignment, Terran Recruits, Operation Retribution, Garda Nua* and *Assignment: Casha-Six*. In between the Paladin triptychs, Aidan has penned two, three book series, *Keeper and his Tiger,* and *West's Ghost Ranch* and a novel, *Fearin' the Banshee.*

Unpublished books in his various series are scheduled for release on a regular basis in the coming months.

Visit *www.RedsInkandQuill.com* or *www.AidanRedBooks. com* for more information on Aidan Red's books and where to purchase them.